HELLCAT

"Oh, God!" Edna moaned. She jiggled the key, pushing hard at the door with her fist. The meow lulled and dissolved into a low, guttural growl. She could see nothing but hellishly black shadows as the wind rustled menacingly through the trees. Suddenly the door burst open so fast she had to catch herself to keep from stumbling headfirst against the threshold.

She groaned, falling halfway to the floor before she was able to brace herself. She frantically groped for the doorknob, her fingernails scraping the wood.

Then it was upon her, hissing and yowling, its breath nearly gagging her with the sour, vile odor of ancient graves. She caught her balance feebly, only to be thrown off balance again. The sheer weight and adrenaline-charged fury of the black cat felled her as it leaped at her like a fiendish missile....

HELLCAT
AMANDA KINGSLEY

To Ann
Happy Reading!
Amanda Kingsley

LEISURE BOOKS   **NEW YORK CITY**

To my mother,
with deepest gratitude.

A LEISURE BOOK®

June 1992

Published by

Dorchester Publishing Co., Inc.
276 Fifth Avenue
New York, NY 10001

Printed in the United States of America.

HELLCAT

Chapter One

It was her birthday.

"Forty years old. The big four-oh," Edna muttered sadly, talking to herself. She'd been doing that a lot lately and guessed it came from living alone.

Feeling a new-found sense of freedom but depressed about being forty, she decided to combat the doldrums by splurging and treating herself to a special day. And why not? She could afford it now, after receiving a hefty sum from James's life insurance.

Edna stared dully into the bathroom mirror, taking in the crow's feet that had started to form around the edges of her eyes and the puffy bags sprouting beneath them. *James has done this to me*, she thought, with an acidic bitterness that even his death hadn't assuaged. The precious years that James had stolen from her she could never get back.

She bent forward to get closer to the mirror. Her hair was so messy, unkempt, and she pinned it up quickly into a bun. Stray wispy strands, speckled generously with gray, floated at her nape. Her skin seemed coarser, drier, mottled with one or two patches that were slightly darker than the rest. Her hazel eyes were still beautiful, large and clear, fringed with thick black lashes.

"I look like Popeye's Olive Oyl . . . on a bad day," she mumbled grumpily, then cackled aloud at this intense inspection of herself and tacked the wild hairs up, vowing to get a haircut. Maybe a really short hairdo, something fluffy. Not so damned *severe*, for God's sake. She didn't want to look like some damned over-the-hill prissy schoolmarm. There were many good years left in her. Oh, maybe she didn't actually want to get married again, but the idea of going out to dinner with a man had its appeal.

But it also frightened her. A lot. The very idea of going out on a date seemed foreign, alien, and immensely daring. She'd do it just for fun, though. She certainly didn't want to be permanently saddled with a package of trouble like James Wilkins had been. Most men were a sorry bunch, but Edna conceded that there might, *just might*, be a handful of decent men out there. Somewhere.

She would definitely get a haircut today. She wanted to go to town anyway, to do some shopping. She'd buy a couple of new dresses, some shoes that didn't shriek "Miss Prim" to the world, and a few paperbacks. Trashy ones. She'd always loved reading and now she had the time. Nothing but time, actually. She had no job and didn't have to worry about getting one, either. Why, she could sit on her rump for weeks, months, a few years even, when you got right down to it, and do exactly as she pleased.

"A couple of thick-bodied romance novels. That's what I'll get," she murmured, slicking back the last recalcitrant strand of hair and positioning it under the bun with a bobby pin. Lightweight books, but they were safer than attempting a real relationship with a man. You could have all the thrills, but none of the chills, none of the bad parts of a relationship. That appealed to Edna, who was frightened of men in general.

She squirted a good dose of super-hold hair spray on her bun so it would endure the rigors of the day's outing and marched into the bedroom to select sturdy walking shoes.

She slipped on a pair of knee-high stockings and a loose flowered shift, eyeing herself critically in the ancient plastic-rimmed floor-length mirror on the back of the closet door.

She could see the tops of the hose dragging crookedly beneath the hem of the dress.

"Damn it," Edna said, yanking open the dresser drawer. She located a pair of regular pantyhose and put them on, easing them up very carefully to avoid pulling a run. She stood before the mirror again, regarding herself solemnly. She looked like a bag lady.

Well, by God, she would treat herself to half a dozen new dresses and toss these damn shoes into a Goodwill bin somewhere. She deserved some new things after all those long, hard lean years of scrimping and pinching pennies like a miser to pay bills. Working two jobs. Standing on her feet all day. Caring for an invalid on top of all that. Well, a pseudo-invalid, anyway.

Whenever she'd wanted anything new, James had balked, becoming petulant and fussy like an evil old curmudgeon. "Why the hell-fire do ya need new panties for? Ya got three or four pairs. So what if they got a coupla holes in 'em? Nobody sees 'em but *me*. You're too goddam greedy, Edna," he'd snort, his nostrils flaring out like a racehorse thudding down the home stretch.

So, intimidated by his uproarious tirades, she'd worn holey underwear. Worn it until it was hanging right off her behind in tatters, until it was so frayed and ancient that it looked like it had been run through a shredding machine.

God forbid if she'd ever been in an accident during those years. An ambulance would have been called, and the paramedics would have loosened her clothing to reveal dishwater-gray faded and torn rags that had passed for underwear.

"New underwear, too," she added, her eyebrows squeezed into an angry knot. All the damned underwear she wanted. At least one pair for every confounded day of the week. Lacy, pretty, frivolous ones.

Hellcat

Who was there to stop her? Who was there to berate her, or even care? Her family was dead and gone, her few friendships dissolved by her heavy load of marital duties which had drained the very life out of her.

Edna's lips tightened as the old, bitter anger coursed through her. Just thinking about James could still make her furious. He'd pretended to need all her attention and coddling long after he had thoroughly recuperated, which was a mean, vicious, devious thing to do.

And it had used up all her years. No time for friends, not a minute to spare. Who had time to waste on long, gossip-filled telephone calls? When you worked two jobs and cared for an invalid—a malingering goddamn invalid—time was a precious commodity. Rare as hen's teeth. So her "friends," such as they were, had fallen by the wayside quickly once old James's ticker had started to fail. She'd never been one to make scads of friends, anyway, never garrulous and outgoing. More the shy, loner type.

So now she had no friends. Nary a one. Unless she counted Helen from the Safeway. Well, there was Jessica, whom she'd met at the Baptist Church, but she hardly counted. She was a dedicated, Bible-packing enthusiast who had no time for anyone hardly, except the church. Edna's very best friend, Christy, had moved away last month to California.

She had no friendly neighbors, that was for sure. It was a secluded street with only one house on it besides her own, and a lot of dark, woodsy areas. Her only neighbor, Janet Mercer, lived directly across the street. Janet was an odd duck, with lots of women friends coming and going at all hours from the red brick rambler across the street. Never any men, just hordes of women. A constant, never-ending barrage.

Edna harbored a suspicion that Janet was a lesbian. Oh, she hated to jump to conclusions like that, but Janet *did* sport an incriminatory short-cropped mannish hairdo. And she certainly *moved* like a man—a weight-lifter, to be exact—with a cocky strut, balled-up fists, and her arms held stiffly out from her sides. She dressed like one, too, forever wearing those God-awful Army fatigue camouflage pants and black combat boots. Even in the sweltering heat!

An occasional, "Good mornin', Miz Wilkins" was practically all she ever said. A great one for keeping to herself. So the street seemed as cold and as isolated as Edna's whole life.

Edna filed off a hangnail with an emery board, then added a touch of pale pink lipstick. She got her black leather purse and tucked her house keys carefully inside the front flap.

When she stepped outside the front door, she turned to double check the lock. You couldn't be too careful these days. God knew there were all kinds of nasty thugs and marauders lurking about, especially in the D.C. area.

She was glad they'd bought the tiny red brick house in Silver Spring, Maryland and not a few miles down the road across the Maryland/D.C. line. Things were terrible there, the District of

Columbia having earned the nickname "Murder Capital."

As she stood in the warm, lazy June sunlight, Edna noticed a stray black cat, fat and glossy, streaking through her salmon-colored azalea bushes at the side of the house. It paused to peer out at her behind the safety of the blossoms, its eyes gleaming fiercely.

"Oh, get outta here! Outta here, you rascal! Off my azaleas!" she shrieked raucously, agitated, moving quickly to the bushes, which flanked the front porch and were her pride and joy. Her full bosom heaved as she loped.

The cat took a tentative step or two out from under the bush, its ears flattened tight against its head, skulking low to the ground. A bit of azalea blossom clung to its underbelly and stray pieces of leaves matted its fur. Edna swatted futilely at the huge cat, taking a good swing at it with her heavy handbag. If she could manage to hit the blackguard, surely the sheer weight of her purse would knock it flat. But she kept missing it by a thin margin and began swearing.

"Don't you come back here, you ugly son of a bitch!" she yelled, her breath chuffing. She spied it crossing the side yard, hunkering, moving soundlessly like a streamlined jungle creature, trampling her beloved marigolds in the tiny rock garden she'd worked like a slave to perfect.

It paused then for an eerie moment, dead still as a statue carved of stone, its great luminous eyes shining magnetically at her as though seriously considering her epithets. It raised its narrow, triangular head and drew back thin slick lips, baring its teeth to hiss at her, a long low cry that was chilling.

Edna felt a strange, inexplicable tremble of foreboding. Her body shook slightly as if she were cold, even though she could feel her armpits making sweaty circles on her flowered shift. Her palms felt moist and clammy.

Those *eyes*. So hypnotic . . . so unusual. Lord, she'd always despised cats. They just had that eerie way of looking at you, looking right *through* you, right down to your very soul, as if they knew your every thought, even the evil, unspeakable ones, thoughts that didn't bear mentioning to another living soul. Cats were strange creatures, not to be trusted. Hateful creatures, sly and cunning. Aloof . . . and not quite real somehow.

She hated all cats, and when this particular cat galloped off across Janet's yard, its large, pendulous body twitching unevenly from side to side, Edna let out a huge sigh of relief, unaware of how she'd been holding her breath with a hard-edged tension.

Ugly damned thing. Something about it made her shiver again as she watched.

"Ahh . . ." Her breath caught in a ragged, hitching gasp of surprise as she saw it turn once more to stare at her, with its huge, luminous freaky eyes. Somehow—impossibly—its slitted eyes had an uneven, out-of-kilter tilt to them. Off-center, one eye was situated a bit lower than the other in the cat's triangular skull, giving it a madly cockeyed, crazy ominous look. Its black fur stood stiffly out from its great plump body, bits of leaves and clods of dirt clinging to its back, adding to its scruffy mangy appearance, like some unholy scavenger of forbidden places.

It made her pulse race unevenly; she couldn't tear her gaze from it. Goose bumps shimmied down her forearms. Why did it stare at her like that? For so *long*?

A creature of the night, a creature of death, was the morbid thought that ran through Edna's mind, shocking her. Her heart thudded dully as the cat continued to stare, boring holes into her with the fierceness of its steady, unrelenting gaze. Time seemed to stand still and a part of Edna's mind whispered that this was absurd, as if they were two small children engaged in a silly game to see who could outstare the other—the loser being the one who broke the spell first by looking away.

It was, by far, the ugliest, most abominable cat she'd ever laid eyes on and she hoped the damnable ragamuffin never came back. It had an unnerving air about it, though Edna couldn't exactly put her finger on it. Something about its *eyes* frightened her so, scared her senseless. Its narrowed intense gaze and its bold, taunting manner sent shivers down her spine.

"Oh, this is ridiculous," she chastised herself aloud, her breath not yet on an even keel. "It's only a cat. An ordinary cat, for God's sake."

She forced herself to put the dreadful animal out of her mind as it finally broke eye contact with her and scampered off. This was her birthday. She wanted to enjoy it. She wanted to shop and have fun. Get a spiffy new hairdo. Get lots of new *underwear*. How did the kids these days phrase it? Edna squeezed her brows together to think. Ah, yes. She wanted to "shop 'til she dropped."

She grinned widely as she stepped across the gravel driveway to get into her old blue Chevy Cavalier, taking great care not to track bits of dirt or grass inside. She did like a clean car.

Chapter Two

"It'll have to have a perm if I cut it short. It's got no body at all, just as limp as a dishrag," declared the bored beautician, fingering Edna's fine, graying strands with barely concealed distaste.

She was a teenager, a stick of a girl, slender as a pencil. Her own thick, bushy black hair stood up like a proud rooster's cockscomb, rising high into the air in a veritable exclamation point of confusion. She wore sluttish patterned black hose, a skin-tight black leather skirt that was embarrassingly short, and some sort of white sweatshirt that hung off one shoulder, making her look like some tawdry hooker.

She looks like a damn fool, thought Edna, *with that hair sticking straight up. A fine one to judge other people's coiffeurs.*

"Then *give* it a perm. I want it short. Short and fluffy." She favored the girl with a stern glare that brooked no difference of opinion.

Edna had been wishy-washy, mealy-mouthed, never able to stand up to James, always letting him boss her around. But since his death, she'd become amazingly assertive at times, even surprising herself.

"Well . . . it's *your* hair." The girl shrugged, rolling her eyes in exasperation.

She jerked Edna's head backward and attacked her hair with a vengeance, using a no-nonsense grip as she sectioned it off deftly and wound it around the tiny pink rods. The stink of the permanent-wave solution was horrendous, and Edna felt as if she was suffocating as the acrid aroma stung her nostrils.

A man in the chair to her right sat sullenly as the beautician buzzed the sides of his head, did the top in a crew-cut length, and left one hunk of hair on the crown about a half-foot long. To Edna's left, a little old lady sat primly, her hair so wispy and sparse you could read a newspaper through it, begging the operator for a lush, Christie Brinkley-type hairdo.

Two hours later Edna left The Hair Cuttery, her head an enormous brown bubble of curls, her nostrils still pinched from the stink of chemicals. She was pleased with the result. The arrogant slip of a girl had done an admirable job, despite her negative attitude. Edna decided she'd worry about "covering that gray" later. Actually, amidst the abundant curls, she could hardly notice the tiny gray streaks on the right side of her head.

She sauntered around the mall, catching glimpses of her reflection in the store windows, shocking herself with her new-found fluffiness. She looked like a different person.

She wandered into B. Dalton's and stocked up on romance novels, tucking them under her arm until she'd collected an impressive pile. A nerdish-looking sales clerk with glasses and slicked back brown hair snickered slightly at her choices. She handed him a fifty-dollar bill and a baleful glare, watching his snicker turn into a fearful gulp of apology.

She sniffed indignantly and snatched up the large shopping bag off the counter. Next she went to Woodward & Lothrop's to select dresses. It gave her great pleasure to shop at Woodie's. All her life she'd had to pinch pennies like a miser, always buying her things from K-Mart or Lerner's. And many a time she couldn't even afford to go there. She'd hunted for bargains at Salvation Army thrift stores. Cheap castoffs from other people, faded and frayed, torn sometimes, or with buttons missing. Never anything decent and certainly never anything stylish. It was time to treat herself.

You're not getting any younger, old gal, taunted the ugly voice in her mind. *Might as well buy some fashionable clothes while you've still got a half-decent body to hang them on.*

She tried on a dozen garments, two of them romantic, flowered lacy dresses, and a smart-looking tailored blue suit. She fell in love with them all. The bill was a perfectly frightening amount, and Edna grinned as she handed the clerk her credit card.

"Buying myself a few birthday presents," she confided, fiddling with the flap of her purse to pull out a stick of gum.

"Might as well. Can't take it with you, honey." The clerk let out a horsy guffaw that ended in a gurgle, a thin trickle of saliva spraying out from between her buck teeth. "Always buy myself a coupla things. My ole man don't even give me a birthday card." She handed Edna the credit card and receipt and winked broadly. "Woman's gotta take care of *herself* these days, doncha know?"

"Lord, isn't that the truth?" Edna agreed, wagging her curly head. She stuffed the plastic card back into its slot in her wallet and zipped her purse shut.

On the way out of Woodie's she passed the jewelry counter, not intending to look at anything, but it drew her like a powerful magnet. She stared down at the beautiful necklaces and bracelets, telling herself she was just browsing. She had never been all that fond of wearing jewelry, except for her opal ring.

Then her eye fell on a gorgeous, gold heart-shaped locket. So old-fashioned and sentimental, it captured her fancy. But it was a romantic bauble, something a husband might buy for his beloved wife. Or mistress.

Filled with a sudden, intense longing she couldn't explain, Edna knew she had to have it.

She stared down at it a long while, like a kid with his face pressed to the window of a candy store, her fingers against the glass, making moon-shaped halos of mist.

The clerk came over and Edna glanced up, her eyes shining like a woman in love. "How much is that locket?" she asked, jabbing a finger toward it.

The clerk inserted a key in the back of the glass display case and lifted the price tag to inspect it. "Six hundred fifty dollars plus tax," she answered. "It's fourteen-karat gold. Do you want me to take it out?"

Round-eyed, Edna nodded as the woman plucked it from its velvet nest inside the case and laid it before her like a sacred offering. The clerk glanced around, eyeing shoppers warily, as though expecting them to shoplift at any moment, while Edna examined the locket.

She lifted it lovingly, reverently, placed it around her neck, and let the saleswoman latch the clasp, quivering with excitement. The slender gold chain draped her neck, the feel of it icy-cold and rich against her skin. Real-live fourteen-karat honest-to-goodness gold!

Goose bumps marched down Edna's arms as she regarded herself in the mirror on the counter, turning in different directions. The small, carved heart looked elegant, just perfect, nestled against her throat. It was as though she had some strange cosmic tie to this inanimate object. Already, in her mind, it belonged to her.

She seemed to hear James's voice drumming

in her ears. "Are you outta your goddamn *mind*, Edna? That fucking necklace is for rich folks." She could see a vision of his face welling up in her brain, sizzling with anger, puffy and florid, a wicked gargoyle of hatred. No, he would never, ever have entertained the idea of buying her a necklace like this. Never in his life. But now his death would allow her to, would pay for it, in fact.

"Oh . . . oh my, it *is* lovely." She sighed wistfully, pushing out James's horrid image from her thoughts. She reached up to touch the locket and ran her fingers over the smooth cool gold. "I'll take it. I can't possibly leave it here," she said to the grinning clerk. She rummaged through her red leather wallet for her trusty credit card.

"It's a beauty, all right. Had my eye on that one myself, but I can't afford it." The clerk sounded envious.

"I'll wear it," answered Edna, loath to take it off. Already she'd grown strangely attached to it. An instant replay of James's hateful face rushed at her, but she ignored it. James was gone. He no longer ruled her.

She left Woodie's, a foolishly happy grin across her lips, fondling the small heart and murmuring, "Thank you, James" softly to herself. For hadn't James actually "bought" it? She would never have been able to purchase such an expensive piece of jewelry without the insurance money. True, James had been irresponsible and shiftless, but he was an incorrigible fanatic when it came to life insurance, insisting on lots of it—a total of $150,000.

So, in actuality, the locket was James's last "present" to her. She considered it to be from him, a last sentimental memento to remember him by. Why, maybe she'd even put his picture inside the tiny heart. But who was she kidding? That would be too hypocritical, since she'd grown to hate him so much toward the end.

God, wouldn't he flip over in his grave if he knew she'd bought a necklace like this? His infuriated corpse would be doing the watusi six feet under. She shuddered at the thought.

Her purchase complete, she strolled through the mall and sat down by a fountain, fingering the golden heart and watching the young girls with their slender, tanned legs and high teased curly hair, and teenaged boys wearing neon-colored shorts so bright they knocked your eyes out to look at them. Most of them had such weird haircuts and half of them wore earrings. They all seemed depressingly young.

She rose and went into a shoe store and bought a pair of black low-heeled pumps and a pair of neutral sandals. Then she decided to have lunch at a Chinese restaurant in the mall, and cracked open a romance novel as she waited for her meal. She blithely ignored the way a rude young blonde punched her date in the rib cage and tittered as she eyed Edna hunched over the paperback.

Bride of Passion was the absurd title of the novel and it was a bit too racy for Edna's tastes. She was positive she was blushing deep crimson as the waiter brought her pork fried rice and pepper steak. But by the end of the meal, she was thoroughly hooked, longing to do nothing more than scurry home, prop her feet up on the couch, and finish it, like a lady of leisure. And that was exactly what she intended to do.

A perfect, sinfully indulgent way to end a birthday. Perhaps a trifle dull but maybe her life would become more lively now that she'd had a complete makeover. She had a new hairdo, new clothes, a whole new persona now that James was gone, and she felt free as a bird, drunk with a heady, carefree freedom. She didn't have to punch keys at the Safeway and stand long hard hours on aching feet.

She could do as she pleased.

Edna pulled the car into her gravel driveway and carefully locked the doors, reflecting on what a wonderful birthday she'd had. A little lonely maybe, but wonderful nevertheless. A pang, just one short bittersweet pang, for the old days rushed through her. The days when her marriage had been young and her love for James had been new and he'd brought her long-stemmed red roses, an unheard-of extravagance in later years. How she'd cried a river over that! He'd been so sweet, so touchingly thoughtful—for about ten minutes! Then Edna remembered the later years, the bitter years full of scathing arguments, of ranting and raving verbal abuse, and of physical abuse, too. She'd never forget the times he'd blackened an eye and dislocated her shoulder, the times when James had turned into a glowering monster. He hadn't given a damn, hadn't even remembered her birthday. And hadn't cared. And had bluntly and cruelly told her so, sniggering in her face at her tears.

She patted her new permanent, enjoying the feel of the tight curls, the springy, zesty way they bounced right back. She hiked her shoulder bag up higher, clutching her shopping bags tightly, her step eager at the thought of curling up with her book.

It would be a little lonely on this birthday, but curling up with a romance novel was a good deal better than suffering another birthday with James Wilkins. Anything was better than that.

For a moment she felt angry with Christy for moving to California, which was silly and unreasonable since it wasn't Christy's fault. Her husband had had a great job offer. She'd gotten a funny birthday card from her yesterday, touting the myriad benefits of having reached forty. And that was basically the way Edna felt. Forty was young.

She had stopped at the 7-Eleven on the way home to pick up *The Washington Post*. She wanted to check the "Weekend" section, to see what singles dances were being held this weekend. Maybe she'd kick up her heels. She needed to get out more, come out of her shell, now that James was gone.

She had been naughty at the 7-Eleven and bought a carton of mint chocolate chip ice cream, too. She couldn't resist; it was her favorite. But if she couldn't be naughty on her own birthday, for heaven's sake, when could she be naughty?

When she arrived home, she approached the front porch, envisioning herself curled up on her old flowered Early-American couch, her legs snugly wrapped in a light afghan, "Entertainment Tonight" pleasantly rolling on the television as she spooned down ice cream and avidly devoured her romance novel. It was a soothing, pleasant image.

Especially after you'd gone to hell and back with a hell-raising sourpuss like James, she thought bitterly.

"Great way to top off a birthday," she muttered, balancing the heavy shopping bags adroitly as she fumbled for the door key.

She sniffed at the June air, loving the faint aroma of the pine tree that stood in her front yard, mixed with the vague lilting scent of honeysuckle that grew abundantly in her back yard and all along the lane.

Ivy crept up the side of the house, twirling around toward the front porch. Its fronds twisted a zigzag path, looping up to the door, its edges beginning to curl around the wood. Edna reminded herself to clip it back soon, before it grew right across the front door. The white wooden door needed painting, too. Such a lot of work to keep up a house. She sighed.

In the dusky twilight a preternaturally early moon had risen across the horizon, pale and huge. In the dim light she barely noticed a rounded, dark mound on her small concrete porch. She paused a moment, clutching her purse and bags to her chest as she leaned down to squint at it, then drew back sharply as the acrid, sour odor pervaded the air. It was a mound of cat turds. Right smack in the middle of her front porch.

"Oh, oh, no!" She grimaced tightly, holding her breath against the horrible stink. She looked around for a twig to brush the mess off the porch. She'd seen no cats around lately, save that hateful, odd creature she'd spied earlier today, trampling through her azalea bushes like a wildcat on a rampage. That destructive, misshapen creature!

She hoped it didn't plan on hanging around the neighborhood, making a damned nuisance of itself. She had enough housework without scraping cat turds off the front porch.

Nothing like shoveling shit on my birthday, she thought, grinning ruefully as she bent to fetch a twig. She leaned down to push the turds off the porch, and took her books out of one of the bags, set them on the steps, and neatly slid the entire load into the empty plastic bag.

"Some birthday present," she mumbled disgustedly.

It was the only one she got.

Chapter Three

Edna scrubbed her hands roughly with soap, rubbing hard to eliminate the lingering foul odor of excrement.

Then in her bedroom she took the tags off her new garments and put them away. The telephone rang as she was changing into her duster. She picked up the tan princess phone on the nightstand. It was Helen Townsend, her former co-worker and friend, from the Safeway.

"Happy birthday," shrilled Helen in a chirpy, overly bright tone. "Thought maybe you'd have gone out celebratin' tonight."

"I've been out all day celebrating. Just got back a few minutes ago actually," Edna said, fingering her new perm, studying her new persona in the dresser mirror near the bed as she chatted.

"Oh, really? Do anythin' excitin'?" Helen asked, a vaguely envious note creeping into her voice. Helen had been green with envy when Edna quit her job at the Safeway a few months ago after the insurance money had arrived.

"Well, I got a perm. And some new dresses. Bought some shoes and a couple of books, too. Kinda splurged," Edna confided, hoping it didn't sound as if she was bragging.

She didn't *mean* to brag. She always tried not to bring up the subject of her new lifestyle, always made an effort not to rub it in because Helen was forty-seven years old, unmarried, and as poor as a church mouse. She shopped at the Goodwill thrift store for used clothes and household items. In fact, that was how their friendship had blossomed. They'd gone shopping together at the Goodwill, each promising to keep it a secret, ashamed to let the others at the Safeway know.

But now things had changed—for Edna, anyway. And she tried not to act haughty and smug, but Helen took offense easily. She could see jealousy shining in Helen's eyes with a hard, ugly brightness. But sometimes she let things slip out. Like right now. And she could hear the raw, burning jealousy envelop Helen like a dark diseased shroud.

"Well . . ." Helen's sizzling envy floated right across the telephone wire. "Sounds like you had yourself a pretty great birthday. How'd the perm turn out?"

"Uh . . . well, it's kinda tight right now," Edna

said, gingerly touching the springy curls with wonder. "I, uh . . . I sorta look like an aging Shirley Temple." She guffawed and Helen joined in with her high, squealing bray.

That laugh got on Edna's nerves. Helen sounded just like a damn donkey. But Edna sternly reminded herself that Helen was the only person in the whole wide world who'd called to wish her a happy birthday. The only person in the *world*, and she did appreciate it. She appreciated it so much that her hazel eyes became wet with unshed tears.

"Ah, I bet it looks real good," Helen declared loyally, gulping down one final snort of laughter. "I'd like to see it. Never seen ya with a perm. You used to wear it all slicked back in that straight, smooth ponytail when you was workin' here." Helen snapped chewing gum with a slurp and Edna winced inwardly at the irritating sound.

"Maybe I'll come down tomorrow . . . Probably scare the hell outta you guys," Edna offered. She stood up from the bed and walked to the edge of the nightstand to push her feet into a pair of blue rubber thongs.

"Yeah. Yeah, why doncha? Ya haven't been in for a long time, Edna. I'd like to see ya."

"Maybe I'll do that. After these crazy curls tone down a little. I look like I stuck my finger in a light socket. Really wild." Edna sat back down on the edge of the bed and leaned against the headboard.

They both whinnied again for a minute, Helen breaking out in a shrill ungodly heehaw, and

Amanda Kingsley

Edna thought how good it was to chat with a friend. She tried to remember the last time she'd spoken to Helen and couldn't. It seemed like a month or so. Maybe more.

"You, uh . . . you datin' anybody?"

Oh, no, thought Edna, *here it comes*.

"No. Nobody. You know it's only been six months since James died," Edna protested.

"Yeah, yeah. I know that." Helen sucked in a deep breath, warming up for her familiar lecture. "But you can't turn yourself into a derned hermit, Edna Wilkins!"

"Oh, Helen, I've had enough of men for a while. I don't care about dates." Edna bounced the blue thong off her heel against the carpet, brimming with exasperation. God, she wished Helen would play matchmaker with someone else. A month ago Helen had coaxed her into a disastrous blind date with a real nice guy from her church, Morton Farley. He had talked about vitamins and himself all night long and took her home at 9:30 so he could watch TV with his mother. At thirty-nine, he still lived with his parents.

Edna had had enough of Helen's Cupid act, thank you very much.

"Well, suit yourself," Helen answered in an injured tone. "I just thought you might be interested in this terrific guy who comes into the store sometimes." She popped the gum with a loud crack.

"I'll pass this time, Helen. Thanks, anyway."

"Well, if somebody snaps him up, you'll be

32

sorry. I swear he'd be perfect for you. And, God, what a doll he is. Got this sexy gray streak in his hair."

If he was so incredibly sexy, why didn't Helen snap him up? thought Edna, brushing her thongs rapidly against the carpet, beginning to wish Helen would hang up and leave her the hell alone.

"Sounds divine. But I'd rather look for my *own* dates, Helen. I'll find somebody myself," she muttered. Someday. When hell froze over.

"Well, I'll be lookin' for ya to come to the store soon. Say, didja get any fascinatin' birthday presents?"

Helen could be a nosy package, and Edna debated whether to tell her about the "present" from the alley cat. She decided it would do poor Helen good to hear about it; after all, how the hell could she be jealous when all Edna had received was a pile of stale cat turds for her birthday? It was rather pitiful when she thought about it. Pitiful and highly depressing.

"Not hardly," Edna snorted, permitting her voice to take on a wounded air, "unless you count the pile of cat doo-doo deposited on my doorstep when I arrived home this evening." She picked at a cuticle, propping the phone against her shoulder.

Helen considered this a moment. "Wh–what did you say?" she then asked, evidently certain she had heard wrong.

"I said cat shit was on my doorstep when I got home tonight. That was my only birthday present," Edna repeated solemnly, containing a giggle.

"A *cat* was on your doorstep you say?" Helen still sounded confused.

"Cat turds! T–u–r–d–s," Edna spelled loudly, irritated.

"Holy Toledo!" Helen shrieked, her voice dissolving into a series of rapid, staccato-like chuckles. "Are you joking?"

"I'm serious. That's the only present I got. Except the ones I bought for myself." And the locket, of course. But she wouldn't tell Helen about that. The locket was her *special* present, the present James had bought her.

"Well, glory be, Edna," Helen said, still fighting the giggles.

"That's right. I spent my birthday evening scraping cat turds off the front porch." Edna reached for the mail off her nightstand and browsed through the envelopes as she continued. Junk mail. A sweepstakes. A coupon booklet. The telephone bill. "But I'm gonna read my romance novel. Take it easy. Eat a little birthday ice cream. Mint Chocolate Chip, nice and fattening. Don't give a damn if it is . . ." She yawned.

"Now *that* sounds more like it." Helen was finally able to speak without whinnying. "Happy birthday, Edna. You come see us tomorrow, now don't forget!"

"I will, Helen. And thanks for calling." Edna was eager to get off the phone. She wanted to give her parakeet, Petey, a little birdseed and fresh water, then scrounge up something for her own dinner.

She replaced the receiver and turned her head from side to side, eyeing the stranger in the mirror warily. Her head looked so damned big.

She looked like a cross between Shirley Temple and Little Orphan Annie, a more mature version, naturally, her hair a mammoth round brillo pad of stiff wiry curls.

"Good grief, my head looks like a damned five-year-old," she mumbled sourly and then started hooting with laughter, falling back against the mattress heavily.

She sobered then, got up and went to the kitchen to hunt for the box of birdseed. Petey fluttered around in the cage, flapping his wings until feathers flew. He was a beautiful sky-blue parakeet she'd bought a year before James had died. She loathed cats and James had loathed dogs. They both hated fish. That was practically the *only* thing they'd ever agreed upon. So Petey had been their compromise.

"All right, all right, I'm coming!" she shouted to him, answering his loud screeches. She refilled his water cup and poured out fresh seed, promising herself to clean his cage out the next day. The floor was scattered with droppings and bits of feathers. Petey could be messy. And loud as hell.

But she loved him anyway, thankful for the company he provided in the lonely house. She put the box of seed back in the pantry and sighed, wondering what the hell to have for her birthday dinner. It was a toss up between a frozen french bread pizza or some scrambled eggs and toast.

She shoved the pizza in the oven, feeling brazen over the prospect of the 2,000-plus calories the pizza and ice cream would provide. But so what? She did watch her weight somewhat, but not diligently. And it was her birthday, she reminded herself, watching Petey take a nose dive into the birdseed with reckless abandon, spewing seeds across the floor.

Edna sobered then as she recalled the cat turds. Imagine the creature doing a contemptible, malicious thing like that! Of course, it could have been an accident, she supposed. Or maybe the stray she'd seen hadn't done it at all. Perhaps it had been another cat. But somehow Edna didn't think so.

She burned the pizza a little, sat down on the couch to eat it, and watched *Tootsie* with Dustin Hoffman. Then she went into the kitchen and got herself a humongous plastic bowl full of ice cream, stuck an old blue candle in the top and lit it. She held it up and belted out a sorry, off-key rendition of "Happy Birthday" to herself while Petey cawed a high-pitched raucous chorus. She blew out the tiny candle and dumped it in the trash.

"Not bad . . . even if I *did* have to sing it myself," she said, taking the bowl into the living room. She ate every last drop of the ice cream, propped her feet up on the coffee table, and got absorbed in her novel.

A little later Jessica called to wish her a happy

birthday and extend an invitation to the Wednesday night Bible meeting, which Edna gracefully declined.

She resumed reading her novel, but every once in awhile her mind strayed, and she thought how very different this fortieth birthday was than the one she'd always imagined. She had always thought she'd be happily married; perhaps her husband would bring her flowers or perfume and take her out to dinner. Or at least plant a big sloppy kiss on her, followed by a fond hug.

Instead, she was spending her fortieth birthday with a damned parakeet, serenading herself, and gobbling up ice cream like a little girl.

Chapter Four

"No dice. She doesn't want a blind date. She doesn't want any dates. I think she's on the verge of joinin' a nunnery," Helen said. "Sorry, Gene. I tried."

Gene was the man with the fabulous gray streak Helen had told Edna about and he'd been dying to be introduced to Edna for months. Helen had promised him she'd fix him up, but she'd struck out, Edna wasn't having any of it—no matter how thrilling Gene and his gray streak were.

Edna was crazy. If Gene Martin was interested in *her*, Helen'd be tickled pink, right down to her toenails.

"Hell, damn and shit," Gene said, breaking his normally polite demeanor. "Oh, I'm sorry.

Pardon my language, Helen. Guess I'll just have to meet her on my own . . ."

"I guess so. It'll be rough sleddin', though. She's such a shy, shrinkin' violet type. Especially with men. She had such a rotten marriage . . . Guy was a real jerk. If I'd been married to a creep like that, guess I'd swear off men, too." Helen scratched her arm and thought. "I don't know what you can do . . . Say, I know a real nice woman from bingo. Lillian, her name is. Good cook, likes to make all those fancy gourmet things. Hell, she's man crazy. Wanna meet her? She'd go crazy over you, Gene . . ." Helen was starting to get excited over the prospect of fixing him up.

"Nah."

He seemed downcast, crushed over Helen's failure to set him up with Edna. The man had nothing but Edna on his mind, it seemed. Maybe it was Edna's big boobs, thought Helen. She did have a great figure. Men were always staring at her.

"Lillian uh . . . She has one of those hourglass figures you're so hung up on," Helen tempted, sure she had him hooked now.

"No, no. I'm not interested. Helen, it isn't just Edna's figure that intrigues me. It's *Edna*. Something about her—and I don't mean her bustline. Something draws me to her." His voice sounded sad and forlorn like a disappointed little boy.

Helen wished she could help him, but what could she do? Edna just wasn't interested, hadn't really gotten over the death of that son of a bitch,

James, yet. Hadn't gotten over that fiasco of a date with Morton, either. Helen guessed she owed Edna one for setting her up with that nerd.

"Hey, Gene, I have an idea. You busy tomorrow? It's not for sure, but I think Edna's comin' down to the Safeway. If you can come, maybe you'll get your big chance." She laughed, juggling the telephone against one shoulder. She was sitting on the couch, one foot hiked up against the coffee table to paint her toenails a shocking red, readying herself for a hot date with Skipper MacLaine. She never went on a date without polishing her fingernails and toenails. She had no problems finding men and felt it was her mission in life to help less fortunate females.

"I'll be there," he said, immediately brightening, his voice quivering with excitement. "Call me when you find out for sure, okay?"

"Will do," she said, amused at how excited he'd gotten. He'd really flipped out over Edna.

"I just hope I can get up the nerve to speak to her. The first time I saw her in the store I acted like a damn fool, opened my mouth to say something, and wound up just stuttering. She hardly noticed me. I'm sure she doesn't even remember me. I got so embarrassed I just turned tail and ran."

"Well, for God's sake, don't do that this time. Just cool it. Pretend you're Cary Grant or somethin'. Or better yet, Tom Cruise. Be real suave," suggested Helen, dispensing pearls of wisdom on a subject she knew a lot about. She accidentally splattered polish against a cuticle and reached for a tissue on the coffee table to dab it off.

"But don't sound too phony. Edna hates a phony."

"Oh, great." He chuckled. "Suave but not too phony. How the hell do you manage that?"

"Ah, it's a delicate matter." She laughed. "You'll think of somethin'. Believe me, as much as you're dyin' to meet her, you'll think of somethin'."

"Well, thanks for your sage advice to the lovelorn," he said.

"Glad to oblige," answered Helen, starting the second coat of polish as she hung up.

Chapter Five

Edna rose at the crack of dawn the following day, as was her habit. She rolled her feet over the edge of the creaking mattress and rubbed at her eyes, then threw off the comforter. A bad dream, dimly remembered, gnawed at the edge of her mind like a festering wound. She strained to remember it, closing her eyes again to concentrate, struck by a sudden premonition that it was somehow vitally important.

The cat. It was some nightmarish, ghastly dream regarding the mangy stray she'd encountered last night. But she couldn't recall any details, only that it was a coldly menacing, haunting sort of nightmare that left her with a gloomy, grim sense of dread.

She sighed, walked to the window in her

thongs, and shifted the Venetian blinds open a bit, blinking as the sharp June sunlight filtered through. It was a gorgeous day, dazzlingly sunny and clear, not a single cloud in the sky, not a day to dwell on macabre nightmares.

The lawn needed mowing; yellow dandelions had sprung up in many spots and tufts of grass dotted the landscape in ragged, uneven heights. Edna squinted and watched two squirrels chasing each other across the small circular rock garden. It needed a little pruning, too. Tall weeds fought with daffodils, red tulips, pansies, and marigolds for space.

She pulled the cord to let the blinds up a little and headed for the bathroom.

"Oh brother . . ." she mumbled, sucking in her breath at the sight of her head as she glanced in the medicine-cabinet mirror. Tortured corkscrew curls spiked heavenward at odd angles like some bedraggled dog that had stuck its poor paw in a light socket. It was perfectly appalling how a permanent looked after you'd slept on it.

She took her time flossing, doing it painstakingly proper, taking no short cuts. She'd suffered through an abscessed tooth last year which ended in a root canal. Then she needed three crowns done and the dentist had cheerfully announced that another tooth was beginning to abscess, making her a prime candidate for yet another root canal soon. She also had a couple of cavities. Major dental problems. One of the delightful little fringe benefits of reaching forty, she guessed.

Hellcat

So Edna flossed diligently, textbook-perfect flossing, doggedly seesawing back and forth through her teeth. She even carried a package of floss in her purse. It was amazing how many teeth she could floss while sitting at one of those long stoplights.

The phone rang. Edna trotted to the kitchen and picked up the white wall phone. "Hello?"

"Oh, hi there, Edna. It's Helen. Comin' to the Safeway today?" Helen sounded a little keyed up about something, but that wasn't unusual.

"Uh, yes. I was just getting ready." Edna pushed a strand of hair behind one ear.

"Oh. So you'll be here pretty soon? I don't want to miss you. I was gonna run home on my break." Helen lived within walking distance of the Safeway in an old run-down apartment building.

"Oh. Well, I'll probably get there about ten. Gotta finish flossing and do something with this hair." She laughed.

"You and those darned teeth. Swear to God, I never saw anythin' like the trouble you've had with 'em. Oughta get 'em *all* yanked out and get yourself a pair of falsies!" Helen chortled loudly into Edna's ear.

"They're probably a pain in the butt, too."

"Yeah, that's true. My grandpa's are always slidin' out at the damndest times," Helen snorted. "I'm thankful I've never had any trouble, only two cavities my whole entire life."

"Count yourself lucky," said Edna.

"Okay. Well, I'll see ya at ten then?"

Helen certainly seemed eager to pin the time down, Edna thought, but then Helen was rather eccentric in more ways than one.

"Yes. Somewhere around ten."

Edna hung up and went back to the bathroom, finished her teeth, then fought with her hair awhile, dampening it with water first. Then she "finger-crunched" it like the hair stylist had demonstrated, squinting into the cracked medicine-cabinet mirror.

"Not bad," she announced after playing around with it, "for a beginner." She applied lipstick, some blusher, and eyeliner, not wanting the old Safeway crew to think she'd gone downhill once she'd quit.

She put on her new blue tailored suit, but it seemed far too dressy for a casual stroll through the supermarket. She pulled it off fitfully and tried the summery blue dotted dress she'd bought at Woodie's. It made her look slimmer, not that she really needed to lose weight, and its puffy sleeves and long, full skirt were feminine-looking as well as cool.

She prepared toast with strawberry preserves, then gathered up her purse and car keys, bidding Petey a fond farewell.

She pulled open the front door hesitantly, peering with caution at the front porch, just in case the wretched stray had left her another "present" during the night. She sure as hell didn't want to step in it.

She locked both locks and glanced nervously around the yard, half expecting the big cat to be lurking somewhere, waiting to pounce and scare the hell out of her. But she saw nothing. The front yard was serene and calm, save the gentle buzz of a bumblebee circling the azalea bushes, and the sweet scent of honeysuckle blossoms hung heavy in the thick, humid June air.

She fervently hoped the creature had found someone else to bother.

At ten-fifteen, the Safeway had only a handful of shoppers. Edna got herself a cart and wheeled it toward the produce section. She might as well pick up a few things since she was there.

She spotted Helen's teased French twist, lacquered to a high sheen, at the "10 Items or Less" express check-out line. Helen seemed caught in a time warp. She'd clung to the old-fashioned hairdo, like a drowning man clings to a life raft, never changing it, never varying it one whit. Old faithful. If there was one thing in life Edna could depend on, it was the sight of Helen's glassy, sleek hair, crowned by a small bubble of precise round curls and a wispy row of perfectly straight bangs across her high forehead.

The grocery cart's left wheel hit a snag as Edna rolled it down through the frozen-foods area. It kept twisting crazily to one side, making an irritating sound: *ba-bump, ba-bump, ba-bummmmmp*. Edna pushed it a bit harder, forcing it to roll forward in spite of itself, and brought it to a tilting, crooked stop in front of the fresh-fruit aisle, where a toothy man in a white apron was laying out clusters of ripe bananas.

God, it's freezing in here, thought Edna, shivering a little. Management always kept it that way. She'd forgotten to bring a sweater to cover the thin summer dress.

There was a terrific sale on seedless green grapes and she grabbed a large plastic bag of them. She inspected it briefly for inferior grapes lurking beneath the cellophane, then tossed it into the contrary cart. Yellow apples next. After ripping off another plastic bag, she selected half a dozen ripe, plump ones.

She pushed the cart but it steadfastly refused to budge, drunkenly lodging to one side like a crippled sparrow.

"Shoot . . ." she muttered hoarsely under her breath and pushed harder, her body shaking. Her fingers felt like ice cubes in the revved-up air conditioning. The cart started forward a little, hiccuping out its irregular rhythm, and then locked its wheels.

"Well, darn it," Edna breathed angrily, giving it a determined shove, putting a little muscle into it. It bounced forward like it had been shot from a cannon and wobbled crazily, its wheels sputtering, plowing directly into a man's buttocks.

"Hey!" He pivoted around to glare at her, dropping the bag of onions he'd been holding into his cart.

Edna turned scarlet and gasped. "Oh dear . . ." she managed to stammer nervously, her hands fluttering at her throat. Goose bumps ran down her arms. The dark-haired man was very attractive, so attractive that Edna was suddenly thankful she'd worn make-up for a change.

Edna could see the clerk in the white apron grinning at her out of the corner of her eye. He placed the last cluster of bananas on the counter and wheeled his cart down the aisle toward the back of the store.

"I—I'm so sorry," she said, smoothing down the lacy lapels of her dress.

His expression of outrage dissolved into a wry grin as he eyed her with a long, slow look from head to toe. Edna's throat felt tight and bone-dry as his cool, sea-green eyes met hers. She lifted a hand and toyed nervously with the locket around her neck, only dimly aware of how his gaze caused her pulse to accelerate. What beautiful, beautiful eyes he had. Golden-flecked pupils highlighted and magnified the coolness of green.

"Nice shot," he drawled in a deep, resonant baritone.

A wide, easy grin accentuated the slight dimple on the right side of his full, sensuous lips. Edna was held fascinated by it, unable to look away.

"Right in the tuckus. Great aim," he added, hooking a thumb into the pocket of his jeans and cocking his head to inspect her more thoroughly.

"I—I'm sorry," she repeated, flustered, aware she was playing with the locket like a nervous, addled schoolgirl. "The cart . . . It has some kind of problem with the wheel. I really should've gotten another, I guess. Really didn't mean to run you down like that . . ."

She felt her heart hammer a little faster as she watched his green eyes drop to her bosom briefly, then return to her eyes. Edna was impressed. Most men were captivated by her ample bosom. Enchanted. Totally bewitched. Edna always told people she could tell what sort a man was by how intently he studied her bosom, and whether he made eye contact. The slugs, she staunchly maintained, spent a lot more time staring at her bustline; they didn't care about her personality.

"I'll get you another one," he offered. "Wouldn't want you to hit someone else in the tuckus."

He grinned rakishly, flashing his dimple at her, and turned on his heel, leaving Edna with her mouth hanging open like a fish out of water, still searching for a reply, her hands aflutter. Forty years old and she still got nervous as a cat when talking to an attractive man. Would she ever outgrow it?

A minute later he appeared with a replacement cart, the charming smile still plastered across his tanned face, his clear green eyes staring eagerly into hers. His dimple, she decided, was intoxicating, the cutest thing she'd ever seen. She wondered if he was aware of the power of his dimple. And she wondered if he normally performed so gallantly for ladies in distress at the supermarket. Or was she special? Edna was a bit surprised to realize that she fervently hoped so.

A teenager with a fat drooling baby on one hip and the cheeks of her buttocks spilling out from beneath a pair of ultra-short cut-off jeans stared

at the man, checking him out as he pushed the
cart up to Edna.

"Th–thank you. And I do apologize. Hope I
didn't, uh, damage your jeans. Or your *tuckus*."
An impish grin creased her face as the words
slipped out. Flirting with a strange man in the
grocery store was way out of character for Edna,
but this man seemed to stir something within
her. She was alarmed to notice that her voice had
betrayed her; she sounded like a timid adolescent
with a crush. She couldn't stop fiddling with the
stupid locket, either, much to her chagrin.

Over the man's shoulder, Edna could see the
teenager checking out his tuckus, then his lush
dark hair with the peculiar gray stripe, while the
chubby baby tried to grab a pomegranate off the
produce counter. No doubt about it, the man
had a great physique with taut, corded arms and
broad shoulders that would make a bodybuilder
salivate.

"Perfectly all right," he mumbled, enjoying her
tart reply. He transferred her grapes and apples
to the new cart as he spoke. "You can hit me in
the behind any time . . ." His green eyes sparkled
with amusement as he pushed his own cart off
toward the frozen foods.

Edna's cheeks flamed with embarrassment
over his suggestive answer, and she stood rooted
to the spot, watching his progress down the aisle.
He was tall and the white polo shirt and faded
jeans emphasized his lean, muscular build. Dark
brown hair streaked with a thin grayish-white
stripe across the left side lent a distinguished,

sexy look to his thick, wavy locks.

Edna forced herself to stop fumbling with the locket. She had to dismiss the incident and get on with her shopping, instead of gaping after him like an idiot. She just hoped Helen hadn't witnessed the encounter. Helen would tease her about it forever. She could hear her now: "Thought you said you were done with men, Edna! Why, bless my soul, you were moonin' over that man like a lovesick calf!" That's what she'd say, and then gloat. And it was true. She *had* been acting like a lovesick calf.

She selected three pieces of kiwi and a half-dozen ripe bananas, then headed for the meat counter to pick out chicken breasts. As she rounded the corner sharply, still feeling ridiculously unnerved by the handsome stranger, a fat woman with pink spongy hair rollers and too much eyeliner swung indiscriminately around the corner, fairly knocking down a display case of saltine crackers. Edna swung her cart quickly to the right to avoid a collision, instead striking an oncoming cart head on. Her face blossomed into a deep dark crimson as she glanced up to see the green-eyed stranger once again.

Kismet, she thought, working to fight off a hysterical giggle that was building inside her like a dam getting ready to explode.

"Oh. Oh, it's you again," she gasped helplessly.

Her hand, with a mind of its own, crept to the security of the locket again, twisting it, like a dog worrying a bone. An icy shiver raced through her, but it was difficult to tell if it was really from the pumped-up air conditioning or the way he was looking at her.

"Hey, do you drive like this on the *road*? This is getting to be a habit with you, you know," he said, full of mock sarcasm, a faint glimmer of merriment lurking in his twinkling eyes. "If you hit me one more time, I'll begin to think you're trying to pick me up," he added in a low, sexy tone, his deep voice raspy as he leaned across the cart toward her.

She became predictably tongue-tied, as she was wont to do in such circumstances, but it didn't matter. He turned immediately, strolled over to the meat counter, and began examining the pork chops.

An older version of the teenager with the baby, in a low-cut tight cotton shift, stared longingly after him.

Edna whipped her head around to glance at the express check-out line at the far end of the store. In the distance, she could see Helen's head bobbing and weaving as she punched keys and heaved canned goods down the tray, with nary a glance in her direction.

Too busy. Thank God for small favors.

Edna patted the back of her perm self-consciously, straightened the lapels of her dress agitatedly, and pushed her cart to the other end of the meat counter. She picked out some chicken breasts, grateful that the man was safely busying himself at the opposite end of the lengthy counter. *The farther away, the better*, she thought.

He certainly had a nerve, she fumed silently, making that impudent remark about her trying to pick him up. Did he suppose every female in the supermarket was out to snag him, or what? Conceited thing. Well, all the good-looking ones were.

She lifted up a big package of split chicken breasts for inspection, noting out of the corner of her eye that he was still preoccupied at the far end of the counter, seemingly in a quandary over the pork chops. Momentarily, he glanced at her, his eyes gleaming with devilment. She gave a haughty sniff and lifted another package of chicken, placing the two in her cart and deliberately turning her back on him.

As she plucked a package of cream-filled oatmeal cookies off the end of a display rack, a finger tapped her shoulder lightly.

"Uh, excuse me, do you know how to cook this thing?"

Edna turned, already recognizing the deep musical baritone. A chill ran through her, and it most definitely wasn't the air conditioning. It was from his gentle, almost timid, touch. The hand that reached out to her seemed so at odds with his arrogant, sure attitude. It was strange. His engaging dimple was in full bloom and he was waving a tremendous brisket in the air, looking baffled.

"Well, it's not difficult," she began, still feeling a bit peevish. She couldn't decide if he was truly interested in cooking a brisket or not. Maybe he just got his kicks out of agitating people in the grocery store. Some weirdo who did this all the time.

"Doesn't sound too hard. I guess I can do it," he said, after she'd finished her spiel. He plopped the fat brisket into his cart. "Do you shop here often?"

The glint of humor came back into his cool green eyes, as well as that slight touch of shyness she'd glimpsed before. Edna found her gaze riveted to his dark mustache, his lips, and the generous sprinkling of soft brown-black hair across his forearms as he leaned casually against the meat counter. He had no potbelly and the faded jeans fit his flat stomach like a second skin.

"Uh, yes. Yes, I do," she gulped, her throat forming a dry knot.

She could smell the musky scent of his cologne wafting toward her. Miss Teenager hovered behind him a few yards away. The bald-headed baby dribbled saliva down onto cartons of chicken livers as the young woman poked through packages of chicken wings, and paddled her hips soundly with its plump, tiny feet.

"Well, maybe I'll see you again then?" He gave her a meaningful, hopeful look like some lost puppydog begging to be taken home, his eyes fixed on Edna's.

The invitation hung there in the air. And then suddenly Edna felt guilt flood through her, like a hot deadly lava that destroyed everything in its wake, rocking her with its overwhelming, gut-wrenching intensity. She should be ashamed of herself, responding to this stranger like some overeager kid with hopped-up gonads.

A terrifying, vivid image rose in her mind of James in his last moment, his glazed eyes fixed accusingly on her, and she felt half sick with the familiar, overpowering guilt. She should be ashamed. What on earth was she doing?

On the other hand, James had been dead for six months; she couldn't mourn him forever. And wasn't it hypocritical, a part of her whispered, to mourn him at all, when she had hated him so much? With every fiber of her being? When she had been a party to his death?

"Will I see you again?" he repeated, his voice wavering with uncertainty.

"Y–yes," she muttered, fighting off the horrible image of James on her mental screen. She fiddled nervously with the clasp on her purse. His very presence seemed to unsettle her, making her nerves tight as a drum.

"And try not to hit me in the behind with your cart anymore, huh?"

He grinned, showing the glorious dimple one last time, a lock of the grayish stripe falling forward over one eyebrow like an aging Elvis Presley. Oh, but Elvis Presley had never, *ever* in his entire life looked half as distinguished as this man did. Distinguished and sexy with bedroom eyes. And that fantastic, wild, unruly hair. Edna was certain that more than one woman's head had been turned in the Safeway this morning.

Her heartbeat fluttered sporadically and she felt foolish watching him saunter down the cereal aisle. He bent and picked up a box of granola bars, and Edna toyed with the idea of following him to strike up another conversation. But what on earth would she say? She didn't want to look as if she were chasing after him. He had asked if she shopped there regularly. Maybe if she came back at the same time next Tuesday, he would be here. Waiting. Him and his dimple.

Edna rolled over to another department and grabbed a package of mozzarella cheese. Her tenth item. That was the limit in Helen's line. She got behind the cart to push it forward and spied the handsome man diligently poring over the packages of cookies down aisle six, checking out the shortbread cookies.

Edna stared at him, brooding, her lips pursed. She was sick of men, fed up with them, yet she'd responded so strongly to this particular one. Was it possible she wasn't as sick of men as she'd thought? Just sick of *James*?

"Do you know where the mayonnaise is?" asked a skinny, ponytailed woman in a tent dress. She had a space between her front teeth and spewed forth a fine spray of saliva as she talked.

"Oh, yes. It's on . . . Hmm, let me think a minute. Aisle three," Edna answered automatically. She still knew the Safeway like a book, even though she'd quit six months ago.

"Thank you," the skinny woman replied, tottering off on thin bird-like legs, her ponytail swinging rhythmically.

Edna pushed her cart into Helen's line in back of a gaunt young hippie with two gold earrings

57

dangling from one dirty ear and a bunch of tattoos on an even dirtier arm. Holes were sliced at regular intervals all the way down the legs of his jeans, giving him a studiedly tatterdemalion air.

"Gimme a book of stamps, too," grunted the hippie, pushing a lock of greasy, frizzy hair behind one ear.

His earrings glinted in the fluorescent store lights, giving him a dangerous, exotic flavor. It occurred to Edna that if he were dressed in the proper apparel, he could pass for Captain Hook in *Peter Pan*. People often reminded Edna of characters in plays or movie stars she'd seen.

And a helluva lot of people looked like animals to her. For instance, Helen was a lot like some perky, chipper sparrow in her body movements. Her laugh, however, was definitely like a donkey's. A constipated donkey, at times. No question about it.

"Sure," Helen answered the hippie, snapping her gum insouciantly.

Helen adored chewing gum, said it gave her something to do to pass the time behind the register. Edna hated to tell her that she looked like a damned cow chewing its cud.

"Whoops, all out," Helen said, pilfering through the drawer. "Be right back." She shut the drawer and ran to get stamps from the other cashier, her slim behind swaying as she sashayed forth. The hippie watched closely, thoroughly entertained.

Edna wasn't a bit surprised. Helen usually managed to attract all manner of low-life slugs.

Never anyone decent. But it didn't bother Helen a bit. She liked all kinds of men, slugs and low lifes included. Anything that wore pants, practically.

"Here you go," Helen said, returning with the book of stamps in hand. She deposited it into the hippie's open palm and popped her gum loudly, letting her orange-lipsticked mouth hang open, not giving a damn who liked it and who didn't. Helen never cared what the customers thought of her. Or the boss, either, for that matter.

The hippie's grin was a mile wide, showing a yellowed snaggle tooth on the left side. He eyed her thin, tight figure appreciatively. Though Helen was quite flat-chested, Edna noted that scads of men thought her petite figure engaging.

The hippie nodded mutely, grasped his grocery bag in one arm, wedged his stamps down into his skin-tight jeans, and swaggered out the glass doors, glancing back to examine Helen's rear once more, as if to fix it in his memory banks forever.

Edna began piling her fruit onto the conveyor, snatching a package of mints off the counter at the last minute.

"Paper or plastic?" cawed Helen like an automaton, swooping the bag of yellow apples and sliding them past her register with a liquid motion born of years behind the counter. Then she looked up to see Edna standing there, grinning at her.

"Why, my Gawd!" she crowed, her mouth dropping open like a trap door, nearly letting the gum roll out. "You look like a different person, Edna Wilkins, so help me!" She rang up the fruit and cheese, punching the keys hard and fast. "Didn't even recognize you for a minute there . . ." She glanced behind Edna and smiled, a sparkle lighting her eyes.

Edna turned to see who she was looking at. It was *him*, a gloating, smug expression of triumph on his handsome, tanned face. He had artfully managed to weasel his way in back of her in the line somehow, though she'd seen hide nor hair of him just moments ago. She favored him with a weak, half-assed grin and immediately turned back to face Helen.

"Let me see the back of it," Helen gushed, leaning way over the counter. "Turn around. Go on."

Edna did as Helen instructed, feeling irritated and more than a little embarrassed.

"It *does* become you . . ." the man behind her stated, putting his two cents' worth into the conversation.

Helen nodded at him with a big, fatuous grin, and Edna could feel her cheeks flaming.

"Why, it looks terrific. You look just like a derned movie star," volunteered Helen, talking too loud. People in the next line turned to look. "You and me'll just have to have a night out on the town, Edna. Wouldn't be a bit surprised if you caught yourself a boyfriend." Helen exchanged glances with the man, then she proceeded to bag the groceries, popping gum, and darting quick, nervous glances at him intermittently.

Obviously, Helen was going through one of her matchmaking phases. Then it hit Edna like a ton of bricks—the gray streak in the man's hair, Helen's obvious familiarity with him. It had to be the same man Helen'd been trying to fix her up with. Edna felt a boiling fury building inside. Of all the goddamn nerve.

"Would *you* be surprised if she caught herself a boyfriend, Gene?" Helen asked coyly, flinging the man's brisket backwards as she stabbed the register keys like a demon, her fingers flying.

She darted another meaningful look at Edna, who was horrified and cringing at Helen's boldness, humiliated by her stop-at-nothing matchmaking tactics. She recalled the phone call from Helen this morning, checking up on her to see *exactly* what time she'd be at the grocery store. Obviously she'd given Mr. Gray Streak the word. And here he was, in the flesh, brandishing that sexy gray streak for all he was worth, sidling up to her to get important info on cooking a damn brisket.

Edna fumed. She kept her head low as she fiddled with her wallet, finally folding it and stuffing it into her purse, which didn't want to close. She felt a rising urge to grab Helen's skinny chicken neck and throttle her. How the hell could she do this? It was so embarrassing.

Shamefaced, Edna stared at the floor like a galled, speechless adolescent. From the corner of her eye she could see the man fairly chuckling at the direction the conversation had taken.

"It wouldn't surprise me one bit, no," he charmingly agreed with a flash of dimple.

His green eyes were riveted to Edna's, carefully watching her responses, one thumb hooked into the pocket of his sinfully tight jeans. Edna caught a glimpse of soft brown hair at the throat of his white shirt and gulped, breaking her gaze with no small amount of effort, forcing herself to focus on how angry she was, not on how exciting she found chest hair on a man.

"Oh, Helen's just kidding, Gene. She has this compulsion to play matchmaker. Don't think a thing of it." Edna's voice was a light banter, but edged with a dangerous tightness. "Well, I'd better be going, Helen. Give me a call."

She shot Helen a deadly look, lifted her bag of groceries from the cart, and stalked smartly to the glass doors. In the background she could hear the man chuckling and it seemed to her that he began to bombard Helen with questions about her.

Edna escalated her walk to a good clip, fighting the overwhelming urge to hang back and eavesdrop. She couldn't wait to give Helen a piece of her mind!

Edna burst through the glass doors and clumped out to her car, dumping the groceries in the trunk, and then after getting into the car rolling down all four windows. It was hot as hell. She wiped fat beads of perspiration off her forehead with a paper napkin from the glove compartment and started the car.

As she headed for home, she did a mental run-through of how she'd tell Helen off—that she was a meddlesome busybody. And manipulative. Sneaky, too.

Edna'd been humiliated, embarrassed beyond words, more embarrassed than she could ever remember being. But she had to admit that, yes, the man *was* terribly attractive. Had a good personality, too, although he had his moments of being insufferably arrogant.

Edna grinned as she decided she didn't know whether she wanted to cuss Helen out—or to thank her.

Chapter Six

Gene stood outside the supermarket on the curb, watching Edna pull off in a dusty blue Cavalier. He couldn't see her face, but he imagined she still looked just as pissed off as she'd looked in the store.

He'd blown it. He didn't know what the hell had gotten into him. One minute he was trying to follow Helen's instructions to act like Cary Grant—or Tom Cruise—and the next minute he'd metamorphosed into a complete asshole, one of those incredibly obnoxious, overbearing guys whom he'd always hated.

And Edna had hated it, too. God, the expression on her face when he'd made that stupid remark about her trying to pick him up! She had looked like someone had struck her across the face. Surprised, dazed, and angry.

From that point on, it had all been downhill. Helen, though he loved her like a sister, had acted just as bad as he had, raving over Edna's hair, practically yelling, drawing attention from the other shoppers. And Edna had stood there, looking as if she wished the floor would swallow her up so she could disappear, a sickish grin on her face.

They'd really botched it. But at least he had her phone number and he guessed after he slunk home to lick his wounds, he would screw up the courage to give her a call. To try one more time.

He wasn't going to give up, especially not now. Because for just an instant there, he could swear there had been some spark between them, some flash of attraction, before he'd dived head first into assholedom.

Hell, she seemed just as shy as he was. She probably hated those smooth-talking, blasè guys, too, which was a good sign because he heartily disliked what he'd done today, pretending to be something he wasn't. The charade hadn't worked. It had turned Edna off and he deserved it if she wouldn't speak to him. He couldn't really blame her. But he'd call her and he'd sure as hell give it the old college try.

He folded the scrap of note paper that Helen had given him with Edna's phone number on it and pressed it into the pocket of his jeans. He pulled out a strawberry mint from the other pocket, and walked across the parking lot to get into his car, plotting a unique, brand-new strategy—being himself. And just praying Edna liked him.

The temperature had risen. The air was thick with a muggy, suffocating humidity. Gene wiped a thin sheen of perspiration off his temples and forehead with one hand as he inserted the key into the car door. His silver Volvo was only three months old and already some rude bozo in some parking lot had scraped the door and put a small dent in the fender. It never failed. When you bought a new car, somebody just couldn't wait to "initiate" it, making it look just as shitty as some old rattletrap.

He cranked it up and put the air conditioner on full blast, cracking the window a little to let the hot air escape. He yanked open the glove compartment to fish out a new roll of mints, his fourth of the day. He was trying to quit smoking and hogging up vast amounts of chewing gum, mints, and candy in the process. But what the hell, he mused, it was better than getting lung cancer.

As he put the car into reverse, he paused to glance backward to check for pedestrians or cars, and his jaw dropped open in surprise, like a loose trapdoor.

"What the hell . . ." he sputtered.

A huge, scruffy black cat was sitting perched on the trunk of the car, calmly looking him dead in the eye, not moving a muscle. It was the biggest goddamn cat he'd ever seen and Christ, was it ugly! Its glossy fur stuck out like some el cheapo fake fur from a dime store, or some atrocious Halloween fright wig. And, either he was hallucinating, or its eyes were *lopsided*, and something was horribly wrong with the very structure of its skull.

It sat there proudly for a moment, its tail switching grandly from side to side like a well-paced metronome, regarding him with a hard, glassy eye that gave him the creeps. Then its head rolled backward and it emitted a long, vibrating mewl that seemed somehow like a vague, ominous threat. It leaped softly to the ground.

Gene shook his head, thinking what an unusually odd, ugly beast it was—just as ugly as homemade sin. He drove the car to the edge of the parking lot and waited for the traffic to clear. He ripped open the pack of mints and flipped a green one into his mouth, tossing the roll up onto the dashboard.

Out of the corner of his eye rose a blurry black shape in a jumble of movement. He whipped his head around to the side to discover what it was, his heart jumping into a quickened patter.

The big ugly cat, just as bold as you please, had run up alongside the driver's door and was now standing on its hind paws, its front paws resting snugly against the bottom edge of the window. Its leering, mocking face was pressed against the glass, its mouth thrown open so wide he could view the damn thing's tonsils, as well as a set of heart-stoppingly razor-sharp long white fangs. Fangs that would do some huge jungle beast proud. Gene's heart ticked faster as he gaped at them. Its cold blank eyes were slitted dangerously. Its whiskers twitched obscenely, like eager, squiggling insects.

Christ, this was no ordinary alley cat, thought Gene as his heart drummed faster. It was ungodly. An abomination. A cold, slick sweat dribbled down his forehead, lined his upper lip, welling up between the hairs of his mustache. He jerked his head away from the sight, gasping, and took a cursory inspection of the road. No cars were in sight.

After one horrible last view of tonsils and fangs—it was still pressed against the window, birddogging him and scaring the living shit out of him, not about to give up—he pressed on the accelerator, stomping it nearly to the floor. The car barreled out onto the highway, leaving the surprised beast in a cloud of dust, yowling at the outrage, a claw lifted menacingly in the air.

It was an ugly bastard, he thought, waiting for his pumping heart to slow down to a normal rhythm. And strange. And it certainly had an awesome set of molars, he'd testify to that. But, still, he couldn't quite fathom his unsettling, fearful reaction to the animal. Hell, it *was* just an alley cat, he reminded himself. But a part of him didn't buy that, claimed that was a crock of shit.

A part of him whispered that this cat was *different*.

It had sent chittering shivers down his spine. Why, its sheer size was beyond belief: Not just fat, but big-boned, larger than any goddamn pussycat he'd ever seen. A great hulking brute of a feline, with a set of choppers that was pure nightmare material.

But its eyes—oh, its eyes—were truly disturbing. They were the one thing that had really rattled him, the thing that had practically caused him to toss his cookies.

He would never forget those stone-cold, vacant, crooked eyes.

Jesus, he wanted a cigarette, craved one. He'd even give his left nut for a smoke. He pulled up to a red light and seized the glove compartment door, rummaging through it until he found a chocolate candy bar. Then he gobbled it up with a primal, animalistic desperation, thinking what a hateful, totally unsatisfying, sorry substitute sugar was for his beloved nicotine.

Talk about your nicotine fits, jeered a small voice inside. *Nothing like a good dose of fear to get the ole craving revved up, to get you howling and begging for a smoke like a sniveling, weak-willed jellyfish.*

But those *eyes* . . . those Godforsaken unnatural eyes.

Chapter Seven

Edna brooded about Gene all the way home and as she stepped out of the car with her grocery bag, it seemed that the June day had grown brighter somehow, sharper, the sunlight a dazzling promise of things to come.

She crossed the driveway, her heels crunching against the white stones, daydreaming of Gene, with the beautiful hair and eyes. Romantic, mushy Hollywood love scenes played in her mind, complete with camera angles featuring Gene's exotic gray streak, cute dimple, and soft brown chest hair.

But a part of her was wary and on guard, too, because she'd learned the hard way what a sorry lot men were. Edna did allow as how there were a *few* good ones, but they were the rare ones, indeed. Few and far between.

She would not allow herself to behave like a damn fool over Gene, despite his fetching dimple, his sensuous lips, and perfectly tanned face.

Edna walked up the sidewalk toward the house, making a mental note to refill the bird feeder that hung from the pine tree. A plump sparrow and a desperate-eyed cardinal jockeyed for position on the plastic tray, which held only a few seeds.

"Damn critters eat like horses," she muttered. It really was amazing how much food a small bird could consume. Of course they wasted half of it, strewing it across the grass in their eagerness.

She looked up at the house and noticed the white shutters on the kitchen windows needed repainting. They were beginning to look tacky, with tiny ripples of paint starting to crack around the edges. Otherwise, the sight of the neat little red brick rambler, her azalea bushes, and her rock garden filled her with pride. A redwood fence circled the back yard with miniature round hedges spaced exactly six feet apart. When she felt especially industrious, Edna set out a few tomato vines in the back yard and grew green peppers and cucumbers against the back of the house. The ever-present magical, sweet scent of honeysuckle crawling across the back fence enveloped the entire yard with its fragrance.

But not on this particular day, thought Edna, a frown creasing her forehead. Something smelled bad. Stunk to high heaven.

Not just bad. Putrid, a powerful foul stench that caused her nostrils to contract. And an eerie, prescient hush seemed to have fallen over the yard, a surreal quietness. Edna could hear no birds gaily chirping, no sounds of distant traffic. The very atmosphere seemed deadened, thick and tense, as if nothing could penetrate it. And it seemed to her that she could feel the presence of someone, some*thing*, close by. Watching her.

Yet she saw nothing out of the ordinary, save the spooky quietude that had descended. On the surface, it seemed a gorgeous June day, Rockwellian in its picture-perfect appearance. Nevertheless, apprehension overcame her, settling around her swiftly, like a suffocating, dark cloak. Her antenna went up, and she could feel the hairs on the back of her neck bristle as if alerting her to some unknown, grave danger. Her palms grew moist and clammy. Her temples began to thud dully, as she felt a nameless anxiety, an indefinable jittery nervousness. Dear Lord, the sour stink was making her stomach grind and churn with nausea now. She lifted her hand and rubbed her aching temples.

"Where the hell is it coming from?" she whispered into the preternatural quiet. Her thin voice seemed to echo and bounce right back at her.

She sniffed tentatively as she moved slowly along the sidewalk, trying to discern the exact direction the foul stink emanated from. Oh, God, it was unbearable, a ghastly rotted odor like overripe moldy fruit, like fumes drifting from an open grave filled with maggot-ridden corpses. A horrendous, bitter reek, far worse than mere cat turds. Hell, this odor made a whiff of cat turds smell like expensive perfume.

God above, cat turds were *nothing* compared to this abominable, gagging odor, Edna thought, her breath hitching raggedly in her extreme effort not to inhale.

"Good God!" she gasped aloud, pinching her nostrils together tightly with her finger. She peered frantically around to find the source, and noticed something strange on the concrete porch. A dark spot. An irregular shape, somehow ominous.

Nervous sweat slicked Edna's upper lip, like a liquid mustache. She loped the last few steps toward the porch, a dark presentiment of terror filling her, the grocery bag bouncing awkwardly against her hipbone, thumping as she jogged. The quiet of the yard seemed heavy, charged with a cruel menace, as if unseen demons regarded her silently.

"Oh . . . oh, no!" she cried aloud at the sight, her voice a thin mewling whine, her stomach lurching crazily with a sickening nausea. Dark red blood was spilled copiously across the concrete porch, a generous sticky trail leading down one side. It was still wet.

Edna's heart raced, skipping a beat erratically, as she took in the front door. Bloody claw marks were scraped across the white wood. A *cat's* bloody claw marks, she was certain. It looked as if it had deliberately left scratches on the door, almost as if it had left its "signature."

A chill of foreboding rushed through Edna at the idea and she fought off a wave of dizziness that threatened to take her. She put her head in her hands and rubbed her temples until it went away. Then she began to feel silly. Jesus, now she was actually attributing *human* actions to a stray cat—a common, ordinary alley cat. Was she going crazy?

She sighed shakily, running a hand to blot the cold sweat off her forehead. Damp tendrils of hair circled her face. She forced herself to bend to examine the blood on the porch, seeking the origin. She let the small grocery bag and her purse slump to the ground beside her.

The bloody trail weaved off to one side of the porch in an uneven, jagged pattern. Grunting, Edna leaned over the porch railing and peered down, shading her eyes from the bright sun. Beneath the azalea bush, lay a huge rat, totally eviscerated. Its steaming entrails had been cruelly gutted, its intestines spilling out of its mutilated body in a blood-ravaged mass. Its head had been fairly ripped from its body, hanging on by a mere thread of stringy skin, a pulpy desecrated stump where the neck had been, bubbling with blood. The pointed, raw snout of its face lay a good foot away from its head. It had been literally torn from the animal's face by the monstrous, savage thing that had murdered it. It was a massacre. Though Edna loathed rats, this senseless bloody slaughter turned her stomach.

She moaned and felt her gorge rise as bitter acidic bile filled the back of her throat. She stumbled backward to the opposite side of the porch, doubled over the wrought-iron railing, and vomited down onto the grass, painful dry heaves that seemed to go on forever.

Once again, the mangy stray had left her a "present," and she felt a cold, numb fear at the inhumane cruelty of the act.

You are not alone. Something is here. It's here— here with you, close by. The thought hummed dully inside Edna's pounding head as she wiped her mouth with the back of her hand. Suddenly she was gripped with stark terror. She wanted to go inside the house. *Right now.*

She tried to tell herself it was silly, tried to tell herself she was just overreacting and that there was nothing to fear. She was just upset over the gory mess and that was understandable. She swiveled her head around to scan the yard. It was empty. Yet the absurd terror-filled paranoia wouldn't leave her.

Edna wiped a dot of spittle from the side of her mouth and turned around to gather up her grocery bag and purse, her stomach still twisting, making an audible grinding noise. She was going inside, damn it. She was going to follow her intuition.

But she was just a heartbeat too late.

"Mrawrrrrrr!" A high-pitched, ululant squeal rang through the still air, blasting Edna's eardrums painfully with its sheer force, standing her hair on end with the shock.

She whipped around, fear seizing her heart in a deadly vise, squeezing air from her lungs, and her eyes widened.

The black cat stood, poised on top of the iron railing on the opposite side of the porch, like some ancient evil gargoyle to be worshipped by demon slaves. Its hair stood stiffly out from its regal body like huge, lethal needles, its tail proudly erect, its claws extended in bloodthirsty anticipation of mayhem, death, and destruction.

Edna met its slitted button eyes and her heart dropped, a woozy vertigo seized her brain, and the world turned fuzzy at the edges. The yard spun around her in psychedelic, mind-bending circles, threatening to cave in upon her. The outline of the cat seemed to ebb and flow toward her in waves like a funhouse trick mirror as her pulse beat in a thready crazy rhythm.

"Oh, dear God, I—I must be hallucinating . . ." she moaned, her white-knuckled fingers gripping the railing behind her in terror. And she *felt* as if she was hallucinating, as if she was drunk or stoned—or just going insane.

Because it was *James's* eyes looking out at her from the cat's face. Just as sure as God made little green apples. And nothing in this world could make her believe otherwise. Hadn't she stared into those same beady eyes for years and years of marriage? Hadn't she stared into them when he lay dying, sending piercing malevolent daggers of hatred up at her?

Now lopsided, insanely out of kilter, set into the cat's thin skull at diverging points, they shone out at her with that familiar, dark, everlasting hatred, a hatred that death had not conquered. Burning, raging, seething with it.

"Oh, God, *James*! It's really you," she croaked, and shrank back against the railing like a feeble old woman. Its glowing, fierce eyes mesmerized her, held her a captive prisoner with their hypnotic gaze. They seemed to take on a complacent, triumphant gleam as she mouthed the words, calling its name, glorying in the knowledge that she *knew*, knew who it really was.

"Hsssssss!" It threw back its triangular, scruffy black head and moaned unearthly acknowledgment at the pale blue sky, like a wailing banshee. Then it turned to glare at her and dipped its head with a strange, quirky nod that caused her body to shake with a long, endless spasm of terror. It had looked almost human, nodding at her like that, as if to say, "Yeah, old hoss, you're exactly right!"

Edna's breath came in helpless chuffs, little bursts of wind escaping her lips in convulsive half sobs, as she watched it leap lithely to the grass and race off across the yard like a streak of lightning.

James had come back to seek his revenge. And Edna cowered before the thought.

Chapter Eight

Gene pulled into the garage of his three-bedroom townhouse and parked. He leapt out quickly, then grabbed the two plastic grocery bags.

He entered the house and quickly went to the kitchen to put away the groceries. Then he worked on his two remote-control cars. His favorite hobby, he liked taking the cars to the indoor track to race them each week on Friday nights.

He might as well, as the forty-one-year-old Gene sure as hell had no hot dates for Friday nights. He had been divorced for two years. His wife, Diane, had decided an accountant wasn't good enough for her. She was the money-hungry type and had ditched him for her boss, a prominent attorney, bald-headed and twelve years older than she. But he had money coming out of his buttonholes and that was all Diane cared about.

It had taken Gene awhile to get over the hurt of the divorce and he'd only dated two or three women since, never becoming serious, keeping it light. He had no desire to make another mistake; if he married again, he wanted it to last forever.

Keeping relationships light had been easy until now. While it was true he didn't yet know Edna, he had a gut feeling she was a woman he could become serious about.

"Mreeeer!" screeched Sylvia, tiptoeing softly around his feet, looking up at him with sorrowful, pleading eyes.

God, she was an adorable kitten, not a bit like that phenomenally ugly beast that had leered into the car window at him. It gave him the creeps thinking about it, and a weird sense of uneasiness. It wasn't a cat, it was a monster.

He left the cars and went into the kitchen and pulled out the silverware drawer to get a can opener, fumbling around before he found it. He'd never been the organized type and his three-year-old townhouse was often a jumbled mess, with books and remote-control car parts everywhere. But the house was spacious, with contemporary furniture, lots of large green plants, and a beautiful skylight in the kitchen. His favorite feature was a huge wooden deck which extended from the kitchen, running the length of the house, with a hot tub built into it and a long wooden banquette.

"How many women ya screwed in that hot tub yet?" Phil at work had asked him today, punching him in the ribs with an elbow, his eyebrows doing a Groucho-Marx imitation with an exaggerated leer.

"Not a one," he'd answered sourly. "Not even my wife . . . when she was still there." He'd smiled feebly, self-deprecatingly.

Phil had eyed him with wonder, as if he found this difficult to believe. Phil was a real go-getter, spending a lot of time earning notches in his belt with the women, always inviting Gene to go bar-hopping. But he wasn't interested. He'd bar-hopped a little in his younger days and even then he hadn't been crazy about it. The music was too loud, the women too easy, and too many goddam lushes for his liking.

He was too serious, too much of a stay-at-home, Casper-Milquetoast type, not macho enough, Phil had informed him knowledgeably. A hopeless fucking case.

But Gene longed for a solid marriage, sacred vows that really meant something, and a woman who was deeply capable of caring and vitally interested in home and family. He wondered sometimes if that type of woman was a dying breed. All the women he seemed to meet these days were ambitious, career-oriented, and didn't give a damn if they had a husband.

Diane hadn't even set a foot inside the hot tub. She didn't have the time. She was working as a legal secretary during the day and going to school at night to become a paralegal. Hell, she'd hardly been aware they *had* a hot tub, let alone indulge in amorous fantasies with him.

He sighed and wound the can opener around a tin of beef and liver, emptying it into Sylvia's red plastic dish. He gently brushed her aside as she tried her damndest to lick at the food before he could even dump it out of the can. "Hey, hold your horses." he laughed. "Jesus, you must be starved." Sylvia bleated.

Gene turned on the portable radio on the kitchen counter and decided to heat up one of the frozen TV dinners. He was too lazy to cook anything. Besides, he was eager to tinker around some more with his remote-control cars. He needed to get the motor fixed for Friday night. That is, if he couldn't talk Edna into going out on a date with him, he thought wryly, and began to rehearse various dialogues with her in his head, determined not to come off sounding like an obnoxious butthead again.

Chapter Nine

After Gene and Edna left the store, things got dull for Helen, but livened up again when the dude with the raggedy blue jeans and the long earrings came back in.

Normally Helen didn't date guys with dangling earrings. Oh, the small ones were all right, the tiny studs. But no long, dangling ones. That was out. That was a little bit *too* weird and freaky even for Helen.

But for this guy, she'd make an exception, since he seemed so taken with her. He couldn't keep his eyes off her, so it was possible, just possible, she might get him to clean up his act. Well, it was worth a try.

She'd give him a chance because underneath

the outrageous earrings and the torn jeans, and the tattoos, he wasn't bad-looking. Skinny, but muscular. That was what she liked in a man. And he had to be crazy about her. That was the most important quality of all, since anyone who wasn't would never put up with her. Helen was the first to admit she was spoiled rotten and liked having things her own way. If she didn't get it, Helen knew how to throw a tantrum that would put the fear of God into someone and make him or her willing to do Helen's bidding.

The guy wandered around the aisles close to the front of the store, keeping tabs on her as he pretended to shop. He stood staring at the canned vegetables for fifteen minutes, sneaking glimpses of her out of the corner of his eye, and then shuffled to the express line with three cans of green beans for a dollar, fixing her with a riveting, desperately smitten gaze.

"Paper or plastic?" she asked, smoothing back a stray hair from her French twist with her free hand. She chewed her gum a little too fast to keep from snickering at the way he was hemming and hawing like a klutzy kid asking a girl out for the first time.

"Huh?" he said, stuttering with nervousness, and plunked the three cans down on the counter, dropping one on his foot.

Jeez, he's a basket case, she thought, and quelled the urge to hoot with laughter.

"I said, paper or plastic? Do you want paper or plastic?" she repeated slowly, forming the words with a seductive pout. His eyes seemed glazed over with lust as he stared stupidly at her Cupid's bow mouth.

"Uh . . . yeah. Plastic will be fine," he managed to croak. He seized a *TV Guide* and threw it down on the counter beside the beans, his hand quivering.

By the time she'd bagged the beans and magazine, she had him hooked. She scribbled down her phone number across the back of the *TV Guide* before she tossed it in the plastic bag and handed it to him with a big grin, suggesting that he give her a call if the TV shows in the magazine proved boring.

He agreed, his eyes aglitter, shaking his head until the earrings bounced up and down, and gave her a long, slow lazy look full of unconcealed, burning passion.

Helen was glad it had worked out.

At least *something* today had worked out. She was afraid she'd made a mess of fixing Gene up with Edna, who had looked as mad as a wet hen before she'd left the store. It was a shame; Gene seemed so perfect for her, too. Helen did hope he got up the moxie to call Edna.

She leaned her string-bean frame against the metal counter, folded her hands across her chest, and stared out the store window.

Thank Christ that horrible cat had disappeared, she thought, blowing a bubble and cracking it. A big black cat had perched on the small stone ledge outside the store window and had sat there the whole time Edna and Gene were in the store. It then left directly afterwards. As if it were following them, almost. Ugly sucker gave her the creeps. . . .

Chapter Ten

After seeing the cat, Edna couldn't get it out of her mind, haunting visions of its strange eyes rising in her consciousness. She knew that it wouldn't give up, wouldn't go plague someone else, because it was James. James's *soul* within the cat.

Those were James's eyes staring hollowly out at her, flat and cold, filled with an almost palpable loathing, stunning in its intensity. Oh, she realized this was a perverse, crazy idea. A sick, *insane* idea, of course. But it was true.

The brash, sure way the beast had stood there, perched on top of the railing, looking right through her very soul, with an intimate knowledge of every fiber of her being, had shaken her to the core.

Naturally, she couldn't confide in anyone. They'd think she was nuts, off her rocker. She could hear them now, down at the Safeway, "Edna's gone bananas now that she's alone. Can't handle being a widow. Completely lost her marbles. Such a pity." And they'd wag their heads in agreement at how pathetic she was.

She tried to file her nails and couldn't even concentrate enough to do that. She jumped up and raided the refrigerator, ate a piece of hot apple pie with melted cheese across the top, and consumed an entire bag of pizza-flavored tortilla chips. Then she paced the kitchen floor for hours, a bundle of nerves and restless energy, her brain teeming with tumultuous thoughts.

She even tried to pray awhile, finding little comfort, and at last she gave up, took a hot bath, and lay down to sleep. But sleep never came as she tossed and turned, writhing restlessly, like someone pursued by demons. She wound the stiff blue percale sheet round and round her body, twisting her legs up in it, then finally kicking it off the bed. She sat up as scenes of James and their marriage flashed through her brain, over and over, like a VCR's fast-forward button gone awry, showing a phantasmagoria of a lifetime together: birthdays, Christmases, their first anniversary, the happy times and then later times, when their marriage had gone sour.

It had been a misery, having to care for James day and night, and working two jobs, too. Totally worn out, she had turned into a lifeless drudge.

As a cashier, she had stood on her aching,

calloused feet all day long, her arms numb from bagging heavy groceries for hours on end. It had been a boring, mindless job she had held for twenty long, sorry years. Years of heaving grocery bags, punching cash register keys, and watching the bunions on her tired feet grow. She had corns and callouses on top of corns and callouses. Days spent telling people where the endless items they needed were located.

A workhorse drone. That's what she'd been. Just a miserable workhorse.

When she wasn't punching cash register keys at the Safeway, she had worked part-time for a doctors' answering service, most of the time listening to a bunch of hysterical whinebags demanding to speak to their doctors after hours, about some piddly, ridiculous problem that common sense could solve without bothering a doctor.

The patients got their shorts in a knot if she didn't hurry up and get the doctor to call them back quickly, and the doctors got miffed if she disturbed them on the golf course or had to call them in the wee hours. A real no-win situation that had been as frustrating as hell for her.

It had got on her nerves, but not nearly as much as James Wilkins had. He had been a good-for-nothing, no-account failure.

After having moved to Silver Spring, Maryland with his parents when he was in grade school, his father got a job with the Government Printing Office as a printer. They'd come from the hills of Tennessee—just a pack of hillbillies from a little hick town—but his father had been bright and industrious. His mother had been a hard-working beautician.

But James had favored neither. He was lazy. He'd been an only child and after his death, his parents, now retired, had slunk back to the rolling hills of Tennessee to be with the rest of their family.

They'd given him every opportunity, yet he remained lazy and unstable, drifting from job to job. Oh, he'd had grandiose plans when she met him during her last year of high school. At eighteen, she'd been eager to believe all his big talk. She'd eagerly swallowed his bragging lies that he was stashing away the money he earned from selling pianos so that he could go to college to become a big-time, rich lawyer. He was going to set the world on fire, by God.

What a fool she'd been! She now mused as she gazed at the ceiling. She'd swallowed that load of crap hook, line and sinker like a gullible little lovesick fool. The twenty-two-year-old James had turned her head with his sparkling dark brown eyes, jet-black hair, and muscular pretty-boy physique. And he had had eyes only for her.

Then that had counted for a lot with Edna, who had never been cherished, had never had a man smitten with her charms, had never enjoyed the extravagant attentions shown by a man in the throes of infatuation.

After a whirlwind, storybook romance, they had married directly after her graduation from high school. She'd chucked her graduation gown

to don a white silk wedding gown with little respite, anxious to rush headlong into a marriage
that would prove to be hellacious by anyone's
standards.

Her mother had tried to reason with her. Her
father had begged her not to "marry that bum,"
on bended knee, his eyes bright with tears, a
shocking thing to behold. Edna was an only
child, too, and their darling.

But she'd turned a deaf ear to their pleas,
full of a bullheaded doggedness that astounded
them. How could their meek and mild Edna be
so insistent? She had seen the puzzling question in their eyes. For awhile, her father had
raised a ruckus and had delivered long, heated diatribes denouncing "that worthless bum,"
then had thrown in the towel, having run out of
energy. He claimed to see facets of James that she
did not, laughing and pooh-poohing the idea of
him becoming a lawyer. Her mother had thought
James a handsome, clean-looking boy, had said
he had his head in the clouds sometimes, and
had a bad temper at times, but she refused to
be too picayune on the subject, declaring that
only Edna knew him best. When she got wind
of the marriage, however, she had delivered a
few stern monologues about how James wasn't
really good enough for Edna, and had remarked
caustically on the microscopic-sized diamond
solitaire James had bestowed on her. He was
stingy, her mother had correctly prophesied.

But Edna hadn't listened; she idolized James
Wilkins, and that was all there was to it. She had

been a hard-headed little idiot. So her parents had given up, and paid for a medium-sized wedding. Her father, an electrician, and her mother, a teacher's aide in a nursing school, had thrown themselves into their work to appease their skittish doubts about the marriage.

For a brief period in their marriage, James had lavished her with the attention she so desperately needed to bolster her flagging self-esteem. A fat, pimply teenager, shy and bookish, she had totally lacked self-confidence.

Two weeks after the wedding her parents died in a fatal car crash, leaving Edna devastated and bereft with a terrible, black grief, worsened by the fact that they'd begged her not to marry him.

James had babied her, spoiled her, comforted her for a few months, until he had grown bored and tired of being a nurturing, caring person and reverted to his normal, self-centered state. James had always been totally wrapped up in himself— a taker, not a giver—and the more Edna gave, the more he demanded. He had rapidly deteriorated from a glorious knight in shining armor to a beer-chugging, gluttonous used-car salesman, having been fired from the music store for pure laziness. He had spent more time flirting with the women passing through the mall than working a sales pitch to interested piano buyers. All his fancy pipe dreams of lawyering were neatly disposed of in one fell swoop. He had begged off going to college entirely, whining that he just wasn't the "bookish" type. He'd squandered the money he'd tucked away for college on a bunch of fishing equipment, a tent, and camping gear.

Not bookish. Oh good Lord, wasn't *that* the understatement of the century! Edna thought as she pulled the sheet closer to her.

The only reading James Wilkins had ever done was to peruse the *TV Guide*, his thick, hairy finger carefully following the words on the page like a first-grader who'd just learned the alphabet. Night after endless night, he would sit before the twenty-five-inch TV, the true love of his life, his pupils wide and spacey like a shell-shocked war veteran, his T-shirt thrown on the floor, revealing a fish-belly white, basketball-shaped abdomen that was not a pretty sight. It had reminded her of a flabby, soft pile of dough that desperately needed to be molded and reworked.

The muscular physique he'd been blessed with in high school had quickly deteriorated into sagging flab. For hours on end, he'd sit in the green reclining chair, a human vegetable lost in a zombie-like trance, his coarse, chunky hand rhythmically dipping into giant bags of potato chips, tortilla chips, chocolate-marshmallow cakes, and swilling down beer by the truckload. The only sounds that passed his lips were occasional raucous bellows for food, food, and more food.

Or beer, which he guzzled down in nothing flat, belching like some vulgar redneck, emitting great booming gusts of air so deep and loud at times that the vibrations had rattled the window frames. And if he wasn't belching, he was farting, letting loose a loud, rumbling rotten-egg odor which had permeated half of their small house, causing Edna to flee, seeking safer ground.

The man had been a cretin, an ill-mannered disgusting *animal*.

The beer-chugging had sickened her. If there was anything she couldn't abide, it was the smell of beer. It reminded her of rank, soured urine.

She also couldn't forget how all the loving affection that James had so generously bestowed on her at first dissolved rapidly into bouts of scolding, cursing and belittling her at every opportunity, undermining her self-esteem. If she dusted the wrong way or made the beds improperly, he would chastise her with long, frantic lectures, calling her names, heaping verbal abuse—and sometimes physical abuse—on her, citing a long litany of offenses.

"Stupid twit" had been one of his favorite pet names for her.

She could hear him even now ranting, "You're a stupid twit, Edna, and you always will be." Then he would chuckle, finding humor in it, like the true misogynist he had been.

Shifting in the bed, she remembered all the times she had thought of leaving him and would be on the verge of doing it, when he would suddenly become contrite, begging her to stay and vowing to change. The periods of verbal abuse would be carefully, cleverly interspersed with bouts of heart-rending affection and maudlin sentimentality.

Just enough to make her feel she should give

the marriage another try, just enough to keep her foolishly hoping.

Then, when Edna had finally mustered enough courage to leave him, James had cleverly managed to have a heart attack, just for spite, filling her with guilt.

Through the years, he'd gained weight from his sedentary lifestyle. He had adored anything fried, anything dripping buckets of grease. He had eschewed exercise devoutly, and had gained a whopping sixty-five pounds since they'd married, turning into a real butterball.

He had liked to smoke, too, to add insult to injury. He managed to smoke an entire pack each night. And he went through another pack at work, sitting behind his desk, or walking through the car lot, huffing and puffing like a steam engine. He had been a pigheaded fool about it— a stubborn bulldog—wouldn't even do so much as switch to a lower nicotine brand even when Edna had begged him to. He had been so hell bent on having his high-nicotine cancer sticks that sometimes Edna had thought the man had a death wish.

At last, to no one's surprise, least of all to hers, James had had the coronary he'd been begging for. And even then he'd been a damn fool, a hardheaded bull of a man who paid no heed to the doctor's stern words of advice to change his lifestyle.

But by then she hadn't given a damn. If he was determined to kill himself off, let him.

Oh, sure, at first she'd fussed a bit with him,

like a good wife, trying in vain to get him to see the light, but it had been like beating her head against a stone wall. Though he would not change his lifestyle, James had been frightened witless of having another heart attack—which made no sense at all.

Soon Edna had grown to despise him. She would bite her lip to keep from telling him off during his endless complaints. Lashing out at him would only make matters worse. It would only unleash a stream of name-calling and abuse from him and a karate chop to the chin.

So Edna had bitten the bullet and had kept her mouth shut, but it had cost her an immense amount of stress and effort that took its toll on her, leaving her worn out and constantly exhausted. Fatigued and depressed all the time, she had lost weight, and had dark circles beneath her eyes.

She thought of the phone call from Andy, James's boss at Andy's Used Cars. He had been very solicitous, telling James to take his time recovering. And so he had.

Then later, when James had said he felt like he could work—at least part-time, *maybe*—he had called his boss, asking if he could return to work. Andy had hemmed and hawed and finally, in a shamefaced, sheepish tone, admitted he'd hired someone else in the interim. He'd recommended that James call the Chevy dealer who was looking to hire.

But he hadn't sounded sorry at all, James had claimed. Andy had insinuated that James was not a shaker-and-mover-type guy, that James was dead wood, with not enough sales ability to sell a halo to an angel. The Chevy dealer had already hired a young man when James called them and he had begun to brood day and night over what Al had said about movers and shakers.

It threw him into a blue funk. He grew despicably fussy and picky. She couldn't do one single thing to satisfy him. Overnight he'd turned into a whining, malingering, *professional* invalid, pathetically attached to his "sick bed," bawling at her at the top of his lungs to wait on him like some hired maid.

God help her, she had had more than enough on her hands. And God help her, there were some days when she had wished him dead and had thoroughly longed for it.

Her fists clenched the sheet as the old anger raged inside her. She had become sick and tired of working like a dog, then rushing home to pamper and coddle him like a spoiled baby, never having five minutes to herself. It had almost killed her. Hell, she had even begun to wish *she* were dead, too. Damnit, at least she'd get a little rest then!

The thing that had finally driven her wild was when Dr. McNamara informed James that he was perfectly able to resume normal activities. Perfectly able to do for himself—perfectly able to work forty hours a week.

Perfectly able to haul his enormous fat ass up off the flowered sofa and look for a job, Edna thought as she seethed with the memory.

Perfectly able to earn a living, like the rest of the world.

Yet he had lain there like a beached whale, indulging himself, with the *TV Guide* as his Bible. (He'd completely memorized the times and stations of most shows.) He'd speak tearfully to her in a quaking, pitiful voice, when he wasn't bawling "Ednaaaa" by the hour, of how much he feared another heart attack, feared bringing another one on by going back to work prematurely.

Edna had felt her own blood pressure rise during those monologues, her head filling with a boiling, churning rage.

One night, they'd had a horrendous, knock-down, drag-out fight. By far, the worst fight of their married life. But James had won, hands down, as he always did. He'd ended the fight, dramatically shedding copious, morose crocodile tears, a beefy hand laid over his poor ailing heart. He'd said in that mock-timid, simpering voice that his chest felt so constricted, insinuating another attack might be forthcoming should she continue to rant and rave like a bitchy harridan.

Oh, but those fake crocodile tears of his hadn't fooled her for a minute! James had been a malingerer at heart, lazy as a skid-row bum, enjoying how she had slaved away to support them, getting a real kick out of her playing nursemaid to him after knocking herself out at two jobs.

Though she had said nothing, throwing up her hands in defeat, she had decided to make the best of a bad situation. Then, when he got better, she had silently vowed, she would divorce him.

As she sat up in bed, propping the pillows behind her, she pictured James and how he had grown fatter and lazier, a foul-tempered, whining old curmudgeon. Impossible to please. Impossible to live with.

She longed to leave him, yet a part of her recalled the time he'd threatened to kill her if she ever did. And James did not make idle threats. Then thoughts of leaving him turned to thoughts of a murderous revenge. Actual visions of killing him danced in her head, much to her horror.

She wanted to make him suffer, like she had, and that urge had become an uncontrollable obsession, usurping all her thoughts.

Edna twitched uncomfortably and adjusted the pillows behind her as she thought of the campaign she'd waged against James.

He was slowly killing himself, anyway, so she had decided to help him along, to help him obtain everything that was bad for him—just as he wanted. Like a good little wifey, humble and obsequious.

Everything the good doctor had said *not* to do, Edna did. To James's immense delight, she became a grinning, sycophantic servant, bowing and scraping, cosseting him like an adored child, the child she'd never been able to have due to her infertility.

When he had whined for fried chicken constantly, she had always bitterly argued with him that it was bad for him. Now she calmly ordered from Kentucky Fried Chicken, twice a week, with a grin on her face.

She had diligently prepared every grease-packed recipe she could conjure up. She made deviled eggs, a favorite treat, with enough cholesterol to choke a horse, and added eggs to foods that did not need eggs, chucking the fake-egg substitute into the trash can. If James wanted cholesterol, he'd *have* it up the wazoo.

And she had hoped to hell it would kill him. As fast as possible.

She had encouraged his other appetites as well. She'd hired the services of a dim-witted, bovine young girl named Nadine.

Nadine, a robust voluptuous creature, had exuded a raw sexuality. She stayed with James during the day, preparing his meals, trotting beers and chocolate marshmallow cakes to the living room, like an obedient puppy dog, and mollycoddling him to an unbelievable degree.

But serving food had been the least of her duties. The main reason Edna had hired her was because everyone knew Nadine was a tramp; her fame was widespread. A rather simple-minded young woman, she couldn't say no to a man. *Any* man.

Edna swung her legs off the bed and headed to the kitchen. Thoughts of Nadine had made her thirsty and she needed a glass of water. As she sat at the table, her mind returned to her instructing Nadine to "amuse" James in any manner that James wished. That is, if Nadine wanted to. At first, she had meekly protested that James was Edna's husband. But after Edna had assured her it didn't matter as long as James was happy, Nadine had agreed.

Edna had often wondered if Nadine actually found James attractive. Who knew? Perhaps the oversexed creature had a thing for basketball bellies.

Nadine had done exactly as requested. Edna now recalled that soon after that James started wearing a silly,vapid grin that seemed to stay with him, lingering, sinking permanently into his thick, coarse features. And she could tell by the way James's eyes always followed the generous curve of Nadine's bosom, the intent way he studied her backside, his dark brown eyes hungry with lust.

And oh, how Edna had burned with a bright, fierce hatred as she watched him. He'd never, ever, no—not even once—gazed at *her* with such a frantic, all-consuming passion. Not even on their wedding night.

Finally, James had become insatiable for Nadine. He began to invent excuses to send Edna out, the few times she was at home, on useless fool's errands, so he could be alone with Nadine, his love.

Simple-minded Nadine, with her pendulous, cow-like breasts that hung nearly to her waist, and her rich wavy long reddish-gold hair that shone like a coppery new penny. Nadine, with her impossibly small waist and big, womanly hips, like a lusty *Playboy* centerfold, but more voluptuous.

Oh, how *her* James had lusted after the simple creature!

Edna grimaced, remembering how truly sickening it had been to watch.

For years he'd romanced other women on the sly, thinking she hadn't known. For three long, hard years he'd allowed her to support them, working her fingers to the bone while he had played at being an invalid. For a year he'd been sleeping with Nadine and Edna had begun to toy with the idea of deliberately catching James red-handed with Nadine. *In flagrante delicto*. She had hoped to hell it would scare him into another heart attack. It would serve the wretched sleazeball right.

Even now, she had to admit it had been a wicked, sinful idea. And she had felt like the scum of the earth for taking joy in it but she had been unable to get it out of her mind. She had tried with all her might to put the sordid thought to rest, but there was plenty of free time for daydreaming while she punched cash register keys and asked folks if they wanted paper or plastic. Unbidden, the terrible thought would come soaring back into Edna's mind, like a hellish homing pigeon, mental images forming in her subconscious, against her will. She had been sure that God would let her rot in hell forever for it, yet the thought would return to the subterranean depths of her mind, like a stubborn, cancerous growth.

She could picture actually walking in on them as they were copulating, standing there gazing at them in bed, filled with fiery rage. She could imagine hurling obscenities, threatening them, acting out the part of the outraged wife with gusto.

And supposing, just supposing, she got James's gun down from the closet? Flashed it around a little, scared the bejesus out of them, pretended she meant to shoot them.

After all the years he'd spent womanizing, going after anything that wore pantyhose, he deserved to die in the arms of another woman. It would be the perfectly righteous, just way for him to kick the bucket, she had thought.

But the part about the gun had been just an idle daydream. She would never have gone that far.

Edna sipped at the water and her eyes flickered to the calendar on the wall near the table. She shut her eyes as she envisioned that ominous day which had changed her life. She came unexpectedly from the Safeway. She had peeked through a small slit in the bedroom door for a second before throwing it wide open, and viewing the sordid scene. Nadine, clad only in a gold ankle bracelet, her huge breasts jouncing and bobbing, sat astride her beloved husband, her rich coppery-red head thrown back like a wanton hussy, while the bed creaked rhythmically like a broken stair in a haunted house.

Edna had fallen back against the wall, white-faced and faint, as her hands trembled.

The sight had affected her far more than she'd ever dreamed it would. She had felt bitter waves of disgust rise within her as she glimpsed

103

James—florid-faced, drenched with a slick love sweat, groaning with ecstasy, murmuring sweet nothings to Nadine in a revolting, babyish cooing tone of voice. His despicable face radiated pleasure; his corpulent body was damp with perspiration. He was naked except for a pair of nasty tube socks with a hole in one toe. Even from the doorway, Edna had smelled that ghastly sweaty-foot smell, mixed with the scent of their lovemaking.

She had thought she would vomit.

Unable to bear listening to their animal-like grunts as they rutted, Edna's hands had covered her ears to shut out the hateful, treacherous sound.

Not once had he whispered sweet nothings to *her*. Not once in their endless, stifling marriage. Edna had felt hot tears stinging her eyes and her throat felt scratchy dry. Her heart had begun to beat like a pounding hammer, letting out a dull achy throb. God, the irony of it, should *she* wind up having the damn heart attack!

Fueled with adrenaline from her fury, she had flung the bedroom door open, sending it crashing against the mauve-colored wall with a loud thunk that had caused both of the culprits to suck in their breath with shock.

Edna's eyes had become a cold, flinty steel. Never had she dreamed she would be seized by such overwhelming, gut-wrenching rage, a compulsion to take some terrible revenge.

"Ha!" she had shouted, fighting against a well of tears that threatened to flood her eyes.

"H–how could you do this? In our own house?"
she had screamed, her eyes bulging wildly, her
chin atremble, quivering with the need to burst
out crying.

Forgotten was the memory of having set it up
herself, in her own house, of urging Nadine to
do the dirty deed. Nothing mattered anymore,
except the devastating sight before her. Her husband lying there beneath another woman, a hulking sweaty mass, his hair standing out from his
head like a plucked chicken, his eyes big round
o's of terror, a trail of Nadine's whorish scarlet
lipstick down his throat, across his chest.

"Edna" was all he had croaked, trying to raise
up on his elbows beneath the burden of Nadine's
lush figure. The mauve-and-gray comforter had
slipped off the corner of the bed into a heap
on the floor, leaving them with nothing at all
to cringe behind.

And the stupid bovine creature had still sat
astraddle him, fool that she was, gazing dully
from one to the other, as if trying to figure
out what the fuss was all about. The ends
of Nadine's coppery hair had hung in damp
tendrils down her back and her smooth ivory
throat had sported a fresh red hickey, courtesy
of Edna's beloved husband. She could recognize
a James hickey, even though it had been years
since she, herself, had worn one! It looked like a
small red tarantula crawling up her throat, Edna
had thought, staring stupidly at it. That thought
had lingered in her memory long afterward, for
some dumb reason. The red tarantula hickey and

James's ridiculously filthy holey tube socks.

"I–I oughta *shoot* you!" Edna had yelled at him in a raspy, gravelly voice, the sound of her own heartbeat drumming in her ears.

"N–no, no, Edna . . . don't! Just calm yourself down now . . ." he had stuttered while his eyes grew to twice their size, huge pinwheels of fear. He had put a hand to Nadine's arm in an attempt to push her aside. She had stared dumbly at Edna, her mouth agape, a string of drool sliding from her lower lip, her mouth swollen and puffy from James's passionate kisses.

Edna had called him all kinds of a son of a bitch then, hardly knowing what she said, just spitting out a stream of vicious epithets in her rage. She had paused briefly then to howl at Nadine through gritted teeth: "You get off my *husband* right now!" Edna's head had lowered, her shoulders hunched ominously, like a rabid bulldog about to lunge forward.

"Oh . . . oh dear . . ." Nadine had whimpered softly. She gulped down feeble sobs, leaped off James's huge supine body at last, and ran clumsily out of the bedroom. She snatched her dress and undies on the way, as tears gushed down her bland face, and her great breasts bobbed furiously, her auburn curls in spirals of disarray.

Edna had continued her heated filibuster, jabbing a finger viciously into the air as she screamed. She had said every bad thing she could think of. She had threatened to shoot his wayward pecker right off—blow it to smithereens—a fitting end for the adulterous, worthless

Don Juan. She had ranted and raved like a shrew, working up a sweat as she raged, holding nothing back, all the years of suffering bubbling up inside her like a hot, roiling liquid from a steaming cauldron of negativity.

She had watched as James's face turned a deep violet-red, his chest heaving like a wounded bird beginning to hyperventilate.

"I'm going to shoot you, James Wilkins. I'm going to!" she had hollered, and actually turned toward the bedroom door as if to fetch the gun. It was an empty threat; she hadn't meant a word of it. What she had wanted to do and fully had intended to do was go into the other room, where he couldn't hear her, and cry her heart out.

But Edna had never made it out of the room.

She had turned her head back for a moment and had seen James's face turning a pallid, cheesy-grayish color as he gasped for breath, staring at her with his eyes bugging out, sweat dripping off his forehead. He grasped the sheet beneath him with one hand, twisting it uselessly, and let out a low agonized moan.

Her mouth had dropped open in pure astonishment and her own heart had begun to pump faster, beating as if it wanted to burst against her rib cage in an explosion of sorrow.

It had only been a game, a daydream of hers, to pass the time at the Safeway. She hadn't really meant it, hadn't really hoped it would happen. But now it was.

James was dying. Really dying!

She had stood frozen and watched in horror,

regretting with all her heart, wishing more than anything that she could take it back.

Gasping for air, James had clutched his heart with a weak, trembling hand, his face an inhuman color, his brown eyes fixed pleadingly on hers, beseeching her to help him.

Edna had stood, rooted to the spot, her feet like clumps of concrete, bitterly remembering how she'd sacrificed her whole life for him, how she'd slaved away as the years stole her youth. She had recalled all the tramps and whores he'd chased and slept with before Nadine. Dozens of them! A tiny part of her had *wanted* it to happen—served him right!—and she could not force herself to go to the princess phone beside the bed to call for help.

His brown eyes, horrified and staring, bulging from their lifeless sockets, had glared up at her as comprehension flooded his last moments.

"Ed—Ednaaaa, help me . . . *pleeeeese*" was his dying croak, a thin trail of spittle running down his chin.

She had jumped as if lightning had struck her and had grabbed the telephone then to dial 911, as if awakening from a trance. This was James. Her *husband*.

She'd endured abusive treatment, years and years of it, but he hadn't deserved to *die* for it. She had then decided to make the call that would save his life, and to let bygones be bygones.

But it had been too late. Before the ambulance arrived he had died at the age of forty-four. And he'd seen the flat, cold hatred in her eyes, minutes before, when she'd been riveted to the spot, just gaping down at him lying atop the damp twisted sheet, his cotton boxer shorts entwined around one thick ankle, his toe peeking through his sock.

He had known somehow; he'd realized that Edna had wanted him to die.

She had got the strange feeling that he had even realized she had set him up with Nadine, egged Nadine on, planned for it, hoped for it.

And now as she sat at the table the knowledge gnawed at her. She couldn't get it out of her mind. The constant feeling of guilt stayed with her and she blamed herself for his death. She had actually stood and *watched* a man die, stood there like a fucking fool! And that man was her own husband. Oh, surely she had earned herself a special corner in hell, Satan's righthand woman.

Even though six months had passed, she still couldn't forgive herself, she thought as she got up from the table and headed for the bedroom. Getting into bed, she hoped now that she would finally fall asleep. But she lay praying for sleep to come, replaying the awful scenes of James's death in morbid obsessed fascination, wishing she could change what she'd done, harshly berating herself, wallowing in self-recrimination and guilt. Then she began to think of the alley cat, thinking what an odd beast it was.

Finally she did sleep and dreamed fitfully of James and the cat. Then she awoke, trying to still her furiously beating heart. All she could remember of one of her dreams was the alley cat prancing around, circling her house dressed in, of all things, the very tube socks James had died wearing. The creature had strutted, sometimes doing the Michael Jackson moonwalk or a hokey soft-shoe number. Its sharp claw had poked right through the hole in the toe of one sock and its feet had a bad odor, just like James's had had. Only worse. A helluva lot worse.

She remembered now as her mind focused more clearly on the dream that it wasn't just a sweaty odor that emanated from the cat's feet. Nothing as simple as that. The odor had been of stinking, molded corpses, coffins filled with slime and squirming maggots. The odor of death itself.

Edna trembled, knowing she would get no more sleep tonight.

Chapter Eleven

"Helen, I could nail you to a wall," Edna hissed through gritted teeth. She clutched the telephone tightly, still filled with fury from the previous day. "You embarrassed me to death in front of that man. My God, he'll think I'm desperate for a date." Edna grabbed the straw broom from behind the refrigerator and swept it across the kitchen floor in a lackadaisical manner as she talked, collecting dust and bird feathers.

"Hah! Oh, Edna, don't be a silly goose!" Helen let out a shrill bark of laughter like a braying donkey. "Why, anyone could tell he was just dyin' to meet you. He was practically droolin' over you, for cryin' out loud. Gawd, you should have seen the looks he gave you when he was standin' in line behind you. Really checkin' out your figure,

Ed. Just about made me blush . . . and ya know it takes a lot to do that. Just thought I'd help things along a bit, that's all. Save time. You're not gettin' any younger, Edna," she teased, and let out a few crass heehaws.

Never mind that Helen was forty-seven and had never married! Edna thought, wincing as Helen popped her gum directly into the receiver. Edna stuck the broom back behind the fridge, and then sat at the breakfast nook on an old cracked vinyl stool.

"Besides, he's a great guy," Helen continued. "Really. Gene Martin comes in all the time. Doesn't fancy me at all, or I'd be out to catch him. But you! I could tell right off he had the hots for you real bad, Edna—" Helen broke off here to emit a brief spasm of whinnying laughter punctuated by small snorts.

Just like a damned donkey, thought Edna, irritated by the sound. She held the phone away from her ear for the duration of Helen's laughing.

"Your phone number," Helen was saying when Edna put the receiver back to her ear.

"What did you say?"

"I said, I hope you don't mind, but I gave him your phone number."

Edna clamped her mouth shut and silently counted to ten as her blood pressure climbed. She grabbed a pencil from the cup on the formica counter and doodled, "God, please don't let me cuss her out" on a tablet three times, willing herself to calm down. She did not want Gene Martin to have her phone number. He was good-looking, but so what? It had only been a moment's infatuation. He would probably turn out to be a package of trouble, like most men. Or like James, she feared.

"Thought ya wouldn't mind. Sheesh, from the way you acted, I coulda sworn you had the hots for him, too. It looked mutual, Edna . . ." Helen paused, sensing something was wrong. "Hey . . . you there, Edna? Say, you're not *mad* at me, are ya?" she asked in an incredulous tone, as if such a thing were inconceivable.

Not mad, thought Edna, biting her tongue to keep it from giving Helen the lashing she so well deserved, *fucking furious*.

Edna usually resorted to saying fuck only when she was hopping mad. Other people might use the f-word in a cavalier, casual fashion, but not Edna Wilkins, who attended church at least once a month and hated movies that had more than a tiny smattering of foul language. Fuck was for special occasions.

"Dear God, Helen what will he think of me?" shouted Edna, snapping the pencil in two, wishing it was Helen's skinny neck instead. She flapped her arms wildly and stood up to pace the kitchen. She just hated it that Helen had foisted her phone number off on this man. It was probably all *Helen's* idea; he was probably just doing her a favor.

Helen was hellbent on getting her a love life.

"He'll think you like him, that's what," Helen promptly answered with an annoying insouciance. "And you do, doncha?"

The gum crackled loudly against Edna's ear and she jerked at the raspy, brittle sound.

"Stop doing that! Could you just stop chewing that damn gum like that? You've no idea what that sounds like over the telephone, Helen. Now what exactly did you tell him? Good God, I hope he doesn't think I put you up to it, like some sneaky conniving witch . . ." She stopped pacing and slumped back onto the yellow vinyl stool, tapping a salt shaker fitfully against the counter.

"Oh, hell no!" Helen's high, reedy voice turned haughty and wounded. "He doesn't think *that*."

"Tell me everything he said. Everything you said, too. Every single word." Edna rose and pried open a small bottle of aspirin standing beside the sink as Helen prattled on. That damn gum-chewing was giving her a splitting headache. She sounded like a damn cow chewing its cud. And the stress of what Helen had done, giving her phone number without even *consulting* her, her crazy embarrassing shenanigans . . . And, above all, the *cat*!

It was too much for her. Excedrin headache # 413.

"Well, he was just askin' me if you shopped at the Safeway regularly, and I said yeah. And he said I seemed to be right good friends with you and I said yeah, you used to work here with me. His face lit up like a damn Christmas tree then. Gawd, don't you think he has the cutest dimple? He said he sure hoped he'd run into you

114

again . . ." Helen paused to clear her throat and went on, a note of pride in her voice.

"So I said, why hope when you can just call her? And I jotted your phone number down right on the side of his grocery bag. Paper one, natch, not the plastic." She snorted, a short staccato grating sound. "I mean . . . it's not like he's a total stranger, Edna. Hell, he's been comin' into the store for ages. We talk all the time. He's an accountant for Beckwith & Sons, up the street from the Safeway in that big tan building in back of the Radio Shack. Divorced. Likes movies and them little racing cars. Y'all sound real compatible, if you ask me. He likes to read, too. You *know* you adore the movies, Edna—and he even likes to cook, if you can believe it! Oh, you could do a lot worse, Edna, mark my words. Men like him don't come along everyday, you know. Most of the rascals won't step inside a kitchen."

During this recitation, Edna finally managed to uncork the aspirin bottle and swill two tablets down with a glass of cold water.

"Claims he's a real stay-at-home, 'cept for the movies and eatin' out occasionally. And you *know* what an old homebody you are, Edna. Hell, sometimes I believe you're half hermit, the way you like to sit at home. I tell ya, you two might be real soul mates." Helen sighed wistfully.

Helen was giving a real sales pitch. Edna figured she must think a lot of the guy, and knew him better than she let on.

"Well, it doesn't sound too bad the way you put it," Edna admitted grudgingly, somewhat loath to let Helen off the hook too easily. She'd had no business giving her phone number out, regardless of the circumstances. "But what will I say when he calls? Will you just tell me that? Jeez, I don't even *know* the man . . . and you know how I clam up around men I don't know . . ."

She cracked open the refrigerator door and rummaged around inside, inspecting the vegetable bin, taking a look in the freezer, and wound up retrieving a day-old deviled egg out of a red plastic cereal bowl.

"Oh, Edna, for gosh sakes, you'll think of somethin', won't ya?" asked Helen.

Helen had probably never had an attack of shyness in her whole life, Edna thought as she closed the refrigator door. Helen couldn't even imagine the untold agonies an introvert suffered when meeting someone new.

"My mind is a blank when I talk to men I don't know. Dumb, isn't it?"

"Well, tell him you like cats, there's a good subject. He has one."

Edna's deviled egg landed with an abrupt splat on the linoleum floor. That did it. They sure as *hell* weren't soul mates.

Chapter Twelve

Still wondering what to do with the rat, Edna was in the kitchen that evening, rummaging through the pantry for the floor cleaner to scrub the bloodstained front porch, when the phone rang, cutting through the quiet of the house with its shrillness.

"Hello?" Her voice sounded awkward and shy to her own ears and when she realized it was Gene, she had an insane urge to ask his advice on the matter of the rat.

But, of course, it wouldn't do to ask him the proper method to dispose of a rat's corpse as an opener. He'd be appalled and, besides, she'd have to explain how it had gotten in her yard to begin with, and then he'd think she was crazy if she told him about the alley cat. It sounded too weird.

Just for an instant, she had the lunatic idea that maybe his cat was the same mangy stray who'd been pestering her. Helen said he lived only five minutes from her house. It was a nutty idea. Nevertheless, she felt compelled to at least inquire what color his cat was, pushed on by an urgent curiosity.

"An orange-and-white calico kitten. She's just a baby, really," he said.

It was obvious how much he loved the cat, and Edna let out an audible sigh of relief. At least it wasn't the stray. And who knew? Maybe she could grow to love his cat if they started dating regularly. She could force herself.

After they'd discussed inane subjects like the weather for a while, Gene got down to the nitty-gritty of the call.

"Uh . . . Helen told me you're a real movie buff, Edna . . ." he began, his deep voice turning timid and a little shaky.

His flustered attitude gladdened Edna's heart immensely. Evidently, he really wasn't quite the suave Romeo-type she'd imagined, all swaggering bravado, oozing self-confidence. A womanizer was not to be trusted, Edna had learned.

"Y–yes," she gulped after a pregnant pause. "Yes, I am." She grabbed hold of the floor cleaner from in back of a big box of laundry detergent and set it on the counter beside the toaster, closing the pantry door.

"Well, there's a good one playing at North Hampton Plaza," he said, his trembling voice gaining courage. "I was gonna go see it Friday.

Sure hate to go alone . . ." He drifted off, leaving the open invitation hanging in mid-air, trying to get a handle on her reaction, she guessed.

She was scared. In fact, she couldn't even speak over the dry lump that had suddenly formed in her throat. It had been twenty-two years since a man, other than James, had asked her for a date. She slumped down onto a stool beside the phone and propped her elbow up on the breakfast counter, shell-shocked. She couldn't speak.

Gene evidently took her silence as playing hard to get, and began to deliver a moving sales pitch.

"It's supposed to be a good movie. *Pretty Woman*. A real good love story," he said, pleading his case, adding the last part as though the fact that it was a love story would intrigue her, compel her to say yes.

Edna remained speechless, her mind in turmoil. She flipped a pen from the cup on the table and chewed the end of it, wondering if she dared say yes. She was frightened, scared shitless. She didn't know *how* to go on a date. She had been out of practice for too long.

Gene took a deep breath and pressed on indefatigably. "Will you come with me, Edna?"

Edna gave a scratchy swallow and emitted a sound vaguely like a snake's hiss, which was meant to be translated as a yes.

"Edna? Richard Gere is in it," he tossed out in desperation, calling upon Richard Gere's incorrigible sex-symbol status as a last-ditch effort to persuade her. His voice sounded forlorn and unhappy.

He was practically begging her, she realized with amazement. Edna grinned, tapping the pen against the formica counter, making a rat-a-tat-tat noise. Obviously, he wasn't just asking her out to pass the time. He actually sounded as if it really mattered to him.

"Well . . ." she paused after clearing her throat. "I *do* like Richard Gere."

Gene burst out with a shaky baritone chuckle of victory.

"How about I meet you there? At the uh . . . theater?" she suggested, feeling a little foolish and hopelessly old-fashioned. Oh, she knew how dumb it sounded, with definite prudish overtones, but she didn't want him coming to her house to pick her up. Not the first time, anyway.

After all, you couldn't be too careful these days. She didn't know him from Adam, even though he sounded very nice. Why, he could be the Boston Strangler or anyone. Just because he'd yakked with Helen a bit or a *lot*—she knew where he lived!—what difference did that make? He could still be a murderer. She worried briefly that he'd take grave offense at her suggestion, but apparently he'd heard this tune before.

"Okay. Great!" he said immediately, brimming with enthusiasm, sounding as if he'd just won the lottery.

She felt a sudden rush of warmth, surprised to discover how much she wanted to see him again, surprised at how glad she felt over his obvious enthusiasm.

Don't act like a fool, Edna, cautioned the pessimistic part of her mind, determined to add its two cents' worth. *He probably just wants to fool around, that's all. Maybe he's just dying to get laid, and you're mistaking that for genuine caring.*

But she didn't really believe that, for his voice had the unmistakable ring of sincerity to it, a shining hopefulness, a boyish excitement.

Edna broke open a cellophane package of almond cookies on the counter and ate two as they decided to go to the 7:30 show on Friday night.

"Okay. I'm looking forward to it," said Edna, thinking what a ridiculous understatement that was. She picked an imaginary lintball off the front of her blue housedress and ate another cookie, dribbling almonds across the countertop.

"Me, too," he said. "Uh, Edna, listen, I just want to apologize for the way I acted in the grocery store. That's not me; it was totally out of character. I'm not some silver-tongued, glib fellow, out to get all the women he meets. I just wanted to tell you I'm sorry. I knew you were embarrassed."

"I—it's okay. Forget it," she answered. She had already suspected as much, particularly after this call. The man was a nervous wreck, stumbling for words and stuttering, full of a boyish awkwardness that spoke for itself.

As they hung up, he whispered confidentially, "Thank God for Richard Gere!" and they both cracked up, laughing like a couple of teenagers.

Edna felt absurdly touched at how important the date seemed to him. How important *she* seemed. It had been a very, very long time since she'd felt important to anyone. A very, very long time since a man had wanted her company, had found her amusing and fun to be with and attractive.

"A date," she rolled the unfamiliar, alien word around in her mouth. "I have an honest-to-goodness, real live date!" she said, a pleased grin plastered across her face.

She folded the cellophane package of cookies securely and skipped through to the living room. She did a short violent shimmy—reminiscent of a belly-dancing class she'd once taken—and collapsed on the green recliner, hugging herself with her arms, while Petey chirped in distress, overexcited by her uncharacteristic jubilance.

"I have a *date*, Pete!" she shouted to him. "First date in twenty-two years!"

Morton didn't count, she added to herself.

It just went to show that there *was* life after James. And Edna intended to explore it—even if it did scare the hell out of her.

Chapter Thirteen

Gene hung up the phone and scooped Sylvia off the living-room rug, holding her close as he twirled around the room as if she were his dancing partner.

"She likes me! She likes meeeee!" he sang, and the kitten mewled softly, blinking up at him with astonished green eyes.

He set Sylvia gently back on the rug and she scampered off.

He'd been nervous as a kid when he'd called Edna, couldn't seem to control his damned voice. It had shaken like a leaf.

He sat on the green-and-white contemporary couch and watched Sylvia chase a dust bunny under a chrome-and-glass table as he thought of their conversation.

Christ, Edna sounded just as painfully shy as he was! They'd be a good match, all right. There had really been no need to explain to her that he'd been putting on an act in the supermarket. It was obvious, because he sure as hell hadn't sounded cool, calm, and collected on the phone.

Even at his age and even though he'd been married, it was clear he wasn't any Clint Eastwood-type smoothie like he'd pretended to be at the grocery. She could tell he was having a hard time.

He grinned. He guessed he'd always wonder if it had been the lure of Richard Gere's on-screen charisma that had finally swayed her.

He thought about working on his remote-control cars, then remembered he had a *date* on Friday night and wouldn't be spending it playing around with cars, or out with the guys.

What the hell! He decided to celebrate by jumping into the hot tub with a margarita on the rocks. It was the perfect night for it, clear and warm.

He put an old Beatles album on the stereo and turned it up loud, then searched through the cupboards for the tequila and triple sec, belting out "Yellow Submarine" with the record.

"Mewwwwwrr—!" Sylvia seemed distraught over something, running in circles around his legs, being a real pest.

"What's wrong with you tonight, girl?" he asked, stooping to pet her briefly. "You've got your bowels in an uproar over something."

He stroked the cat a little more until she calmed

down, then washed his hands and prepared a salt-rimmed cocktail glass for the margarita. Sylvia couldn't be hungry, he'd already fed her when he first arrived home. Just having growing pains, he guessed.

He deftly juggled the cocktail glass and a couple of towels out to the deck. He lowered himself slowly into the soothing water, then leaned his head against the ledge, resting his arms along the rim, the cocktail glass within arm's reach.

God, the hot tub was nice. He should use it more often, he thought, shutting his eyes and relaxing.

Chapter Fourteen

Edna stood on the front porch in her blue duster, dishcloth in one hand, and wearing rubber flip-flops. She scowled down at the dead rat, wondering what the hell to do with its body. Its fetid stink filled the night air. She'd already worked herself to a frazzle scrubbing the bloody claw marks off the front door.

A light, ominous chill had crept into the June night that was unnatural for the season, and a slow, whining wind whispered restlessly through the sycamore trees by the curb. Edna's arms were cold in the sleeveless housedress.

"Hey there, Edna, what's up?" Janet hollered, leaning her short-cropped spiky blond head out the window of her maroon Caravan as it crawled to a stop in front of Edna's house.

Her neighbor wore a puzzled, quizzical expression and Edna realized she must look strange, standing there, her arms akimbo, clutching the dishcloth, her feet planted wide apart like some stand-up comic doing a lousy impression of Yul Brynner in *The King and I.*

"Oh, uh . . . why, I'm just getting a breath of fresh air," Edna improvised cagily, sniffing a little as if to demonstrate that it was true, but not so much as to inhale the rank odor of the rat's body.

She stepped hastily off the front porch and moved a few steps down the sidewalk, just in case Janet hopped out of her van and trotted a little closer. Edna certainly didn't want her to come up close to the porch and get a snoot full of the ungodly smell. The slight wind was picking up the smell of blood and death, whistling through the trees, distributing it everywhere. She was surprised Janet hadn't already caught the scent.

Janet idled the van, still frowning at her, the muffler rattling loudly, the back end spitting out a dark cloud of pollution.

Edna wondered when she'd last had a tune-up.

"I have to go back inside, Janet. I'm sorry . . . don't mean to be unsociable," she fixed her with a big, shit-eating grin, "but I'm uh, expecting a phone call any minute now." Edna hated to lie, but she didn't want Janet skipping up closer to the house and seeing the dead rat.

"Well, see ya." Janet nodded, easily accepting

the explanation. "Like your new perm. You look like a new woman." She sniggered a bit, making that birdlike tittering sound that was so annoying, and pulled the wheezing van down to her own driveway, leaving a trail of black smoke in its wake.

Edna went back up the sidewalk to the porch and peered over the railing at the rat. The small porch light threw yellow shadows across the terrible mess and Edna shivered. What a dirty job this was going to be. She guessed she'd discard the thing by putting it into a heavy trash bag. A double-duty one would probably do the job. Maybe a couple of them, to lessen the phenomenal stink somewhat, and then she'd just put it in the trashcan. Her poor trash man would probably reel from the putrescent scent, but what could she do? She sure wasn't going to *escort* the damn thing to the city dump. Chauffeur a rat? A dead rat, at that. Forget it.

A bold, orangey-red sliver of moon shone down across the front yard as Edna turned to go to the kitchen after the garbage bags. She climbed the three concrete steps up the porch and the gleam of the streetlight flicked on behind her. It struck the front door with sudden illumination, transforming the stones in the gravel driveway into a tombstone-white. It provided a lot more light than the tiny, dim porch light.

Edna's hazel eyes fell instantly on the claw marks and she sucked in her breath with horror, making a whistling shriek, dropping the dishcloth, her eyes widening with alarm. A tight, steel band of fear constricted her chest and it became difficult to breathe. She blinked stupidly, as if this were some ungodly vision she'd only dreamed that might disappear when she opened her eyes again. It had to be some weird hallucination—had to be!

But what she saw was still there. She squinted hard and blinked. Still there.

"No! Oh, no, no! It's not there. It can't be there!" she gasped, her voice sinking to a croaking growl. A cold, clammy sweat broke across her brow, her upper lip, despite the chilly breeze, and the sight fairly swam before her eyes like a vague, ethereal vision. Her hackles rose and a trail of goose bumps raced down her arms as her mind rebuked what her eyes clearly saw.

"No . . ." she mumbled again, her voice cracking, "this isn't happening . . ."

She stepped forward and bent to examine the front door more closely, praying she was wrong. After all, she hadn't seen the indentations when she'd cleaned away the blood on the door. She ran her fingertips slowly across the prints the cat had made and beads of cold sweat trickled in thin threads down her forehead even as the cool air brushed against her skin. The putrescent odor of rotting flesh assaulted her nostrils. She saw spots dancing before her eyes and felt as though she would faint.

"Oh God! Oh, dear sweet Jesus," she said, sinking back on her heels to a sitting position on the porch to gape at it, her blue thongs squeaking against the concrete.

Her eyes went hollow and vacant with fear, and she wagged her head slowly back and forth in futile denial, as the wind flapped through her thin cotton housedress.

But there was no denying it. The cat's claw prints formed an almost-perfect letter *J* scrawled across the white wooden door. Right smack in the center of the door, well placed, so she would be sure to notice it. Painstakingly printed.

"For James . . . of course," she murmured, and covered her face with both hands as a shuddering spasm of terror shook her.

The shrill wind whined through the clammy night air, singing a song of maleficent night creatures, damnation, and death.

Chapter Fifteen

Gene lolled back in the hot tub, enjoying its soothing warmth. But after a while, he noticed Sylvia standing on her hind feet against the inside of the glass patio doors. She was taking small, agitated leaps up against the glass as if trying to get his attention. It looked like she was mewling, too, but he couldn't hear.

He cocked an ear and listened. Yes, she was screaming her little lungs out; he could hear her now. Something was bugging her tonight, but he couldn't figure out what. Maybe she was just lonely.

He'd go inside, shove a steak into the stove, pet her a little, and then come back outside for a few more minutes. After that, he'd let her snuggle up with him on the couch and watch TV.

A little "bonding," that was apparently what she needed. *Just like a baby*, he thought as he grinned and shook his head. He stepped out of the hot tub and wrapped a towel around his waist, shaking the excess water out of his hair.

"What is your problem?" he said sternly to the kitten when he opened the glass doors. He reached down and gathered her up into his arms. She was shivering.

"Hey . . . Christ, you look like you're scared to death," he said, puzzled. "What is it, baby?" He gently nuzzled the ball of fur with his cheek.

She cried in baleful, lugubrious tones, then sniffed at his mustache. He gave her a pat and set her back down on the kitchen floor, promising to come in shortly and to curl up on the couch with her.

"Want some milk?" he asked. Maybe that was it. He poured out some milk in a small dish and set it down. She eyed him tentatively, then took a few small sips and sat down to watch him mournfully.

He took out a thick steak, put salt and pepper and some tenderizer on it, and pushed it into the stove to cook. His baked potato had been cooking for half an hour, so it was nearly done.

Just a short dip in the hot tub and I'll come back in, he promised himself, *and babysit Sylvia*.

"See ya soon," he said, edging out the doorway

and closing the glass before she could squeeze through.

She scampered toward the door as quickly as her small steps would allow and stood looking at him sullenly, bereft over his desertion. Then she started mewling again, tiny wails of despair that made him feel guilty.

"Shit, Sylvia, you're *worse* than a baby!" he said, walking around to the steps at the side of the hot tub.

He laid the towel down on the wooden banquette and stepped carefully down onto the first step of the hot tub, and a windy breeze rippled his hair. It *was* getting a little nippy out, a little too cold for hot-tubbing.

He glanced down. Where the hell was his drink? "Must be losing it. Guess I took it inside," he mumbled. But he didn't *remember* taking it inside.

He edged down the last step into the tub, as the warm water swirled about his waist, then let out a blood-curdling yelp of pain.

"Aaaah! Oh sweet Christ!" he screamed. Something had hurt his foot, something had sliced into it like a sharp butcher knife and the water in the hot tub had a pinkish swirling cloud of blood in the vicinity of his heel when he looked down.

He lifted his foot up, hopping on one leg, still moaning. He grasped his injured foot at the same time, squinting down into the water to see what the hell it was that had pierced his foot so brutally.

The glass . . . It was pieces of the goddamn cocktail glass. He guessed that he'd somehow knocked it off the ledge when he'd gone inside, though he didn't remember bumping against anything. He could swear it.

He hopped back up the two steps and slumped down on the ledge of the hot tub, lifting his foot up to inspect the cut. It had cut his heel, carved a two-inch niche in it. It was bleeding freely but it wasn't all that bad. He'd live.

What bothered him though was the fact that he didn't really remember knocking the glass over. He held his foot up and peered down into the water. The glass lay in three or four jagged pieces across the bottom step.

That was strange, too. If he had walked by and bumped the glass over, wouldn't it have fallen a lot more to one side of the hot tub, rather than where the center steps were?

He didn't see how it could have fallen where it had. It seemed impossible, unless someone had practically kicked at it. And if he didn't even remember hitting it at all, how the living shit could he have knocked it over *that* goddamned hard? Hard enough to make it land on the steps? It made no sense at all.

He sat there for a minute or two, still holding his foot, shivering in the night air. The wind had picked up and it was quite breezy now. He decided he must be losing his marbles. Maybe Sylvia's little neurotic act had gotten to him to the point where he didn't remember about the placement of the glass. He got up, grabbed the towels, and prepared to hop over to the glass patio doors. He'd worry about the broken glass tomorrow, when he could see better in the daylight.

He took three awkward shaky hops and looked up to see two yellowish glowing eyes focused on him. That was what he noticed first—the eyes.

Then, a moment later, as it rushed past him in a mad frenzy, like greased lightning, he saw that it was a huge black cat, scruffy and fat, its fur filthy and matted with dirt. The same black cat that had leaped up at his car window. His good buddy, back again.

It paused on the edge of the redwood deck and twisted its great skull to look at him before it leaped away. Gene's heart triphammered with a pounding that threatened to explode his rib cage into a thousand aching fragments as he met its eyes. Then he knew, beyond a shadow of a doubt, that the beast had knocked the glass into the hot tub during his trip to the kitchen. He couldn't say *how* he knew this, only that he did.

He stumbled to the glass doors and slid them open, then shut. Sylvia stood by the door as if guarding it and he suddenly understood why she'd been behaving so strangely. She'd been instinctively aware of the black cat.

"It's okay, girl. It's gone now," he said, hobbling toward the bathroom to wash the cut and put some alcohol on it. The acrid smell of burned meat and potato wafted toward him and he remembered the food, too late.

"Hell!" he swore. He grabbed the dishtowel, and yanked the oven open to reveal a crispy browned-black piece of meat, sizzling with a tiny trail of smoke coming from it. The potato was also shrivelled.

The cocktail was ruined. Now his dinner was ruined, too.

He guessed he'd just make a ham-and-cheese sandwich and drink a diet soda. He set the steak and the potato on the top of the stove and headed back toward the bathroom to tend to his wound, which was dripping a little bloody spot on the kitchen floor.

He hopped on one leg into the bathroom adjacent to the kitchen, washed the cut with soap and water, then uncapped the rubbing alcohol and dribbled it across the cut. It stung like hell.

Sylvia crept cautiously to the doorway to watch him, big-eyed and silent, as if she knew something bad had happened.

"You knew that black sonofabitch was out there, didn't you, Syl?" he asked the kitten. It regarded him solemnly, its head cocked to the side. Adorable, he thought. Just the opposite of that horrible black cat; it was almost as if it were a different species.

"Jesus, if I see that black bastard again, I'll wring its neck!" he swore, knowing the oath was an empty one.

It had just been a coincidence, seeing the cat

in the grocery store parking lot and now at his house. To think anything else would be acting like a paranoid pantywaist, thinking maybe it was out to get him or something, which was ridiculous.

Hell, it was only a little pussycat.

Chapter Sixteen

Edna took a small garden trowel and pushed the rat's snout and heavy, stiffened corpse into the trash bag, averting her head, trying not to inhale the pungent, sickening odor.

Its skull wobbled weakly on the slender stalk of ripe flesh that had been its neck, then broke completely off, dribbling oozing blood in its wake, sending a tremor of revulsion down Edna's spine.

"Oh Lord," she moaned, bending to scoop the pulpy, messy ball that was its head onto the trowel. She dumped it unceremoniously into the trash bag as her stomach rumbled with nausea, rolled it shut rapidly, and fastened it with a strong wire tie, wrapping it round and round several times. Then she slipped the macabre burden inside two more trash bags in a vain effort to alleviate the treacherous stink.

She'd brought out a large shoe box that had contained a pair of knee-high leather boots, and shoved the whole ugly parcel into it, cramming the lid shut tight. Her stomach churned with nausea. She pushed a hand through her hair and stood gazing down at the package with a saturnine expression.

"A boot box for a coffin. You poor sorry bastard." She sighed, shaking her head. A chill breeze fluttered her hair. For good measure, she pushed the entire thing into yet another trash bag.

"*J* for James," kept running through her mind like an insidious, dark melody, and she fought to push the thought away. The wind whined against the back of her neck, raising goose flesh.

Edna ran inside the house after she'd shoved the bag deep into the trash can and shook the dirt off the trowel. She took a hot bubble bath, scrubbing her body hard as if trying to wash away the lingering scent of death from the rat.

Feeling relieved that the gory chore was over with, she slipped into a cool cotton shift and shoved a chicken salsa TV dinner into the stove and cut up some fresh fruit to eat with it. She used to confine herself to purchasing only cheap TV dinners, but she'd moved up in the world since James died. The insurance money had allowed her to chuck the inexpensive prepared food and move to the more expensive one.

J for James. Edna shivered as the thought

intruded into her consciousness. The paring knife slipped off the fat yellow apple she was slicing and a bright-red drop of blood spurted to the surface of her hand.

"Damn it," she whispered softly, turning on the cold water and holding her hand beneath it.

She stared down at the blood. It reminded her of the rat which reminded her of the cat, and then James—those hollow, accusing eyes filled with murderous hatred. But it was insane to think that the cat could actually *be* James . . . wasn't it?

A maelstrom of thoughts assaulted Edna as she fought to convince herself she'd just imagined it all. She tried to tell herself it was just an ordinary, scruffy black cat. Perhaps tomorrow or the next day it would lope off down the street and find someone else to bother. Someone else to torment.

J—for James thrummed through her brain.

"You're being ridiculous," she said aloud. In the corner of the kitchen, Petey squawked in agreement and Edna laughed. She turned off the cold water and shook her hands. It was only a tiny laceration and the blood had already coagulated.

She went to the bathroom, dumped a stream of hydrogen peroxide over the cut, yelped a little, and then returned to the kitchen. Petey had his head buried in the seed dish.

"I'll read, that's what. Get my mind off it. It's driving me batty. I'm *not* gonna let that little bugger do this to me," she vowed, raising her voice and shaking the dishcloth at Petey, who remained unimpressed as he continued to root around in the food dish.

She put on an oven mitt and cracked open the oven door to check on her frozen dinner. Almost done. The aromatic, spicy smell of chicken wafted upwards and Edna's taste buds shifted into overdrive. She prepared a tall glass of low-calorie iced tea and dumped half a tray of ice cubes into it.

She cranked up the old box fan onto its highest setting, pushed it around to face the couch, and plopped down onto the flowered Early-American couch. The three other books she'd bought were on the coffee table. She lifted them to peruse the back-cover blurbs. She'd finished *Bride of Passion* and it had whetted her appetite for more.

"No junkie like a romance junkie," she muttered with a wry grin. She tasted the iced tea and set it back down on a coaster. A bit weak, but it would do.

Prince of My Dreams sounded like a winner. She decided to begin it after eating. Keep busy. That was the ticket. Keep busy, so she wouldn't have time to entertain sick fantasies. It was very, *very* sick to think her dead husband's spirit resided inside some damn cat. She would force her mind from it, reject the notion before it reduced her to a babbling idiot.

Prince of My Dreams. What if Gene Martin turned out to be the prince of *her* dreams? Well, she wouldn't rush into anything, no matter how princely he seemed. She feared being saddled with another man like James.

She went back into the kitchen to retrieve the TV dinner and flipped on the tube to watch a show as she dined.

After dinner, she got energetic and decided to take advantage of it by cleaning out Petey's messy cage. Then she dusted the old-fashioned rolltop desk in the living room, the end tables, and the glass etagere.

"I'm on a roll now, Petey," she cried.

She watered the snake plant and her small cactus collection on the wicker shelves beside the fireplace and gave her aloe plant on the bedroom windowsill a little drink. Then she collapsed onto the couch and read six chapters, got totally hooked on the book but too sleepy to continue, and decided to pack it in.

She flossed and brushed diligently, and then set the digital clock radio on the nightstand for seven-thirty. As she drifted off to sleep, she was seized by an idea.

A stupid idea, chastened the pragmatic voice inside her head, but it was an idea, nevertheless. Since she couldn't rid herself of the absurd notion that the cat was James's spirit, why not lay a trap for the dangerous beast? Give it a "test," so to speak.

Edna curled up in a fetal position, the light comforter across her feet, half-dozing, and considered the merits of this. But what kind of test? It was a dirty shame that Nadine had moved away. She could have gotten Nadine to hang around the house and see what happened when the cat showed up. If the bugger seemed partial to Nadine, well then, wouldn't that lend some credence to her suspicion?

Stupid, dumb as dirt, cawed the nagging practical half of herself.

It was too bad Nadine had moved to live with her cousin in Buffalo, she thought as she toyed with some ideas, but rejected them. Then it hit her and she jerked upright and hugged the pillow to her chest, giggling a horsey nervous laugh.

What if she laid out a big plate of those little chocolate-marshmallow cakes on the front porch? See if the loathsome beast came running, with its tongue hanging out? Or tunafish.

She rolled over on top of the pillow and stared at the dim outline of the aloe plant against the Venetian blinds. Of course an ordinary cat would go for the tunafish. But those gooey chocolate-marshmallow cakes?

Those suckers were a horse of a different color. What feline in its right mind would eat one of those? Such a chocolatey, sickeningly sweet mess. She didn't think it likely any cat alive would gobble up such a concoction once it got a good sniff of it and saw what it was, even if the creature were half-starved for food. Surely it would turn up its nose at it, unless it was some weird psychotic beast.

Edna cackled, on the verge of hysteria, letting out a loud crow of delight. "Chocolate-marshmallow cakes, that's the ticket," she mumbled, twisting the mauve comforter about her legs, drifting off to sleep in spite of her churning mind. "They were his favorite."

Right before sleep overcame her, she got a sudden bolt of inspiration. So long as she was giving the damn thing a little treat, why not lace it with rat poison? A little extra goodie.

It would be a snap. She could whack the ends off the cylindrical little cakes and slide a few of the green pellets inside, then ease the pieces back together. No fuss, no muss. And maybe that would get rid of the stinking cat forever.

She began snoring lightly, visions of the black cat, its whiskers caked snowy-white with marshmallow filling, an evil grin on its angular face, dancing in her brain.

Chapter Seventeen

"There. See how you like that!" cried Edna. She bent down to set a cereal bowl heaped high with fresh chocolate cakes on the porch. She then set a bowl of plain tunafish adjacent to it.

A normal, red-blooded American cat would devour the tunafish, naturally. She only hoped the birds didn't chow it down before the cat got its chance. The damned birds would eat anything they laid eyes on, regardless of how trashy or unhealthy. She was afraid either the birds would get the food, or those fat greedy squirrels that were becoming so remarkably bold these days. She'd read an article just last week in *The Washington Post* about some park being closed because of overly aggressive squirrels. One feisty squirrel had actually attacked a child who'd dropped a chicken nugget. When the toddler bent down to retrieve it, the ballsy squirrel rushed her for it and bit her hand. The little devils were over-stepping their boundaries, turning into vicious mongrels. She hoped they didn't like cake.

Edna looked around the yard. Today would be a good day to mow the lawn. It was dry and clear, with the sun shining brightly. She'd wait until the cat showed up—until it had scarfed up the poisoned cakes—and then get out and mow it before the grass grew up to her butt.

"Also pull a few weeds out of that rock garden," she said. The weeds were in danger of strangling the beautiful flowers.

She hoped the cat came for its treat before the mailman made his rounds. He'd think she had flipped out, setting out a bunch of snack cakes on the porch. More important, she hoped the stinking cat didn't get suspicious of the poisoned cakes.

"Here kitty, kitty, kitty. Come and get it, you ugly son of a bitch," Edna called softly, cupping her hand around her lips. It was just appalling how she'd taken to cursing like a sailor lately.

She had the uneasy, spine-tingling feeling that the beast was lurking in the vicinity of the house, watching her. There was no logical reason for it, the feeling was just there.

The air was heavy with the sweet, cloying scent of honeysuckle, and the sun sparkled across the gravel driveway.

Gnats buzzed around the azalea bush beside the porch and Edna swiped them away from her face. One lone robin pecked avidly at the seed in the bird feeder, then took flight suddenly as if it had received some private message of impending doom. Across the street at Janet's house, squirrels played tag across the sloping, neatly mowed lawn and tore through her hedges and rose bushes, shaking the petals off them in their play.

Edna fingered the gold locket around her throat nervously, glancing around the yard. The cat was probably just waiting for her to go inside the house so it could pounce on the dish. There was a sizzling electrical tension in the atmosphere, a sense of something about to happen in the odd silence. She couldn't rid herself of the feeling it was watching her from some secret subterranean lair. *Licking its chops, probably salivating all over itself from the sight of those goddamn snack cakes*, mused Edna. Watching and waiting.

The skin on the back of Edna's neck began to crawl and she felt a choking dryness seize her throat, suffocating her.

She walked back inside the kitchen and hiked up the Venetian blinds just a bit, intending to spy on the creature. She could wash the dishes and clean up the kitchen with one eye riveted on the porch. She wanted to see exactly what it did, even though the idea of seeing it again was unsettling and made her half sick. She became distraught at the prospect.

She boiled rigatoni spirals for a salad later, stirring it one-handed while she propped open the book she'd been reading with the other. It was quite engrossing, though the silly heroine was behaving like a young fool. Any dimwit could see her current boyfriend was a married man, a real slimeball. He refused to take her out at night, made flimsy excuses for not giving her his telephone number.

Edna hoped the heroine'd have sense enough to give him his walking papers soon and save herself a lot of heartache.

She parked the book face down on the counter while she chopped onions and green peppers. When the rigatoni was done, she dumped onions and peppers and a can of tuna into the mixture, adding a huge dollop of low-cal mayonnaise. A splat of mayonnaise dropped off the spoon and fell onto her houseshoe. She bent over, grunting, to wipe it off with a paper towel.

"What a klutz I am," she mumbled absently, aware of how she was talking to herself more and more these days. She supposed it was that hellcat, stressing her out, stretching her nerves to the breaking point.

Or maybe it was simply because she lived alone, with only a parakeet for company. You did need to hear the sound of a human voice occasionally, even if it was only your own.

She rubbed at the shoe, but the sticky mayonnaise didn't want to come out of the fluffy material. Suddenly she got that crawling sensation against the back of her neck again, that feeling of being *watched*, that feeling of another presence nearby. Besides Petey, who had stopped his song in mid-chirp as if strangled, and was now fluttering wildly around the cage, going berserk.

"Petey, what the hell—" She stared at the cage and then raised up from the floor, depositing the paper towel in the trash. As she lifted her eyes, she gasped and her heart quickened into a ragged, irregular thumping. The sound of it seemed to fill her ears, drumming loudly, pulsing with its frightened uneven rhythm of terror.

Petey let out a long, piercing blast of frightened caws, then hopped to the floor of the cage and huddled there, with his feathers shivering.

"Oh God!" Edna panted. "Oh dear Lord . . ." Her breath came in hitching, uneven gasps and her heart beat a wicked tattoo.

The cat's pyramid-shaped black skull was pressed close to the outside of the kitchen window, not three feet from her own. Edna's eyes bulged at the sight.

"Hssssss!" it shrieked ominously, giving a battle cry, its thin, blood-red lips peeling back to form the sound. Its shining white fangs looked lethally sharp, impossibly long. Its twitching whiskers appeared to be tinged with red and Edna wondered if it was blood. It lifted both claws and raked furiously at the glass, as fast as it could, setting up a scraping noise that was akin to chalk against a blackboard.

Petey let out a howl, then fell silent.

Edna sucked in her breath, trembled convulsively, and stumbled against the counter, one hand before her in a protective gesture, even though the windowpane separated her from the creature.

What was a little glass? she thought. If the monster wanted, it could take a flying leap and charge right through it, big as it was. Shit, it must weigh at least thirty pounds!

"N–no, get away from me . . ." she whimpered.

For an instant it held her gaze, its harsh eyes flat and cold. The look it gave her held an eerie familiarity, a ghostly duplication of James's eyes. Then it threw back its scraggly black head and howled a thin cry that made her blood run cold and her hair stand on end. There was a reddish streak under its neck, too. It definitely looked like blood. Its ebony pupils were tiny pinpoints as black as a witch's hat. Edna's heart plummeted into her stomach when she gazed into those wicked, crooked eyes. There was something so *deranged* about those goddamn fucking lopsided eyes. So . . . soulless.

As if it were some carnival freak, some freak of nature that didn't really exist. Just a frigging *clone* of a cat, and not a real cat at all! Some aberration a malicious deity had assembled haphazardly in nothing flat, resulting in its very structure being crooked, its very skeleton a jumbled up mess, a crime against nature.

"Go away, you—monster," Edna moaned as she hung onto the counter for support.

It regarded her fearlessly through the glass, the familiar eyes mocking her terror, taking pleasure in the power it held over her. Reveling in it. Wallowing in it.

She fancied the thing flashed a quick grotesque grin at her, and knew she must be going insane.

"Oh . . . James," she whispered, half-choking over a rising sob. The hairs on her forearm prickled.

It grinned again, wider this time, and it was like gazing into the gaping jaws of hell.

It's gloating, gloating. It's really enjoying this. Getting a real charge out of it, toying with me, Edna thought, panicking. It realized she was scared witless.

The thought filled Edna with a great, burning fury. She leaped into action, raised a dishcloth high into the air and snapped it smartly against the windowpane, not even giving a hang if it was possible for it to shatter the pane. The only thing that mattered was frightening that gloating, smug revolting creature that faced her.

Its low-set ears shot up, on the alert now for danger, no longer smug and complacent. It kept its round, button eyes fastened securely on her, carefully watching to see what she would do next.

In the background, Petey trilled a bold tune, as if congratulating her show of bravery, cheering her on.

What the living hell will *I do next?* she thought frantically, her heart thumping in an irregular pattern like a run-down clock. What would she do for an encore?

She couldn't quit now and leave the goddamn gargoyle-faced thing grinning at her obscenely from the other side of the glass, waiting for her to revert back into a quivering gelatinous mass of fear.

Show it you're not afraid of it, Edna, came advice from some hovering guardian angel. *Show it you're not afraid, or it will go for your jugular next time. Open the door.*

Before she could falter and chicken out, she grabbed the doorknob and yanked the kitchen door wide open, so hard the white curtains fluttered on the rod against the back of the door. She swallowed her quaking fear and stepped outside, her eyes darting around for the dreaded enemy.

"Get out of here you—you hellion!" She swiped at it wildly as she took a few steps out on the porch. She gesticulated maniacally, flapping her arms and hollering in a quavering, hoarse voice that wouldn't scare an ailing chickadee.

She took a deep breath and commanded herself to conjure up a raw, throaty scream that would scare it. "You get outta my yaaaarrrd!" she bellowed until her vocal cords rumbled with a humming vibration, summoning up reserves of courage she didn't know she had, even as her skin broke out into icy goose bumps of terror.

The creature was undaunted; it was far bolder than she'd imagined in her wildest dreams. It leaped lithely as a jungle cat, full of grace and sleekness, off the windowsill and down onto the porch. It stared at her, transfixed, its malevolent hatred a palpable thing in the heavy, still air.

Edna flailed desperately at it, pinwheeling her arms in the air. She felt a heady rush of victory as the dishcloth connected smartly with its backbone, charging the air with an audible crack. From inside the house, she heard Petey squawking as if he were in mortal danger.

"Hah! Go on, get away, you dirty bastard, or I'll give you another one just like it!" Edna was absurdly proud of landing a good solid blow, her face suffused with pleasure. She had finally managed to hurt it!

"Rawwwrr!" the cat screamed, stung. Its thick dirty black body slumped like an old sack of laundry.

Edna could see more blood smeared on its back and wondered what the hell it had been doing before it came to her house. What hellish havoc had it wreaked? What kind of bloodshed? Had it fought another cat—or a human being?

It shrank back from her for a second, mewling pitifully, its ears flattened tight against the oddly shaped skull. Then it seemed to lurch forward, gaining a new momentum. In the twinkling of an eye, it sprang forward at Edna, a tightly coiled, living ball of malevolence. It clawed savagely, mewling a blood-curdling wail of rage as it tore at her, biting and scratching with its treacherous claws.

"God in heaven . . ." Edna groaned, panting for breath, her lungs screaming for air.

She struck out crazily with her hands, pummeling at it desperately to land another solid blow against its backbone. She kicked furiously, her houseshoes drumming helplessly against the concrete, but the cat pounced back on her immediately, undaunted, attacking her legs. It tore and ripped at her tender exposed flesh, driving its lethal filthy talons deep into her and leaving an explosion of white-hot searing pain behind.

"Meeerawwwrr," it uttered, the guttural, low growl dissolving into a hissing sound like a wild panther from some atavistic jungle.

The nasty black fur stood ramrod straight along its hunched, misshapen back. Gnats from the azalea bush at its left side buzzed around its bloody, matted fur, sniffing at the scent. Its dark bullet-hole eyes glittered with a vengeful malice, terrifying in its enormity.

It paused and then sprang at her again before she could move, sinking its huge, knife-sharp claws into Edna's right calf. Blood spurted copiously down her leg in red ribbons, sweet and sticky, filling her houseshoes with its sickening warmth. Petey's mad squalling, the cat's demon screeching, and Edna's frantic wails all combined in a hellish cacophony of harsh, jarring sound that seemed endless.

"Ooooh!" Edna screamed, sinking down further into a sitting position, huddled over, her legs aflame with a stinging fire from the force of the cat's tearing, ravaging claws.

"Oh, dear God! James, don't! Oh, James, forgive me!" Edna cradled her injured leg, weeping as she watched rivulets of bright-red blood stream down her leg, landing in a pool on the concrete porch. The scruffy houseshoes were already soaked. Shoes James had given her for Christmas three years ago.

James, she thought, disoriented, clutching her leg protectively, bracing herself for another onslaught from the beast. It was useless to fight it; she hadn't the strength anymore. Her forearms were streaked with wet blood smeared from clasping her leg. The creature tried to leap up onto her chest, taking a quick, energetic lunge. She balled up one fist and pushed at it weakly, feebly, with draining strength, but it didn't phase the animal. She hit it harder as she saw its jaw drop open, ready to bite, and managed to connect a stabbing punch to its jawbone. It flattened its ears backward and moaned.

Edna laughed hysterically. "Good!" she cried, and balled up her fist, ready to sock it again if it approached her. *Ready to knock James's teeth right down his goddamn throat!*

"Get the hell out of here, James—while you can!" she yelled. She raised up a little on her elbow to see if it was going to run. It perked up its ears at her, hissed, and snaked a claw down her anklebone.

Before she could even cry out, the black cat emitted a high, thrilled shriek of conquest and blood lust, then turned tail and ran. Its black coat twitched from side to side stiffly like a tremendous porcupine, its fur drizzling blood as it galloped off down the street, its long claws leaving a faint bloody trail on the sidewalk.

"I called it James," she whispered, putting her head into her hands, trembling.

She drew a deep breath and swiped damp tendrils of hair back from her face. Insects buzzed at her ears, her nose, and she slapped them away, still watching the creature hurry away down the street. It moved swiftly down the middle of the road, not looking back, not pausing, its head hunched low, its body close to the ground, a true hunter.

"Oh, you bastard." Edna sighed, her breath hitching. "You bastard . . ." She inspected the wounds it had inflicted cursorily. She was a bloody mess. She looked like she'd fought a dozen cats. "I'll kill you, I swear it! I killed you once, James—and I can do it again," she promised softly, certain that it would somehow hear, even though it had trotted off into the distance.

She was aware that she sounded like some deranged madwoman, but she no longer cared. Because she was certain in her own mind of what the cat was.

As she dabbed the caked blood off her houseshoe, her mind swam dizzily and white dots flashed before her eyes. Her jaw dropped open woodenly when she looked down at her leg. No, there was no doubt at all, for there was new proof now. The unholy animal had carved its initial into the yawning flesh of her calf.

In three downward strokes, the claw marks formed a perfectly clear, well-carved J. It had carefully outlined it not once, but three times.

Edna sucked in a gulping sob, making a dry whistling sound, and began to whimper and keen like a small child. She hobbled to her feet, weaving unsteadily, catching hold of the black wrought-iron railing for support. The air was still and an odd otherworldly calm seemed to have enveloped the entire street.

Edna picked up the dishcloth off the porch—it had tiny splatters of blood on it now—and turned to go inside.

"Oh, almost forgot," she said, and glanced back down at the two cereal bowls.

The tunafish bowl was completely empty. Bone-dry, in fact.

The chocolate snack cakes had been totally untouched and atop them had been deposited a good-sized cat turd, moist and smelly in the summer heat. Flies and gnats buzzed around it, having a field day.

The sly bastard had somehow *known* about the poison.

And it was jeering openly at her naivete.

Chapter Eighteen

The following day was a miserable one, just about as miserable as any Edna could remember. The sky had dawned gray and overcast, the kind of gray day that made your soul feel dead. It was Wednesday, two days before her movie date. And here she was, sporting a huge scratch on her calf. She had gone to the doctor earlier that morning, just to be certain the vile beast hadn't given her rabies or some dreadful deadly infection from its dirty claws.

"My God, Edna," Dr. Henson had said, his pale watery blue eyes round with shock, "how in the world did you get this? You look like a tiger attacked you!" He set about cleaning and dressing the injury with gentle, experienced hands.

"Just an alley cat, believe it or not. Pretty vicious son of a gun," she had answered nervously, trying to shrug it off in a cavalier manner, hoping he wouldn't press her for details.

"Well, that alley cat was certainly a bloodthirsty thing. Can't believe a regular kitty-cat would attack someone this viciously. Those cuts are pretty deep . . ." He frowned at her with a skeptical, questioning look, as though he doubted her tale, slathered an antiseptic over the injury, gave her a tetanus shot, and dispensed a prescription for tetracycline. Edna had nodded mutely and slunk out of the office. Now she guessed she'd have to wear slacks to the movies. Otherwise, Gene would be sure to ask questions if he saw the bandages. She didn't want to talk about the cat with Gene, didn't really know him all that well yet, was afraid he'd think she was some half-baked weirdo.

In fact, she didn't know of anyone she could confide in. She didn't trust blabbermouth Helen. If she told her, why, an hour later it would be all over the damned Safeway and out of the store, too, since garrulous long-winded Helen yakked freely to all the customers. Then the Safeway crew would spread the word to *their* friends and soon everyone in Silver Spring, Maryland would know just how daft Edna Wilkins was.

So that left her with no choice but to keep her lip zipped—and to go quietly insane.

Edna settled down on her flowered couch with her novel and looked at the worn ten-year-old piece of furniture. It was slightly tattered on the arms, and the stuffing threatened to billow out in two small spots. She really made an effort to switch ends periodically when she sat down, but the hollowed-out, rump-shaped indentation on the right side, her favorite place, was clearly visible.

She'd have to get a new sofa. That's all. She kept forgetting that she could afford it now.

Her leg occasionally throbbed a little and she propped it up on the coffee table to rest it as she read. It was several hours later before the heroine, a blind fool, realized what an unscrupulous blackguard her lover was. "About time . . ." muttered Edna peevishly.

But while she read, she kept thinking about the cat, seeing its claws and fangs as it tore at her, trying to think what to do. Along about the time the heroine met what surely had to be the real "prince of her dreams," Edna got a severe attack of diarrhea, complete with a bloated, roiling, churning bellyache.

"Oh God," she moaned, carting the book with her to the bathroom. She nearly managed to polish off the book sitting on the throne, in the throes of pain.

Later that afternoon, she changed the dressing on her leg and tossed a low-calorie tuna lasagna dinner into the stove, then hobbled back to the sofa, taking care to switch ends. She watched the news as the dinner cooked, and ruminated over how dreadfully cunning the cat was, not to have touched the little snack cakes.

How could it possibly have known? she wondered for the millionth time. It was spooky. She wondered what other frightening, bizarre powers it possessed.

Helen called then and naturally the first words out of her mouth were, "Has he called yet, Edna? Huh? Has he?"

Snap, crackle and pop went the chewing gum, and Edna gritted her teeth against the annoying sound.

"Yes. The other night," she answered, stifling a low groan as she carefully propped her leg up on the couch, rearranging a few newspapers first.

"Do ya like him?" Helen wanted to know, eager to learn if her matchmaking had been a success.

"Well, he does sound nice. Actually . . ." Edna paused theatrically, "we have a date." She dropped this juicy tidbit of information oh so casually, just as though she had dates every night. She laid her head back against the blue-and-white afghan that lay across the top of the couch and chewed a fingernail, another new bad habit she'd acquired, courtesy of the cat.

"Woo–woo, all *right*!" Helen gushed, sounding so excited you'd have thought it was she who had the date. "Way to go, Ed . . . Toldja he was a terrific guy. Where y'all goin'?"

Edna loathed it when Helen called her "Ed." She quelled the urge to ask her for the millionth time to stop, and cracked open the *TV Guide* to inspect it as she talked. "To the movies. My God, Helen, don't have a cow, for Pete's sake. Besides, he has a cat, you know." Edna's voice took on a sour note.

"Well, so what?" Helen barked fitfully.

"Helen," Edna explained patiently, as though talking to a small child, "you know I loathe and despise cats." *Especially now*, she thought grumpily.

"Oh. Yeah. I forgot." Snap, crackle, pop went the gum.

That took the wind out of Helen's sails. Then she brightened. "Well, maybe he'll get rid of the damned thing. Just tell him he has to choose— you or the stupid cat. Oh, I'm sure he'd choose you, Edna, the way he was makin' cow eyes at you in the store." Helen tittered with delight at the memory, the chewing gum sloshing around noisily in her mouth.

"Helen, I will do no such thing. I barely know the man! Don't you think that would be just a little bit presumptuous? I mean, we might not even get along." Edna spotted a movie starring Goldie Hawn. Sounded pretty good and Edna liked Goldie. Maybe she'd watch it if she could get Helen off the phone by then, a major feat. Helen was a real talker.

"Oh, hockey puck. Of course you'll get along. I saw how you eyeballed him, too, Edna Wilkins. Besides, I'm talkin' about later on, when you get engaged and all." She let out a thin heehaw which trailed off into a gurgling snort.

Edna felt herself blushing crimson. It was true. She *had* ogled him. God, she hoped he hadn't noticed, hoped he didn't think she was some eager tramp, ready for a one-night stand, ready to leap into bed with him as soon as he gave her a nod. She tossed the magazine onto the coffee table beside a clay pot with pine cones in it.

"Okay, Helen. That's a good idea. Maybe I'll say that to him *if* we ever get serious about each other," she agreed, just to shut Helen up on the matter. For God's sake, she already had them engaged.

Edna'd missed half of "Entertainment Tonight," and her dinner was probably burnt to a crisp. So there was no point in hustling Helen off the phone.

"I'm sure he'll take you over that ole pussycat any day, Ed." Helen sounded smugly omniscient, the gum sliding around in her mouth as she spoke, making an ugly wet smacking sound.

"Hey, what about you, Helen? Any new love interests?" Edna deftly put herself out of the limelight and took a big drink of iced tea.

"Me? Well, hell's bells, hon, I'm *always* interested in love!" hooted Helen, working up to her phenomenally irritating horse laugh once again.

Just like a damn donkey, Edna thought as she held the phone a foot from her ear and let Helen cackle all she wanted while she watched the stars' birthdays portion of "E.T."

"Got me half a dozen dudes on the line," Helen confided proudly after she got herself under control. "Always got me a spare, just in case. Goin' out with Freddy on week nights and Skipper on weekends. And if one of 'em craps out on me, I just call up Earl. You know, Earl down at the

Amoco? Worships the ground I walk on. But I told him a long time ago he'd hafta give up drinkin' that rot-gut whiskey if he wanted to have anythin' regular goin' with me. It's me or the whiskey, I says, just like I guess you'll hafta do with Gene and that derned cat of his."

Helen was on a roll now, and Edna felt her stomach give a nasty grind, hellbent on reminding her who was in charge. Apparently she was up for another bathroom run shortly.

"Uh, I've gotta go now, Helen. My dinner is burning, I can smell it. Listen, I'll call you on Saturday. Give you a full report, tell you where we're gonna honeymoon and everything—"

Helen snorted out a loud booming sound like a heifer in distress. "Okay, okay. I'll be waitin'— and don't do anythin' *I* wouldn't do," she cautioned, coyly snickering.

Which leaves me a clear field to behave like a wanton, brazen hussy, thought Edna, cattiness seizing her.

"Okay. 'Bye, Helen."

She slammed the phone down on the end table, nearly knocking over a small brass unicorn statue, and hobbled hurriedly to the toilet, tucking the dog-eared book beneath her armpit, just in case it was a long sojourn.

Her stomach churned and gurgled and she moaned aloud, wondering if this was just a run-of-the-mill case of the shits or had she eaten something spoiled? Maybe the stomach flu was making the rounds.

About an hour later her stomach behaved itself once more. As she replaced the roll of toilet tissue, she recalled James's complaining about the skimpy amount of tissue on the new rolls, and conceded that he had had a point.

It was extra hot and muggy tonight and Edna figured she'd better leave the kitchen and living-room windows open. Either that or suffocate. The house had no air conditioning, only two antiquated old box fans, one of which had a blade missing. First thing tomorrow morning, she was going to buy an air conditioner. After all, she could afford it now.

She hopped over to the windows, limping like a crippled sparrow, her leg aching dully, and raised them all the way up.

Remembering the supper she hadn't eaten, she opened the stove door and grabbed the brown-blackened casserole with an oven mitt and slung it into the trashcan, scowling. She wound up eating a scallion-and-cheese omelet and two pieces of toast, topped off by a bowl of mint chocolate chip ice cream a bit later.

"What the hell! I'll work off the extra calories by mowing that lawn tomorrow afternoon," she told Petey as she licked the last taste of ice cream off the spoon. "That is, if this leg feels better."

That made her think of the damn cat again, meditating on what avenues of recourse she had. The rat poison had flopped; the son of a bitch had been too clever. And what the hell else could she do? No way could she actually catch it. It was far too sly and canny to allow itself to be trapped, or to permit her to approach it. Too damned smart.

And asking for help was a stupid idea. As savvy as the creature was, it would run for the hills if a cop or dog catcher showed up on the premises.

Then she thought of the gun. Her stomach clenched at thought of using it. She probably couldn't even aim straight. She fell back on the couch, eased her leg up onto a cushion, and turned her thoughts to Friday night, wondering what Gene would say and what she would say. Or, more important, what he would do and what she would do.

"Roseanne" was rolling across the TV screen, but Edna was barely aware of the sitcom's plot. Her mind was focused on Gene Martin. The prince of her dreams?

She chuckled aloud at how absolutely juvenile, how extraordinarily silly it all was to have first-date jitters when she was forty years old.

"My God, I thought I was past all that forever," she murmured.

Chapter Nineteen

After work the next day, Gene put on his swimming trunks and a pair of old rubber-thonged sandals to retrieve the broken glass from the bottom of his hot tub.

He waded down the three steps and went beneath the water to grasp the jagged pieces, feeling around the concrete floor carefully to make sure he got it all. He didn't want to cut his foot a second time.

As he emerged from the water, he shook his head vigorously and wiped his face. On the ledge where his cocktail had been was a shaggy black hairball. Cat's fuzz. Evidence that the black cat had, indeed, knocked the drink over. If he needed any.

He picked it up and looked at it. Jeez, it stunk

to high heaven, an old musty smell that made him half gag. Damn thing should've hopped into the tub and washed itself a little, instead of going around knocking drinks off the edge. Would have done it good.

He found another hairball across the deck and some tiny droplets of blood.

"Probably from my damned foot . . ." he said to himself, flipping a lock of dripping wet hair out of his face with one hand.

His foot *had* bled quite a bit. But the bloody droplets did not follow the same path to the sliding glass doors that he had taken. It veered off to the left, toward the wooden banquette along side the deck. Gene frowned and walked over to the banquette. There was a larger wet splatter of blood there, and a wispy black hairball in the center of it.

"Christ, it looks like it smeared the blood all around," he muttered, "deliberately." He got the strange, quirky feeling that something wasn't kosher about this. It was bizarre, odd. It seemed as if it had been *staged* somehow, which, he quickly thought, was ridiculous.

His nylon swimming trunks dripped water down onto the redwood deck as he stood there, squinting at the blood, the sun pulsing down on him, suddenly feeling too bright. The smell of the blood and the filthy hairballs was getting to him; his nostrils contracted at the stink and he felt himself growing strangely dizzy, woozy, like he was half-drunk.

He found himself remembering how he'd gotten the distinct feeling that the black cat had meant to harm him, had wanted him to cut his foot—or worse! It was a stupid notion, but he couldn't shake it.

And now, staring down at the smeared blood, he could swear it looked as if the damned beast had deliberately tried to paint a *J* in the blood. The initial *J*.

What did it mean? It certainly had no significance to Gene, but he felt a nervous quiver run through his body and got the sudden, intense feeling it was important, meaningful somehow.

Chapter Twenty

Edna awakened the next morning to the pitter-patter of raindrops pounding against the roof and gusts of shrill wind howling and rattling the blinds.

She threw herself out of bed, flinging the sheet aside, and jumped to close the windows she'd left open. Puffs of wind blew raindrops through the window screens, leaving droplets on the Venetian blinds, and making the aloe plant tremble on the windowsill.

Before slamming one of the windows shut, she noticed a hole in its screen. Now how had that happened? She shrugged and closed the window and thought she saw a streak of black fur dart to one side, quick as a flash. Cat-shaped fur.

"Oh, terrific," she said, "now I'm seeing cats

everywhere. Getting paranoid." A tremor shook her body and she slumped down on the edge of the bed.

She eased the wilted gauze pad off her calf and took a look at the wound. The gashes were fire-engine red. A frisson of fear rippled through her again as she stared at the clearly-formed *J* carved carefully into the soft meat of her leg.

Even Dr. Henson had commented on it. "Looks like the damn thing was trying to carve its initial on you, Edna," he'd teased, remarking that it looked just like a *J*. His eyebrows were squeezed together into a questioning knot, as if waiting for her to explain how that was possible. But she'd just flashed a weak grin at him.

She looked up from her leg to the window.

Her aloe plant was soggy with rainwater, some of it spilling from the pot onto the edge of the windowsill. Edna got up from the bed and went into the kitchen to get a cloth. She returned to the bedroom and mopped up the mess, took the aloe into the bathroom and poured out the excess water in the sink, then replaced it on the window.

"Oh Lord, not again," she moaned as her stomach rumbled and knotted together suddenly like a clenched fist. She hoped she wasn't in for another bathroom session today. Hadn't she suffered enough last night? But she realized that her stomach was only rumbling from hunger pains.

She pushed her feet into the scruffy blue houseshoes and went into the kitchen to prepare an English muffin and scrambled eggs from the substitute egg mixture. Couldn't be too careful these days about watching the old cholesterol count like a hawk. She didn't want to end up like James.

"Ah, Lord," she said as her eye fell on the calendar above the kitchen table. She had a dentist appointment at ten this morning and hadn't even remembered. Her plan to get an air conditioner would have to wait until tomorrow. After seeing the dentist, she'd be in no shape to go shopping.

Ever since the cat had entered her life, it seemed she'd become alarmingly absent-minded.

She was in no mood for suffering through a dentist appointment, what with her stomach acting up, but she supposed she'd better go. She flipped the eggs over with a rubber spatula and salted them.

Dr. Sorenson had said she needed another crown. He'd also hinted that the tooth had the beginnings of an abscess.

"In fact," he'd grinned, "a couple of your teeth are wavering on the verge of an abscess." He seemed proud and pleased at this announcement.

God knew she didn't want *another* abscessed tooth. She'd had one on the upper left last year and it was more than enough, thank you very much. The pain was excruciating. So Edna guessed she'd better quit crying the blues, eat her eggs, and bustle on down to the dentist's torture chamber.

She sat down at the breakfast nook and ate, then toasted another English muffin.

Better eat a lot, she thought sullenly, *I sure won't feel like eating after I come out of the dentist's office.*

She washed the dishes quickly and shuffled to the bedroom, listening to the rain drumming down on the roof, still brooding about the dim streak of black she'd glimpsed through the bedroom window.

She'd tried her best to crane her neck to get a better view out the window, but it was raining like blue blazes and she couldn't see very well. It had been nothing but a vague black cat-shaped fuzzy blur, hurrying off through the soggy wet grass. Perhaps it had just been a squirrel, she told herself. There were a few black squirrels around. But if that had been a squirrel, it sure as hell was the fattest squirrel she'd ever seen. Some kind of king-sized *mutant* goddamn squirrel.

Edna shivered. There was no use obsessing about it.

She dressed hastily in slacks and a blouse, redressed her wound, and went to the dresser for her watch and gold locket. She fastened the watch around her wrist and snatched up the telephone bill and credit card envelope, searching for the locket, thinking maybe she'd tossed the mail down on top of it. She'd laid it down right beside her watch.

But the locket was gone.

"It's got to be here somewhere," she said, push-

ing aside sales ads from grocery stores, a sweepstakes envelope promising a chance for untold
riches, and a coupon offering two pizzas for the
price of one.

Gone.

Edna's heart leaped, revving up into an
unsteady, jagged skipping rhythm. She swallowed hard, telling herself to be calm, not jump
to conclusions. But a voice nagged at her, telling
her the dresser was directly beside the window
where she'd spotted the huge black streak of fur
hurrying off through the driving rain.

The window had been open all night and there
was that hole in the screen.

Edna's head snapped around, her heart pounding erratically, to stare at the screen. She went to
the window and lifted the Venetian blinds a little
higher. The large, ragged hole in the bottom of
the screen looked like—a cat-sized hole.

Edna touched it, her temples thudding with
anxiety, and ran her fingers softly around the
jagged edge, tracing its outline. A nauseated feeling pumped upward from her stomach when she
noticed a few drops of rain leading toward the
dresser. They weren't actually cat's paw prints
but it showed *something* had indeed made its way
toward the dresser during the stormy night.

She'd dubbed the locket a present from James
when she'd bought it. A fortieth birthday present
from James. *Now James had taken it back from
her*. Confiscated it, you might say. He hadn't
wanted her to have it. But how had he known
her intent when she'd bought the necklace?

Amanda Kingsley

Edna's mouth sagged open listlessly, the sting of bile filled her throat, and her knees knocked together like skeletons dancing in a boneyard at the gruesome implications.

Chapter Twenty-one

On the way to the dentist, Edna tried to be rational about the cat. She tried to convince herself it was mere coincidence about the locket.

Why, the black streak of fur could have been a damned woodchuck, a squirrel, or anything. It didn't necessarily have to have been a cat, for God's sake.

She knew she was obsessing again, getting paranoid about cats, that's all. Getting hung up on them since she'd encountered the stray. After all, with buckets of rain coming down, visibility had been severely limited, and it could have been a lot of things besides a black cat.

But, she reminded herself, the locket was gone. Why did it have to be the stinking *locket* that was missing, of all things?

She pulled up to a red light and a fat yellow bumblebee zoomed into the driver's window and Edna swatted it frenetically, batting her hands back and forth like a windmill. She was morbidly afraid of bumblebees.

"Shoo! Go on, get out of here!" she cried, swiping at it, but the wretched creature doggedly remained, flitting into the back seat to escape her badly aimed flailings.

Edna pulled over abruptly to the shoulder of the road and hopped out, throwing open all four doors of the car. "Damn it, get out! I'm going to be late!" she yelled, flapping her arms, oblivious to the curious glances she earned from people in the cars whizzing past her.

Fifteen minutes later the bee buzzed out of the car, circling Edna's new perm several times. Edna screamed loudly and ran in circles around the car in an effort to throw it off her scent. Finally, the insect flew away.

As Edna resumed her drive, the rain cleared and the sun burst brightly through the remaining clouds, peppering the sky with its radiance as the humidity climbed.

"That one on the upper right might need a root canal, I'm warning you." The dentist grinned, with his too-white teeth, obviously dreaming of his hefty fee. He loomed over her with one of those nasty, torturous picks in his hand. "Starting to abscess a little already," he said, clucking his tongue.

"Oh, dear," wailed Edna pitifully.

"I'm going to make a crown for this one on the left today," he continued, eyeing the X-rays. "It's in bad shape, Edna. Then we'll take care of the one that's abscessing."

His plump jowls trembled slightly as he bent over her and stuck something that resembled a Q-Tip into her mouth, parking it between her molar and the skin of her cheek. He turned to load up the novocaine needle and Edna cringed inwardly, staring up at the ceiling at the cutesy photo of a couple of poodles with pink ribbons in their hair.

Why did her dentist think it would make a patient feel better to stare at that kind of tripe on the ceiling, when he or she was going through sheer hell down here in the chair? Anyone with any sense kept his or her eyes closed, anyway. Unless you were some kind of masochist, and actually wanted to *see* what the dentist was doing to your mouth.

Edna squeezed her eyes shut when he came at her with the hypodermic. She imagined his gray eyes were glazed over just a bit with sadistic mischief. As he sank the needle into the soft, vulnerable flesh of her mouth, she wondered what kind of person would actually aspire to be a dentist. How did it feel to spend your life hurting people each day? Having people dread coming to your office? It seemed neurotic. Warped.

The dentist waited ten minutes, but Edna's jaw staunchly refused to get numb. She wiggled her tongue around inside her mouth with ease; it didn't feel like a chunk of concrete as usual.

"Hmmph. I'll give you another shot." He sighed, holding the killer hypodermic aloft, the semi-sadistic gleam still shining brightly in his eye.

Edna clenched her hands together tightly, twisting her opal ring round and round, her nerves jangling. She fancied the dentist looked a little like Gene Wilder in *Young Frankenstein*. That same crazed, glittering eye.

She fought down a mad urge to bolt from the chair, paper bib and all, and run screaming out the door to the safety of her little red brick rambler.

He administered two more novocaine shots to her mutilated mouth and they waited. Then he attempted to drill again and Edna let out an involuntary squeal of pain, causing the dentist to flinch and jump with surprise.

"Ouch!" she yelped, clutching at the arms of the chair to refrain from letting out a full-blown scream. "It hurts! I—I'm sorry, but it just doesn't feel numb at all."

The dentist stepped back and blinked unbelievingly at her, like a great stunned toad, as though wondering if she was joking. His drill was poised in mid-air. She'd already had four shots of novocaine.

"Guess I'm your problem child today. May I please have another shot?" she begged pitifully, holding her jaw, pain shining in her hazel eyes.

"Well, sure. I can make you numb until next week . . ." The dentist wagged his head, bewildered. "It's rare. But every once in awhile this *does* happen. Novocaine just doesn't take effect. We'll have to try again." He loaded up his weapon with a grim expression.

Edna gulped, twisted her ring around, and stared up at the hateful, grinning dogs on the ceiling. She fancied the little bastards smirked.

And why not? Dogs didn't have to go to the damned dentist.

It took six shots finally before Edna's jaw was numb enough to endure the drilling. As he worked on her mouth, the poodles grinned beatifically down at her. When she staggered out of the chair forty-five minutes later and paid him for torturing her, her jaw felt like a slab of solid granite.

Edna had her doubts she'd even be able to open her mouth by tomorrow night to converse with Gene. At least he'd think she was a good listener.

She was a complete wreck. Her mouth felt like a Mack truck had run over it. Her legs had been savagely clawed by that hideous beast. What else could possibly happen before their date?

Edna laid the magazine she'd taken into the dentist's office down on a table and walked out into the bright sunshine, feeling rather dazed from all the shots she'd received.

"Oboy," she muttered sullenly, rubbing her jaw, "I hope Gene doesn't mind dating one of the walking wounded."

She tried to grin, but couldn't lift her lip.

Chapter Twenty-two

Edna sat, cupping her sore jaw in one hand, a novel in the other, her legs thrown up on the couch with a cushion beneath them. A glass of iced tea and a bag of potato chips were on the coffee table, within easy reach.

She was becoming a real die-hard romance reader and a dedicated couch potato, too—a thing she normally regarded with no small amount of disgust.

By evening she'd finished the novel and begun a third, *Secret Love*, and had plans for going to B. Dalton's to stock up. Her leg still hurt and her jaw ached and she certainly wasn't up to bustling around doing a lot of housework. And, besides, reading kept her mind off the cat.

But as she read, occasional half-baked schemes

popped into her brain. True, she hadn't managed to poison the evil beast, and she had thought about calling the Animal Shelter and the dog-catcher or whoever the hell was in charge of getting troublesome, dangerous beasts off the streets. But she had already dismissed that as wishful thinking.

What good would it do? The cat was no dummy. The shrewd son of a bitch would take off like a bat out of hell at the very first sign of interference.

It was *her* that it wanted to tangle with—literally.

But then there was always . . . the gun. But Edna shied away from thinking about it. She knew she didn't have the guts to use it.

Chapter Twenty-three

Thursday night Gene felt slightly sick to his stomach and had a sore throat.

He chugged down three vitamin C tablets and drank a jug of grapefruit juice, hoping that would help to stave off a full-blown cold or virus or whatever the hell it was that he was catching.

"I'm going on this goddamn date if I'm half-*dead*," he muttered to the walls, sniffing. His head felt stuffy and plugged up, too. Just his luck to get sick when he'd finally found a woman he really wanted to date.

He called Edna at eight-thirty to confirm the date for the following evening. She was reading and they discussed books for a while. His voice went off into a ragged croak once or twice and she asked him if he was feeling all right.

"Ah, it's nothing. Little hoarse, that's all," he rasped, trying to clear his throat without making it seem obvious.

"Are . . . are you sure you still want to go? We don't have to if you're sick. We can make it another time." Her voice sounded disappointed and Gene felt his heart swell with hope.

No way was he cancelling! Not even if this piddly little cold turned into double fucking pneumonia.

"No, no. I'm fine, perfectly fine," he said quickly, praying his voice didn't betray him by going hoarse as a bullfrog again.

He made it through the remainder of the conversation, sneezed three times the instant he hung up, and then flopped down onto the couch to rest.

"Ah, shit," he groaned, admitting to himself that he felt miserable.

He slept fitfully for a while and then got up. His head was pounding, and he swallowed another vitamin C tablet. He'd read somewhere that if you took a lot of vitamin C at the onset of a cold, it would stop the cold dead in its tracks.

That is, if I don't overdose on the damn things first, he thought sourly, and then let out a booming, blustery, window-rattling sneeze. He trotted back into the kitchen to get the box of tissue and honked his nose twice, thinking how he was going to go on this date come hell or high water.

Chapter Twenty-four

Friday morning dawned dreary and overcast, with massive gray-black clouds bunching up into dark, threatening clusters. The weatherman, playing eternal optimist, claimed it would clear by evening. Edna just hoped it would be nice weather for her date.

Already she was a quivering bundle of nerves and feeling silly for allowing a date to affect her this way. It was dumb. She was a grown woman, for God's sake.

She'd planned a jaunt to look at some air conditioners and to the bookstore in hopes that the excursion would take her mind off the date. And the cat, of course.

She cranked the old box fan on high and left the living-room windows open only a tiny fraction, certainly not enough to let a fat black cat weasel its way inside. Then, just before she left, she stood in the living room, twisting her fingers nervously together, and changed her mind altogether, running from window to window to lock them all. When she reached the bedroom, she realized she'd have to replace the screen. Another chore to add to her list.

"Oh, jeez, Petey, I hope you don't burn up," she said, returning to the kitchen and staring at the bird cage with a worried frown. Even if she bought the air conditioner today, it would still be a few days before it was delivered.

She took his water container out and filled it to the brim. It would be a blistering hothouse in here when she returned, but at least she wouldn't have to worry herself sick about that hellcat wedging its body inside to pilfer among her things—and maybe attack her again. Or attack Petey.

Edna left the house and drove to the mall with all the car windows rolled down. Her car was a seven-year-old clunker with no air conditioning. Being a hot-blooded soul, it was a mystery to her why she'd bought a car with no A/C. Then again, she remembered, seven years ago she hadn't been able to afford such a luxury. She'd still been pinching pennies.

Now Edna began to toy with the idea of buying a new car, but the Cavalier was in fine condition, with never a mechanical problem, so it really was unnecessary.

"Just hot as hell-fire, that's all," she said, and grinned.

She wiped a thin moustache of sweat off her upper lip with the back of her hand and pulled into the mall parking lot. The dark clouds had magically dispersed and the bright sun strained to break through, bolts of brilliance piercing the clouds at intervals.

Edna stopped off at the appliance store, bought the screen and the air conditioner and was told it would arrive in a week. She sauntered into the bookstore then and selected half a dozen contemporary romances, a couple of thick-bodied historical romance novels, and two mysteries. She stepped up to the register to pay and a sleek-haired dumpy woman behind her smirked as she eyed the titles surreptitiously.

After leaving the bookstore, Edna hitched the heavy B. Dalton bag up around her forearm and milled around the mall, idly window shopping and enjoying the blessedly cool air conditioning.

"Perm's not bad-looking," she murmured to herself, noticing her reflection in a shop window and the way a man stared at her briefly. The tight corkscrews had toned down a little into smoother waves.

She bought a couple packages of pantyhose in the drugstore and left, suddenly eager to get home. God knew how long it would take her to prepare for her date. It had been so long since she'd gotten really dressed up, she'd half-forgotten how. James had never taken her out, even early in their marriage. James's idea of a big evening out was shuffling on down to the bowling alley, wearing a pair of nasty ancient jeans and a sloppy flannel plaid shirt. And after his heart attack, he hadn't gone anywhere at all, except to the refrigerator and back, and not even then, when he could get Nadine or herself to wait on him. His big event had been stepping out on the porch to get the mail.

When Edna cruised into her driveway, Janet came loping up the front lawn in that mannish, galloping strut. She swung her arms aggressively, like a long-armed ape, and stood grinning at Edna as she hopped out of her car. Janet wore her perennial uniform of Army fatigues and black high-laced combat boots. Edna couldn't believe it. In *this* heat. It made Edna sweat just looking at them.

"Hi, Edna. Wondered if you could do me a favor?" Janet said, running her fingers through her inch-long spiky hairdo.

"Uh, what is it, Janet?" Edna bent to pick up a paper cup off the floor of the car, took out her packages, and then locked all four doors, double-checking them.

"Well, I'm taking a little vacation. Goin' to Ocean City for a week or so and I just wondered if you could take my mail in for me. That is, if it wouldn't be too much trouble." Even Janet's voice was mannish, deep and husky. She kicked at the white gravel in the driveway with the steel toe of her boots, reminding Edna of a restless little boy.

"Why, of course not. I'd be glad to, it's no trouble at all, Janet." Edna glanced across Janet's broad he-man shoulders, where she spied Janet's girlfriend, lolling up against Janet's van in a sluttishly sexy pose. "It's wise not to let your mail pile up so people know you're away. Can't be too careful these days, you know. It might tempt someone to break in," Edna said, crushing the paper cup to put in the trash.

Janet nodded her head and dug the toe of her boot deeper into the gravel, giving Edna a puckish grin. "Oh, thanks. I appreciate it a lot, Edna," she said.

"How can you stand those boots in this heat?" Edna asked, the question popping out suddenly before she even realized she was speaking.

Janet hooted with laughter for a second, then answered, "Ah, the heat doesn't bother me much." She wedged her toe deeper into the gravel. "Get good traction with 'em." She laughed, a tough, mannish guffaw.

"My feet would be sweating like crazy. Well, have a good time at the beach, and don't worry about the mail," Edna said, turning to go inside. *Good traction. Really*.

"Oh, I *will*." Janet's eyes took on what Edna perceived as a lustful glint. "Carol's going with me." She grinned from ear to ear then, the impish face splitting wide apart, and Edna felt her cheeks flush with embarrassment.

In the background Carol struck a seductive Marilyn Monroe-ish pose, pursing her lips and lifting her head high. She had a thick mane of frizzy shoulder-length hair and wore those skin-tight biker pants that were just as good as being naked, topped by a stretchy tank top that managed to display both midriff and cleavage. She looked tacky as hell.

"Thanks again, Edna," Janet said, fairly sprinting down the driveway in those combat boots with the great "traction," like a randy man about to join his mistress. Her boots splayed the gravel with a loud crunching sound.

Edna shook her curly head and heaved a long-suffering sigh as she fumbled with the door lock. Her handbag, the screen, and the book bag flapped against her side as she jiggled the key and balanced the paper cup.

She propped the door open and went inside; the air smelled stale and thick.

"Well, of course it's stale, you idiot," she said aloud, "you shut and locked all the windows." It was hot as an oven and Edna could feel the sweat welling up instantly, beading her forehead and upper lips generously.

But it was more than that. There was a strange odor, more than a mere staleness. It was a musky, heavy animal smell that pinched her nostrils with its acrid bite. Edna sniffed again tentatively, putting her nose in the air like a bloodhound staking out a fugitive, trying to identify it. She tossed her bags and purse down on the couch and propped the screen against the leg of the couch.

"Lord, it smells like wet dog's fur. Or something. Something funky," she whispered, and glanced apprehensively around to locate the source. But she could see nothing wrong.

The living room with its tattered couch, the reclining chair, sporting a faded cracked vinyl arm, the dime-store ginger jar lamps, rolltop desk, wicker bookshelves, fireplace, and cheap tan carpeting seemed perfectly undisturbed. Nothing wrong.

Edna chewed her bottom lip, still riddled with the feeling something was out of place, not right.

What is wrong with this picture? She thought of that game in the children's magazines where you had to spot the flaws in a picture. There sure as hell *was* something wrong with this picture, some flaw. She just couldn't find it.

Then something caught her eye, and she glanced down to discover stray wispy black hairs on the carpet to the left of the front door. Short and black, they were scattered randomly, accented by one small, quarter-sized tuft. The stink of death and terror emanated from it, assailing her nostrils like a deadly nerve gas.

Edna's eyes bugged out as she squinted down at the bit of fur, then darted fearfully around to check out the room, imagining the creature would suddenly jump out at her and brutally attack. Her hands felt cold and clammy with a chilly, slick sweat. A vertiginous, disoriented sensation swept over her.

"Oh, this is impossible. Impossible!" she shrieked, and wondered if she was going mad. She *felt* like she was going mad as the room seemed to swirl dizzily around her head and she sagged weakly down onto the sofa.

It couldn't have gotten inside. There was no way.

From the kitchen, Petey whistled a tune, apparently in good spirits. At least it hadn't gotten hold of him and torn him to bits! And why hadn't it?

She pressed her hands to her head and swiped at the dripping sweat, half-delirious with the boiling, raw heat. Poor Petey, trapped inside a hothouse like this. It wasn't fair!

Edna crossed the room to open both the windows, and spied another tiny hairball on the floor close to the door. The fresh air felt good and she backed up one of the box fans close to it and clicked it on, to draw the air inside. She picked up the screen.

The cat could *not* have paid her a visit and that was all there was to it; there was just no way it could have gotten inside. Case closed.

She went into the bedroom, replaced the torn screen; then, except for the living room, she locked every single window tight. And bolted the door.

The hairballs had to be a figment of her imagination.

Chapter Twenty-five

Gene rolled out of bed Friday morning with a groan and stood scrutinizing himself in the full-length cheval mirror in his bedroom, not liking what he saw.

Sylvia leaped up to the bottom of the mirror and pawed her image, fascinated. Gene sneezed so loud that the vibrations shook his whole body and sent Sylvia running for cover, frightened by the sound.

His nose was red, his cheeks sallow and his eyes watery and bloodshot. *Jesus, I look like I've been on a week's drunk*, he thought, and scratched his head. He needed a haircut, too. He'd get one right after work at that small barber-shop close to the building where he worked.

It wasn't as crowded as The Hair Cuttery in the mall.

He was going on this date, if it stinking well *killed* him.

If it wasn't their first date, he'd have no compunction about cancelling out, but Edna was so damned gun-shy and wary of men to begin with . . . Christ, if he cancelled, she might just say the hell with the whole thing and never give him another chance.

He took an antihistamine, hoping it would dry up his sinuses, and gargled with a cup of hot, salty water, an old-fashioned remedy for sore throat that his grandmother had sworn by.

Maybe he'd feel better as the day wore on. He just hoped he didn't sneeze his head off at the movies. Then Edna wouldn't want even to be near him.

Chapter Twenty-six

Early that evening, Edna tried on three different dresses before she made a decision, stewing and fussing over which was best. First she tried a feminine-looking, flowered one trimmed in white virginal lace at the throat and cuffs. Too sweet and vulnerable.

She unzipped it and hung it back, eyeing the neat row of dresses in the closet. She yanked out a conservative, severely tailored maroon number and put it on. It had long sleeves and buttoned clear up to her chin. Too damned businesslike. She looked like she was going on a stuffy secretarial job interview, not a date.

She stalked impatiently back to the closet, replaced the maroon dress and slipped back into the pink-flowered lacy dress once again, scrabbling the material up so she could zip it in back.

Pink, the color of love. But she didn't want to fall in love, did she? Or did she?

Wasn't that what the dating game was all about? To at least encounter the possibility of love?

She liked the summery look of the small pink flowers on the white background, liked the way the white lace surrounded her throat, giving her whole demeanor a soft gentleness. God, the heart-shaped locket would have been perfect with it.

"Hang it all, I'll not think of that damn cat tonight. Just this *one* night . . ." she mumbled, determined to extricate it from her consciousness.

But visions of black cat hairs floating among the rug hairs in her living room swam through her mind in a dizzying phantasmagoria of claws, fangs, and the mangled dead rat. Her heartbeat leaped into an accelerated, ragged pattern, the familiar uneasiness cloaking her mind like a dark dense shroud.

"I won't!" she said, squeezing her eyes shut for a moment, and shaking her head. "I will *not* think about it tonight." She opened her eyes, blinked, and rubbed her temples.

She ripped open a new package of flesh-colored pantyhose and carefully inched them up over her hips, easing them over the top of the gauze bandages. It made a slight bulge, but she didn't care. It still looked better than going bare-legged. Besides, the flowered dress hung half a foot below the knee, covering most of the bandages.

She focused her mind on Gene, thinking of his thick, unruly hair with the gorgeous movie-star white stripe, like some exotic rare bird. She found herself wondering what it would feel like against her fingers.

Stop the romantic bullshit, part of her said, *he'll probably turn out to be a creep. Don't get your hopes up*.

But she didn't really believe that.

She sighed and yanked the pantyhose up further around her waist, letting the soft material of the dress fall back down around her legs. She opened the closet door to gaze at herself in the mirror. The two white gauze bandages still stuck out like a sore thumb, even though the dress covered a lot of it. Too bad.

Gene would be bursting with questions. And maybe she'd even tell him about the cat. He *had* a cat, didn't he? Perhaps he understood the nature of the beast. Perhaps he'd tell her there was no cause for alarm, tell her the cat wasn't really out to get her, like she thought.

Then again, maybe he'd think she was an odd duck, obsessing about a harmless cat, and not ask her out again.

Well, she could decide later. After she'd talked with him awhile, she would decide whether to entrust him with her strange tale. And maybe he would even help her—save her—to figure out what the hell to do about the situation.

Edna regarded herself critically in the mirror, liking the way the dress looked, then hurried to the bathroom to fix her hair. She wet the ends of the perm and fluffed it up with her fingers, scrunching it tight like a real pro now. She reached into the bobbypin box to select two tiny gold barrettes, wondering if he would think she looked silly.

"Barrettes are for little girls" was what Helen always said with a sneer. "*Infants* wear barrettes. Grow up, Edna!" In Helen's astute opinion, women over eighteen did not wear barrettes, bows, headbands, flowers or any sort of ornaments in their hair. "Too babyish," she declared. A "real woman" eschewed ornaments and slicked her hair back into a tight French twist, or let it all hang out.

"I don't care," Edna said, glaring in the mirror at her scowling face. She pulled back the sides of the perm, daringly hiking one side back and up farther than the other, and inserted a barrette firmly into it.

What the hell was babyish about a perfectly plain brown barrette? It had no silly insignias like a panda bear or a butterfly or other ridiculous doodads on it.

"It looks sexy," she murmured. The hiked-up side gave her a dashing, risque appearance. Like a woman who was longing to fall in love? She grinned, her hazel eyes dancing with mischief and excitement, and grabbed the hair spray, proud of her handiwork.

"Oh, you've missed your calling, Edna Wilkins.

Should've gone to beauty school, I do declare," she said, adopting a silly Southern accent and rolling her eyes, as she sprayed her hair.

A small, furry-legged spider inched its way across the side of the medicine-cabinet mirror, pausing briefly to inspect the small area of cracked glass, and crawled hastily into the safety of a corner crevice of the ceiling.

"Aaah!" She let out a piercing, high-pitched squeal. It was right smack in the corner where she couldn't get at it to swat it with a newspaper or anything.

Edna brandished the hair-spray can like a lethal weapon, both her hands clenching it tightly. Spraying the little varmints when they were in hard-to-get-at corners always worked, she'd found.

"You're not getting away," she called to it, letting out a good blast of hair spray, holding the can up above her head. Its small, plump black body convulsed and quivered as though it had been drenched in deadly tear gas.

She gave it one final squirt to be certain and its tiny hairy legs curled up and were still. Then she tore off a piece of toilet paper, smashed it, flushed it down the toilet, and washed her hands thoroughly with soap.

Lord, how she hated spiders. Even the little ones. If you were fool enough to let the little ones escape, you just had to worry whether they were skulking around your house, busily growing into huge disgusting tarantula creatures. The thought was enough to give you nightmares.

She gave her hair another shot of spray and walked out of the bathroom, thinking how she didn't like to brag, but she really did look great.

She stood in the bedroom and applied some pink lipstick to match the dress, then added mascara and a dab of pale blue eyeshadow, something she rarely wore. Except on special occasions, and this definitely qualified as that.

She picked up her purse and car keys and locked the front door, double-checking it carefully. Paranoiacally, she looked feverishly around the yard, hardly aware she was half-expecting to glimpse the scraggly black cat.

It was 7:03 and the movie started at 7:30. That was when Gene was supposed to meet her in front of the theater. He probably thought she was eccentric and way too old-fashioned, not permitting him to pick her up at her house but she didn't care. You just couldn't be too damned careful these days. And her nerves were shattered enough as it was, what with the cat, without inviting more stress by allowing a strange man to come to her home.

He *could* be a goddamn serial killer, for all she knew.

Chapter Twenty-seven

Gene popped a vitamin C tablet into his mouth and took an antihistamine just as he was leaving work. He felt a little better. His throat wasn't raw and burning anymore, as if someone had stuck a hot poker down it. And he was merely a little congested. His sinuses ached and he still had a runny nose, but hopefully the pill would take care of that.

He jumped into his car and rushed home to take a quick shower and put on black pants, pleated in front, black leather loafers, and a white cotton shirt. He put his watch back on and squirted a good shot of cologne, then ran down the pearl-gray carpeted steps to the first floor to give Sylvia her cat food.

"Be good, girl. See ya later," he said, and petted her a little, but she was too interested in her dinner to care.

He grabbed a box of tissues off the dining-room table, deciding he'd better take it with him, and gave his pink-tipped nose a good honk before he went out the door. When he passed through the living room, he checked his hair in the large mirror that hung in back of the green-and-white sectional couch, raking his hand backward through it.

"I look like a damn skunk," he muttered, staring at his dark hair with the chunk of grayish-white centered in one area, as if it had been painted on. If the gray hairs were equally distributed, fine. But all in one spot like that. He looked just like a skunk and he hated it. And when it got too long, like it was now, it tended to stand out above his head like some weird nimbus.

He shook his head, tucked the tissue box under one arm, and hurried out to the car. He'd stop for a hair cut at the small barbershop close to where he worked.

After parking the car, Gene entered the barber-shop and sat in the chair. The barber cut and styled his hair and after wrestling with the gray stripe to make it behave, Gene tipped him generously.

"Hey, thanks, Skunk," Lew said, grinning as he looked down at the bills.

The barbers at the shop had nicknamed him Skunk, and had laughed about how he was too young to have all that gray, and how it wasn't fair to have it all centrally located. He had told them he hated it; that it was a mixed blessing with women. They either seemed to hate the gray stripe or else be turned on by it. It was weird.

"You gotta hot date tonight, huh? That why you gettin' that skunk stripe all gussied up?" Lew chortled, palming the bills into the pocket of his white jacket uniform. He flashed Gene a big grin and winked.

"Uh, yeah. A real hot date," Gene agreed. He jerked a tissue out of his pocket and blew his nose hard and sniffled.

"Thought so. Got some kinda fancy cologne on, too. Smells expensive." Lew picked the hairs out of a comb as he talked.

"It is," Gene said, and honked his nose one more time for good measure. "But she's worth it."

The other men in the shop laughed, and Gene exited into the crackling bright sunshine. A suffocating dry heat wrapped the atmosphere in its snug, stifling arms, and Gene's forehead dotted with big droplets of perspiration in just a few seconds. He wished the damned heat wave they were having would let up.

He stood on the curb for a few minutes, blinking into the hot sun, and noticed there was a flower shop right across the street. It was open, too. An old woman with a big pink hat waddled inside with a huge shopping bag on her arm.

He wanted to get Edna some flowers. He hadn't bought flowers for a woman in years, actually, not since he'd dated his ex-wife, Diane. He wondered if Edna would think it was stupid, like some love-sick high-school kid. But didn't all women love flowers? Besides, he just wanted to. He didn't care if it made him look sentimental.

And he wanted to get roses.

He knew that roses cost a small fortune these days; prices had risen, of course, since *he'd* last bought any. But what the hell. Maybe he'd just get half a dozen. He didn't want to bowl Edna over, or make her think he was weird, splurging on roses the very first time they went out.

He plunked his soggy, wadded-up tissue into a trashcan on the street corner and waited for the "Walk" sign. It was a busy little shopping area with popular stores on both sides of the street and several tall office buildings, one of which was his own. He'd parked almost directly in front of the barbershop at a parking meter, and left both windows rolled down to let in the cool air. The sign blinked on and off, and people hurried across the busy intersection.

Gene cut across toward the flower shop, in long strides. It was 7:05. He had to hurry. He was meeting Edna at 7:30 at the theater. It wasn't far, maybe two miles, but who knew how long getting the roses would take?

Just before he reached the other side of the street, he squinted and shaded his eyes with one hand. He thought he'd seen a cat in between shoppers hurrying by. A big black cat.

212

He stepped up on the curb and turned around to scan the crowd. Several people went in a bookstore, a few walked into the drugstore beside it. A small knot of women studied fashions outside a women's clothing store. A man on the corner stopped to put a letter in a mailbox and a teenager was fooling with the parking meter in front of his green car.

No cat. He could've sworn he'd seen it, crossing the intersection as the crowd did, hurrying along, keeping stride with the shoppers, as if it didn't want to be noticed, didn't want to make itself conspicuous.

And it looked like the ugly bastard that had tipped his margarita over in the hot tub. Either that, or he was losing his mind. True, he hadn't gotten a good look at the animal, but it was big and it was black. He could tell that much. How many black cats in this city could be *that* fat? It was mangy, too, looked like a tattered ruffian, a vagabond wanderer of a cat that belonged to no one. He shivered. Damn, he wished he'd gotten a look at its eyes. There sure as hell couldn't be two cats alive with those same fucked-up, lopsided eyes! At any rate, it had disappeared into thin air now.

Gene shook his head and went into the flower shop. He bought half a dozen long-stemmed roses with a spray of baby's breath, and went back to his car, checking his watch anxiously. "Jesus, 7:20 already!" he cried.

He shouldn't have stood on the street corner, gaping around, looking for the damn cat, just wasting time. He was getting a real complex about that animal, and he had to shake it off. It was ridiculous.

He reached through the open window of the car and laid the spray of flowers down on the seat gently, then loped around the opposite side and got in. Christ, he hoped he wasn't late.

He leaned to look in the rear-view mirror at his hair and patted it down a little. "Not bad—for a skunk." He grinned and then inspected his teeth, too. He clicked on the ignition and pulled out of the parking spot hastily, eager to be on his way, suddenly filled with anticipation like a kid going to Disney World for the very first time.

Chapter Twenty-eight

Edna drove slowly to the theater, eschewing the beltway, taking small side streets instead. It practically gave her anxiety attacks to drive on the beltway. Whenever she had taken it, she became horrendously nervous, gripping the steering wheel in a frantic death clutch until her knuckles turned sheet-white. She was too scared even to change lanes and was petrified by the high speeds at which some of the drivers rode. The exit ramps scared her silly, too. Cars merged so damned fast and recklessly. But the theater was only one exit away so it was just as quick to take side streets, really.

She debated possible topics of conversation to pursue with Gene. It had been so long since she'd been in the company of a man. That is to say, just her and a man and on a date.

She worried, hoping she didn't clam up. She was shy and reserved until she got to know a person, and it had been so long since she'd had to entertain a man she hardly knew what on earth to talk about. Suddenly the idea of spending an entire evening with Gene seemed frightening and tension-filled instead of fun.

She could feel her hands becoming slick and moist with apprehension.

"Thank God we're going to a movie," she breathed, steering the car to the center line a little more to make room for a biker. At least that was some help. It would use up two hours of their time without having to talk. No doubt he'd want to take her for a cup of coffee or something afterwards, maybe a sandwich. Then she'd be forced to entertain him probably for a whole hour or so. Maybe more.

Why had she gotten herself into this? It was all that nosey, meddlesome Helen's fault.

She stopped at a red light, got a peppermint candy from her purse, and glanced over to her left. A greasy-haired youth grinned at her from his beat-up jeep, showing dirty yellow teeth, and one skinny pale white arm laid across the steering wheel as he tapped his fingers restlessly against the dashboard in a fitful, hyperactive motion. He winked lasciviously and his eyes dropped unabashedly to Edna's bosom. His hair was spiky platinum-blond and he needed a shave.

That's where they always look first, trying to size up your boobs right off the bat, thought Edna. *So long as those boobs are good and hefty, why then, most men don't give a damn if you have a face like an old hound dog.*

But Gene was different. Gene had looked her square in the eye after the most cursory glance at her figure and she liked that in a man.

Edna looked over at the kid again. He was still staring, his eyes lowered and hooded. Edna turned scarlet and pretended to study the scenery. Damn it, would the light never change? Finally it did and the kid took off, laying a rubber patch, his muffler chugging loudly. A black polluted cloud of smoke issued from his tailpipe.

"Oughta get a damn tune-up instead of out drag racing," Edna muttered indignantly. She peeled off another peppermint, zipped the roll back into her purse, and accelerated. It was 7:10.

The closer she got to the theater, the more nervous she felt, fighting off an urge to sneak back home and relax. Maybe she could call up Helen and admit what a chickenshit she was and ask her to go on a double date with her and Gene. Helen could ask that fellow, Freddy. That way there would be four people to talk to and she could get to know Gene gradually.

She wasn't ready for this. Going out on a date felt stupid when you were forty! But it was too late to back out. Gene would think she was a jerk if she stood him up. An inconsiderate jerk.

She eased into the crowded parking lot at the shopping center and took a last, careful glance in the mirror on her visor. She added a little more lipstick and pulled a few curls down into place around her face, then walked up to the theater. Her new shoes felt too tight and squeaked a little as she walked.

Part of her wished she was at home, bare-footed, with a juicy romance and a big cool glass of iced tea. But another part of her couldn't wait to see Gene , a small kernel of hope blossoming deep in her heart, hope that he was "the one," someone she could love and who would love her in return, someone she'd wished for all her life.

There was that slim chance—and as long as there was—why then, she'd go on this damnable date and see what happened. If he turned out to be just another creep, so what? At least she had her romance books to fall back on. And Petey for company.

A group of fifteen or twenty people were in a single file to buy tickets. A bushy-haired young black man lolled up against the side of the marquee, slyly studying people as they strolled past. Edna thought he looked suspicious. He was stringbean-thin with corded muscles and bloodshot, hooded eyes that studied every inch of her when he glanced her way.

Edna crossed quickly in front of him, wincing a bit as the new shoes pinched her toes, and stood at the opposite side of the theater, as far away from him as she could possibly get.

His ogling had unnerved her and she hoped he wouldn't approach her. She turned to study the marquee, which extolled the virtues of *Pretty Woman, Home Alone, Robin Hood* and three others.

She flipped another peppermint into her mouth and noted the price of tickets had gone up again. It was practically seven dollars now, and Edna wagged her head, lamenting the old days. Hell, you'd think the avaricious theater owners were making enough money off the snack stand inside without charging a fortune for the tickets, too.

Popcorn was three dollars a bucket; sodas almost two dollars. By the time you went to the movies and got yourself some popcorn and a drink you'd spent enough money to go to a half-decent restaurant. Movies used to be the cheap entertainment, but those days were gone.

She sucked the peppermint and cast a worried eye at the young man, who had begun pacing a little, to and fro, in tiny hectic strides. He was mumbling to himself distractedly and taking small, useless punches at the air with one fist.

God, she wished Gene would get here. She didn't know whether to be angry with him or concerned. She pushed her bangs back from her forehead and inspected the marquee a minute longer, then turned around and spotted the bloodshot-eyed punk studying her behind. She wheeled back to face the marquee once again, gazing at it with renewed dedication. She glanced

219

down at her wrist to check her watch. 7:25.

She felt irritation building, a tight angry spiral moving upward from her stomach. Gene really should have been here by now; it was inconsiderate as hell. She wondered for a moment if she'd managed to get hooked up with an insensitive brute like James again. Oh surely, not *twice* in her lifetime! It wasn't possible.

She'd read that book, *Smart Women, Foolish Choices*, and paid particular attention to the part about how some women chose the same damned man over and over, always picking a loser. She'd read it and tried to understand and felt a spark of hope at the notion that she didn't have to pick a James clone. She'd felt a shaky confidence building, that maybe—just maybe—someday she'd be capable of picking a decent man, one who would treat her well. Someday.

But now, here was Gene Martin, already behaving in quite a Jamesian manner, rude traits surfacing, and on their very first date. Had she made another foolish choice? Was she doomed to repeat the same foolish choices concerning men?

The thought made her feel close to tears. Down deep in her heart, Edna knew she didn't want to spend the rest of her life alone. Yet she didn't want to spend it with someone like James, either. She'd rather be alone than suffer that kind of marriage again!

She twisted her head around and again noticed the man eyeing her with a brooding, lustful expression as he hopped agitatedly from foot to foot. Edna watched for a second and it made her feel uneasy. Wasn't that what they referred to as the "junkie shuffle?" She recalled reading something to that affect in some article.

He rolled his eyes in her direction and muttered something unintelligible. God, she hoped he didn't think she was trying to get picked up. She *was* dawdling, just loitering like a woman in search of a man. And it was Gene's fault.

Wasn't that just like a man? Inconsiderate.

Damn it, the picture was beginning in five more minutes, and she wanted some popcorn, too. The popcorn line was a mile long. She could see it through the glass windows. One slow, fat pimply boy worked the counter alone, taking his good old time, shuffling tediously between the popcorn bin and the counter as if he had all the time in the world.

Edna began to feel churlish at the thought of missing the beginning of the movie. Often important things happened in the beginning, things you needed to know to understand what in the hell was going on later. Crucial information.

Edna checked her watch again and twisted her opal ring around nervously. The suspicious-looking character took a few tottering, aimless steps in her direction. He'd gotten a toothpick from God knew where and had inserted it between two grimy yellow teeth. It wobbled up and down in mid-air as he nibbled at it, narrowing his eyes in concentration.

He was clearly approaching her, and Edna grew nervous. All the people had gotten their tickets and were safely inside the theater. She brimmed with aggravation at Gene. It was now 7:40.

"Oh, the hell with it," she whispered softly, and gulped. She stuck her chin high into the air, hoping it would deflect the man, and marched primly to the ticket counter, setting her handbag on top of it. She didn't intend to be stuck outside here with some young spaced-out punk eyeballing her like that. She wasn't going to take a chance on getting mugged—or worse—raped.

Edna didn't care if it did make Gene angry that she'd already gone inside. *She* was the one who had a right to be angry. It was already 7:45! He'd caused them to miss fifteen minutes of the show. Also, it was humid and hot as hell out here, nice and cool in there. She could feel perspiration dampening her armpits, no doubt ruining the pretty delicate pink dress. And her forehead was all sweaty, like a worked-up lumberjack, dampening tendrils of hair around her face. She felt like a wilted, day-old petunia.

The heat seemed to hang suspended with a palpable heaviness that made her feel drowsy and suffocated and waspish.

"I'd like one ticket for *Pretty Woman*, please," Edna said, thrusting a ten-dollar bill at the blond teen behind the window. She collected the ticket and her change and glimpsed the black man at the side of her, looking deflated as he gnawed on the toothpick. His slitted dark eyes scanned the bills as she stuffed them quickly into her purse.

She twisted to the side and opened the glass doors. She'd wait in the lobby for a while. Maybe Gene had been in an accident or something. But maybe he'd stood her up. Maybe he was sorry he'd ever asked her out.

She gulped and, to her horror, tears stung her eyes. She blinked rapidly before they threatened to flood her eyes, and stared outside at the street to see if she could spy him pulling up into the parking lot.

The tight shoes were making mincemeat of her toes, and she shifted from one foot to the other. Then she sat down on the edge of some orange-cushioned seats near the window. At 7:50, after fidgeting and peering anxiously out the windows, Edna had had enough.

The buttery smell of hot popcorn was intoxicating. At last she decided to buy a small cup, to wait just a few more minutes, and then to go inside the movie to wait. She could always watch the film and keep an eye out for Gene. She'd get an aisle seat near the back of the theater. That way, if he came in, she would spot him immediately.

His inconsiderateness, though, nagged at her. There was no excuse for his being this late and on a first date, too, unless he had a really good reason.

It reminded her of James. Even on their first few dates, he'd been late, shown up when he pleased, with some piddly stupid excuse. Then the little incidents of inconsideration turned into bigger ones. Like knocking her around the kitchen when she'd added a little too much garlic to the spaghetti sauce, bellowing a mad stream of curses and insults, treating her like a dog. "Christ, Edna!" he'd shout, with a puffy red face, "are ya deliberately trying to give me heartburn with that shit? What'd ya do, dump the whole fuckin' bottle in, fer Chrissake? I'll have the back-door trots all night!"

Edna trembled, remembering how he'd shoved her up against the stove and the handle of the refrigerator. Her arm had been black and blue for two weeks from the bruise. And the lousy son of a bitch had broken down sobbing then, begging her to forgive him, and then begging her to stay with him. She had been mute and silent and he'd threatened her then—told her he'd kill her if she ever left him.

Edna shuddered at the memory.

But *this* wasn't James, she reminded herself harshly. She had to remember that. She had to give Gene a chance. Maybe he had a good reason for being late. Maybe he'd had a flat tire or a dead battery or something.

By the time she went inside the darkened theater, Richard Gere was firmly besotted by Julia Roberts. An unlikely story of a hooker capturing a slick millionaire's fancy, it was nonetheless quite engaging, just the kind of fairytale romance Edna adored, the kind you only found in books and movies.

She dug into her popcorn and glanced up eagerly at each person who came down the aisle. She'd taken an aisle seat all the way in the back so she could spot Gene easily, but she saw no handsome man with a dazzling streak of gray slashed across his hair.

Edna told herself she didn't give a damn that he'd stood her up, but that was a bald-faced lie, of course. When she finished the popcorn, she ducked out into the lobby, just to check one last time, feeling like a silly fool. But he wasn't there.

Face it, she told herself bitterly, *he isn't coming*. He'd dumped her before they had even got started. He was probably off guzzling martinis on a barstool with some young blonde.

She returned to her seat and slumped back down into it to watch the rest of the movie, ignoring the hot glaze of tears that misted her eyes. Richard Gere's luscious silvery locks reminded her of Gene's hair a little.

Julia Roberts stuck to her guns and demanded marriage from Richard. *Smart girl*, cheered Edna silently. She stood right up to him. Told him she wanted "the fairy tale," and didn't want to be his crummy mistress. Refused to play second fiddle. Julia was no dummy; Julia didn't make foolish choices.

"That's right, Julia, you tell him," Edna whispered, not caring that she was talking out loud. So what? No one was nearby. Everyone, it seemed, had dates to snuggle up with or a friend to talk to.

She wept at the end when Richard pulled up outside Julia's tawdry abode in a white stretch limousine with flowers and the sun shining down on his magnificent silvery head. After mulling it over, wearing that brooding, sensitive expression which made Edna drool, he'd come to his senses and accepted Julia's no-nonsense terms. Marriage. The fairy tale.

"Go for it, Julia," mumbled Edna, wiping at her eyes with a soppy tissue. Oh, Julia was wise, all right. She knew she wouldn't have those long slender legs forever, nor that unlined face. Better she should make her demands now, before she lost her looks. Before she married some penniless, philandering abusive fool—like James.

Edna blew her nose loudly, patted her eyes with the tissue, and wadded it up to push it into the side compartment of her purse. She inched her toes along the floor, seeking the high heels she'd taken off, punching her feet back into them against their will. She couldn't wait to get home and yank them off. Her little toes probably had blisters on them by now. The credits rolled across the screen, along with the catchy "Pretty Woman," tune, and she snatched up her purse and went for the door, still feeling weepy over the sentimental ending.

Before exiting, she glanced around just to see if she saw that creepy punk again. She didn't want him following her to her car for a sneak attack.

But he was gone. Probably busy preying on some other helpless female who looked vulnerable, she thought to herself.

Edna minced along to the parking lot, moaning as the shoes pinched her toes. She would've worn her flats and been comfortable if she'd thought he was going to stand her up. Then a huge wave of disappointment washed over her again and she found herself wiping warm sticky tears off her face as she got in the car to drive home, thinking of Gene and wondering why he'd done it. Why had he pretended to like her, to be attracted to her, only to stand her up?

She supposed that busybody Helen had foisted her phone number off on the poor man. Perhaps he hadn't actually been interested in her, after all. But he had seemed interested in the grocery store and on the phone, too. It didn't make sense.

God, she'd made such a fool of herself, wearing this foolish sentimental flowered dress, like a young hopeful teenaged girl. She guided the car one-handed and dug into her purse for a tissue. When it was sopping wet, she tossed it onto the passenger seat and pulled more out of the glove compartment, crying into them until they were a soggy mess. It was stupid to bawl like a baby over it.

"When will you learn?" she cried, beating a hand against the steering wheel. "When will you learn that men just let you down? There's only a handful of good ones around—and they're all taken."

She came to a stop for a red light and pulled the visor mirror down to look at herself. The mascara had run below her eyes, making her look like a raccoon. Not a pretty sight.

She blew her nose with a loud snort on her last tissue and debated stopping for a cheeseburger and fries, but decided she was too full of buttered popcorn to bother.

Dark thunderclouds were gathering above, like an unspoken threat of doom. A tiny slice of moon peeked through a hazy mist of cloud and then disappeared in the thick darkness, leaving the night silent and gloomy, like an endless black abyss, matching her somber mood.

She wondered where and what Gene was doing right now, then pushed her mind away from thoughts of him and stared sullenly at the road ahead, looking for the turn-off.

She wondered where the cat was, too, and a prickly sensation of goose bumps jitterbugged down her forearms. She turned onto her street, Holloway Road, and a thick heavy blackness engulfed the car, as if it had been swallowed up into a bottomless pit. Inky-black clouds dotted the sky, like ghoulish corpses dancing across the heavens.

Edna began to feel tense, a prescient anxiety overwhelming her swiftly and completely. *Stop being so nervous*, she told herself silently.

Holloway Road was long and lonesome, with only the two houses at the end. A small, two-lane back road, dogwood and pine trees were on one side, and a lot of tall weeds interspersed with forsythia bushes and honeysuckle were on the other.

"God, it's really dark with Janet gone," Edna murmured, thin beads of sweat rising across her forehead. A narrow, silvery piece of moon reappeared briefly and then was lost again in the dense desolate black clouds. It was so dark that Edna thought she couldn't even see her hand in front of her face.

Edna trembled as she was suddenly stricken with that unsettling, niggling sense of foreboding once again. In the distance, something gave a piercing wolf cry that caused her heart to leap and the skin on her nape to crawl. Just like a wolf baying at the moon. But there weren't any wolves around here, were there? Her heart thudded dully, skittishly.

The car windows were down and the cloying scent of honeysuckle bombarded the air with a sickish, pungent odor that made her think of rotting cadavers. Her upper lip broke out into fresh droplets of slick sweat.

Something is watching me.

The thought intruded urgently, demanding her attention. She gulped and pulled into the driveway of her house a bit too fast, suddenly frantic to get out of the car and safely inside the house.

Something is watching. . . .

Her brain buzzed with the nonsensical, crazy thought and she felt flushed, her nerves zinging. She threw the shift into park and glanced nervously around at the thick blanket of darkness. She was thankful she'd left the tiny porch light on, even though it provided little illumination.

"Better than nothing," Edna whispered in a raspy, dry voice.

The street appeared uncommonly dark and

deserted, like some lonesome forsaken grave-yard. Usually Janet had her porch light on, which was far more brilliant than Edna's. Also, Janet was in the habit of burning every damned light in the house when she was at home, so her absence created a yawning, black hole, plunging the street into an almost surreal darkness.

The thought grabbed at Edna again: *Something bad, something terrible terrible terrible is going to happen*! She swallowed again, her throat transformed into a dry husk. She clicked off the ignition and pushed the headlights knob off, throwing the car into sudden near-total darkness, the puny radiance from her own porch light like one drop of water in the middle of an ocean. A prickly chill crept up the back of her neck as a sudden coil spring of tension pervaded the air. She threw the car door open and the atmosphere felt stiff, suffocating, prescient with a malicious danger.

I'll run, she thought, wiping clammy sweat from her lip. *I'll run like hell to the door, that's all*.

She was seized with a dark presentiment of foreboding and again the thought hit her like an iron fist punching her in the gut: *Something is watching*!

Her eyes darted quickly across the front lawn, her heartbeat shifting into overdrive with a fast, irregular thumping. Stygian black shadows loomed everywhere, wavery and mysterious, changing shapes with a frightening swiftness. Pitch black. Like the cat!

Oh God, how could she ever see it in this gaping darkness? Its fat black body would blend right in with the darkness of night, the perfect foil to shield it from her eyes until it was too late.

She hitched her handbag up high on her shoulder and leaped out of the car, not even bothering to lock it this time, not giving a damn, because something didn't feel *right*, because she was terrified. She could feel hairs standing up on her forearms, despite the warm, humid night. Her new shoes crunched against the gravel like clacking bones, the toes biting ruthlessly at her feet.

She had to get inside. *Now*.

"Better go inside faaaast, Edna, ya stupid twit!" jeered James's taunting voice inside her head, and Edna quivered with fright, wondering if the message had been telepathically sent from the black cat lurking nearby somewhere.

She could *feel* its evil presence and tried to run, but it was impossible in her heels. Her foot twisted and she cried out in pain. Then she loped, stumbling across the driveway toward the safety of the tiny porch light, shining like a beacon of salvation, her purse bumping heavily against her hip.

The porch light was so small. Why was it so damnably small? It offered no more light than a child's tiny nightlight. As her high heels crunched drunkenly through the drive, Edna had the eerie, distinct feeling something was following her now. Watching her, coming after her, hot on her trail.

She whipped her head around, her hazel eyes large and full of fear, her heartbeat thudding crazily, her breathing stertorous and labored. But nothing was there, save the ominous silence.

Her car keys jingled and bounced together like a specter's burdensome chains as she tripped up the three concrete porch steps and inserted the key into the lock. She jammed it in with a vicious desperation, the cold fear pricking her like needles of ice. Her hand shook and the key fell out of the lock.

She was breathing like a winded, overweight jogger, her lungs laboring, as though the devil himself had pursued her. Something *was* chasing her. She could feel its unholy presence though it remained invisible. It was here, in this yard, with her.

"Oh, God save me!" Edna prayed as she wiggled the recalcitrant key in the lock, but the door stubbornly refused to open.

The night air seemed charged with a thick, electric intensity, a palpable evil. Something was coming for her; she could feel it in her bones. Her legs started shaking as a soft, faint meow whined through the night. Then it grew slightly louder, reverberating through the empty street, more irate, more demanding and dangerous, the sound of a predator stalking its helpless prey.

"Oh God!" Edna moaned. She jiggled the key, pushing hard at the door with her fist. The meow lulled and dissolved into a low, guttural growl.

"Come on, open. *Open*, goddamn it!" she hissed, her breath huffing. "Come *on*!" She rammed the door harder, aware that the whining, moaning cry of a cat sounded very near now.

She heard it again. That low, triumphant death growl somewhere across the lawn. She could see nothing but hellishly black shadows as the wind rustled menacingly through the trees.

"Oh, please, God," Edna cried, thumping at the door with her balled-up fist. Suddenly it burst open so fast she had to catch herself to keep from stumbling headfirst across the threshold.

"Oooh," she groaned, falling halfway to the floor before she was able to brace herself. She frantically groped for the doorknob, her fingernails scraping the wood.

Then it was upon her, hissing and yowling, its hot, rank breath nearly gagging her with the sour, vile odor of ancient graves. She caught her balance feebly, only to be thrown off balance again, huffing as her purse tumbled off her shoulder. The sheer weight and adrenaline-charged fury of the black cat felled her as it leaped at her like a fiendish missile.

Edna lay on her back sprawled half in and half out the front door, her limbs askew like an awkward, broken marionette. She lifted her head to look at the creature. Its snarling, pointed feline face loomed only inches above hers, a gargoylish mask of burning, flaming hatred. It sprayed stringy hot saliva onto her pink flowered dress as it hissed at her, showing enormous, lethally jagged fangs. Sheer terror knifed through Edna.

"Dear God. James! James, don't hurt me!"

Edna sucked in her breath audibly as she met its milky glazed eye. "It—it's really *you*, James," she gasped, trembling with shock.

Its hooded eyes shone with complete knowledge, as though it knew her inside and out, as though it had known her all her life. Its eyes regarded her in that accusing, malevolent manner and she knew with every fiber of her being that it was the very same eyes she'd watched as James lay dying. James's eyes, burning down at her, through her, into the very depths of her soul, sucking the strength and life out of her.

Her heart quickened with terror at the horrible sight and even the air felt as if it were bristling with a hot, burning maleficence.

It wants to kill me, she thought dumbly. *He wants to kill me—just like I killed him.*

She groped and pawed for her purse before the animal could tear and lunge at her, but she was too late. As her fingers twitched and raked at the carpeting for the purse handle, she could feel a hot, searing pain rip through her thigh muscle, gnawing, mercilessly raking and slicing at the soft flesh of her leg with its long, razor-sharp claws.

The purse weighed a ton. If she could just reach it, she could slam it against the bastard, knock it unconscious if she got lucky.

The cat whined and hissed with an eerie keening as it tore at her again and again, hellbent on its blood-thirsty savage revenge. Its pointed fangs glinted like razor blades as the tiny porch light shone across them.

"Oh, dear God, please help me . . ." Edna murmured, sobbing, blinded by tears. She kicked helplessly at the fiend, jackknifing her body halfway, simultaneously closing a hand around the purse strap. She clutched it tight and raised it above her head, grunting like a worn-out sow, to send it crashing down upon the beast's right ear.

"Mmrawwwwrrrr!" It screamed in outrage and lifted a claw, hissing its foul nasty breath at her, breath that reeked of blood and massacre. A foamy, putrid spittle seeped from its mouth in glistening wet strings.

"Good!" Edna screamed.

She raised the purse high again and struck it across the buttocks, a good hard blow. She kept flinging the purse at it, viciously slinging it with all her might on the downstroke, kicking at the monster, desperate to keep it at bay until she could manage to inch her legs across the threshhold and lock the door.

Its heavy weight on her chest was like a suffocating vise. It sunk its claw into her left arm, but only made a surface scratch as she jerked her arm away and lifted the purse to clobber it again. Its hot rancid breath made her stomach heave, her head swim dizzily from the sickening stink.

"So help me, James, I'll break your backbone if I can!" she yelled.

It sprang into the air and raked a sharp bloody claw across her calf. She dropped the purse clumsily outside the door, but managed to drag her legs inside the doorframe at last, grunting with the hard-won victory.

"You son of a bitch! Oh, you son of a bitch . . ."

Weeping uncontrollably, she slid the bolt home and fixed the chain, with her fingers trembling so bad it took three tries. She was afraid to push the tiny white window curtains aside, afraid she'd see that hideous spooky black face pressed to the window like some terrifying grinning death mask.

Waiting for her. Waiting for her, just biding its time patiently, until she was fool enough to open the door again. It wanted to kill her. She realized that now. It was growing sick and tired of fun and games. It meant to kill her!

Slowly, stealthily, her heartbeat triphammering with trepidation, she inched the wood door open and snatched her purse inside, her eyes rolling wildly from side to side to see if the cat was crouched nearby. Then she slammed the door.

The cat was miraculously gone as suddenly as it had come. She'd seen hide nor hair of the beast. The night was dark and serene, as if the attack had never happened. But it had left behind a little "souvenir" of their escapade. Something bright and shiny was carefully linked around the purse strap, winking up at her with a familiar brilliance.

Edna gasped with horror. It was her heart-shaped locket. She bent to untwine it from the purse strap and held it in the palm of her hand, gazing down at it, unaware her eyes were brimming with horrified tears.

Once more, the cat had left its ineluctable "signature." It was taking no chances. It meant to be dead certain she knew its identity.

As if she had any doubts.

Chapter Twenty-nine

Gene was barrel-assing down North Court Road, popping orange-flavored mints into his mouth, wishing he had a cigarette. He clicked open the glove compartment and pawed through its contents to see if he'd stashed a pack in there, but no such luck.

He clicked the radio on to an FM station and listened to Cher belting out something about turning back time. If anybody could do that, it was Cher, all right. At forty-five years old, she looked like a gangly teenager.

It was already 7:25, but he'd be okay. Hell, it was only about a half-mile away now. Three or four more stoplights and he'd have it made in the shade. He gobbled down the rest of the mints and peeled open a package of soda crackers that had been in the glove compartment. Without the cigarettes, it seemed that all he could do was eat, eat, eat.

He warbled along with Cher a little in between bites of cracker, and pulled up to a red light.

Something made a rustling noise in the back of the car.

Gene swallowed the rest of the crackers and cocked an ear to see if he heard the noise again. He wondered if cigarette withdrawal included hearing things, jumping at shadows, and imagining you saw black cats everywhere.

Christ, he wished he had a cigarette, he thought, laying his left arm on the window frame. The date with Edna was making him a nervous wreck, as well as thinking he'd seen that damn cat back there at the intersection.

A Madonna song was on next and Gene whistled along with it, tapping the window frame of the car with his fingertips.

It was 7:28 now.

Gene hit the accelerator harder. He was only two stoplights away, but they were far apart. The scent of roses filled the car. He hoped Edna liked them. Then it occurred to him how stupid it had been of him to buy them. He was meeting her at the theater. What the hell was she going to do with roses at the movies? The flowers would have to stay in the car and wilt while they saw the show. He shook his head and laughed.

Then he heard the strange rustling noise again.

He hit the brakes gently as he came to a stoplight. There were several issues of *The*

Washington Post in the back of the car, as he remembered. Was that the source of the rustling?

The light turned green and Gene accelerated as he twisted his head backward to get a glimpse of the papers.

They *were* moving. They were wiggling around like an earthquake had struck, in fact. Gene's mouth dropped open like a fish out of water gasping for air, as the newspapers rose high into the air.

The last thing he saw before he rammed the car ahead of him was a flash of brutal fangs and yellowish hate-filled eyes as the black cat lunged at him.

Chapter Thirty

Edna wept awhile, gulping down hitching shaky sobs, then stopped, examined her flowered dress, which was forever ruined, and fresh tears started.

"Goddamn you! *Damn* you, James!" she cried, fully aware of how insane she sounded, cussing out a cat whom she believed was possessed by her dead husband's spirit.

She dragged herself off the floor and staggered into the bedroom to take off her dress, careful to avoid the mirror. Ribbons of smeared sticky red blood were ground into the beautiful material. The white lace was spotted with uneven bloody patches across the cuffs and neck.

"Might as well trash it. It'll never come clean,"

she mumbled, her voice catching. She took off the white lace slip, which had a huge bloodstain across the hem, tossed it into a heap on top of the dress, and fell onto the bed moaning.

Her face stung from the scratches and her legs screamed with pain, like thousands of tiny needles jabbing her skin, and her thighs ached dully. The demon had pulled and yanked at her hair and it stood out wildly in a bedraggled scarecrow's nimbus about her head. The blood from her legs was probably staining the mattress, she thought. She supposed she'd better get up.

She rubbed at her temples and rolled to a sitting position. She had to get up, get moving. She couldn't let this throw her into a blind panic.

She peeled off her shredded pantyhose, weeping at the sight of her torn screaming red flesh, then took off her panties and bra. A good hot bath in Epsom Salt, that was what she needed. Badly.

She groaned and crept into the hallway to search through the linen closet for the Epsom Salt. Finding it, she dumped it into the filling tub and then sank into it minutes later as it continued to fill with hot steaming water. Every bone in her body ached. Even though she'd wiped her face and legs before getting into the bath in an effort to get the blood off, the water was already turning a pinkish color.

Edna raised her legs up to rest on the edge of

the tub, and leaned over to pull a length of toilet paper from the roller. She pressed a folded piece over the wounds to stop the bleeding. Her legs looked like they'd been ground through a paper shredder.

Oh, how good the hot water felt. She wanted to stay immersed in it forever, the hot liquid a safe cocoon against a world gone crazy.

She let the water rise high in the tub, moaning thinly, and closed her eyes, her head lolling back against the salmon-colored tile wall.

She had to get a grip on herself, make a plan. Make *some* sort of plan, though her brain was spinning like a whirling dervish. She couldn't let the cat terrorize her like this. It wanted to destroy her and she must think of some way to thwart it. Surely there was a way!

But the cat was sly, full of a dark, supernatural cunning, and she was scared to death of it, afraid to leave the house now, terrified it would attack again.

Briefly, she toyed with the idea of inviting Helen to stay with her for a week or so, but she dismissed it rapidly. For one thing, Helen got on her nerves. She'd have to listen to Helen chattering like a magpie day and night. And the donkey laugh, of course, would have her climbing the walls. Besides, Helen was allergic to bird feathers, so with Petey around it was out of the question. She'd be wheezing her fool head off with an asthma attack.

But most of all, she didn't want to put Helen in the position of possibly being endangered. If the cat attacked Helen and hurt her, Edna would never forgive herself.

She didn't even want to *tell* Helen about the cat. She would blab to everyone that Edna had gone crazy, was scared stiff to leave her house just because a common ordinary alley cat had taken to prowling around the premises.

No way, Jose. Helen was out. She would think of some way to get rid of the son of a bitch herself. Maybe the gun wasn't a bad idea, after all. She pulled the plug out of the tub and eased herself out gingerly, blood still running in tiny pinkish rivulets down her calves. She gasped at the sight of her reflection in the full-length mirror on the back of the bathroom door.

God, she looked like she'd been mauled by a dozen alley cats, not just one. Her body was bruised and battered, with pinpoints of caked blood dotting her calves and arm, highlighted by two long, mean-looking scratches down one cheek.

Edna clenched her fists together tightly as a white-hot anger exploded inside her. It thought it could intimidate her. It thought she would knuckle under to the terror like a scared rabbit. She was glad that she'd at least managed to zap it with her purse, at least managed to show it that she would fight, not run away like a bawling baby.

"I'll get you, James. I swear I will. I'll find some way!" she vowed fiercely, spitting the words out, the thought of using the gun getting stronger by the minute.

She opened the medicine cabinet to look for cotton balls and hydrogen peroxide. She lavished the liquid onto a cotton ball and pressed it against the wounds on her face and body, watching as it foamed into a frothy white mound, then cocked her head.

The phone was ringing.

"Hell."

She pushed her feet into her rubber thongs, grabbed a peach-colored towel to wrap tightly about her torso, and went into the kitchen, her hair dripping, wet puddles forming around the damp thongs.

"Uh . . . Hi, Edna . . ." Gene said, sounding sheepish and guilt-ridden.

The very sound of his voice exasperated her. She dabbed at her wet hair with the corner of the towel and replied in a frosty, stiff voice, "I am taking a bath. Or *trying* to." She grabbed a paper towel with her free hand and mopped up the puddle of water dripping beneath the thongs.

"Oh, Edna, please *listen*," he begged, his voice cracking.

"Give me one good reason why I *should*," she felt like saying. She chewed her lip and wondered if she should give him a break. He sounded miserable and weary, as if something had happened to him.

"If you didn't want to come, why did you ask me out in the first place?" Edna inquired peevishly. No sense in letting him off the hook too easily. "Was it Helen's idea?" Her voice had acquired a slightly shrewish whine, but she didn't give a damn. He deserved it, the swine.

Her wet perm dribbled cold droplets of water down her spine and bare legs and she trembled beneath the towel. Petey hopped onto the bars of the cage, his webbed feet splayed, eyeing her with a quirky expression, fluttering feathers out on the kitchen floor for her to sweep up.

"Edna, I—"

"I don't want to talk to you, Gene Martin," she hissed, squirming around to pull the towel tighter.

One of Petey's feathers flew at her nose and she gave a choking cough. Why should she give him a chance? A date was a date, damn it. Just because he was wildly attractive, he probably figured he could just stand her up and then come crawling back with some half-assed excuse. *James* had walked all over her like that, and no way was she ready to go through it again with another man!

"Now, damn it, Edna, let me explain!" Gene's apologetic tone suddenly turned ornery and self-righteous.

"Did she? Did Helen put you up to it?" Edna demanded, halfway ready to cry. She was on a roll now and couldn't stop, all the disappointment metastasized into hot, bubbling anger. "It's okay, Gene. You can confess. I won't bite your head off. After all, it's really not *your* fault," she growled curtly. Helen was the culprit; Gene was more or less an innocent bystander.

"Calm down, Edna. Granted, you have a right to be mad. I stood you up. But I *do* have a good reason, if you'll just let me explain." He paused to clear his throat. "Edna? You there?"

"Y–yes," she answered in a wary, suspicious voice.

She clutched the terrycloth towel about her middle and slumped down heavily on a yellow vinyl stool at the breakfast nook. The damp towel made a wet, squishing noise. She was trembling, ashamed that her eyes were misting with tears, ashamed that she should care so much that this virtual stranger had a reason for standing her up, apparently a half-decent, valid reason, from the sound of his truculent voice.

"I . . . I'm listening," she whispered hoarsely, wiping at one eye with the tip of the towel.

She took a pencil out of the cup on the counter and doodled on a yellow post-it pad, wishing she hadn't sounded so harsh and unforgiving. He probably thought she was a bitch.

"Okay." Gene cleared his throat and began, his voice gruff and nervous at the same time. "I, uh, I was in a car accident, Edna. Oh, I know how damn phony that must sound . . ." His voice trailed off, trying to gauge her response.

"Yes, it does," she immediately agreed, squiggling zeroes and loops on the pad.

"But I really *was*," he nearly shouted, as if to allay any residual doubts she had. "Some idiot cut in front of me and, well I sort of, uh, lost control of the car . . ."

He sounded like he was lying! Edna thought angrily.

"I plowed right into him. I'm in the Emergency Room of Suburban Hospital right now. I didn't have my seatbelt on, like a fool, but the other guy's all right. Damn it, Edna, if you don't believe me, call the hospital and check it out!"

Edna considered this for a moment, mulling it over, trying to judge the truthfulness of it. For a second there, he'd sounded like he was lying, but mostly he sounded sincere. A car accident. Such a trite, hackneyed excuse. Then again, if he'd truly meant to stand her up, why the hell would he even bother to call her with this elaborate excuse? *And* invite her to call the hospital Emergency Room?

She decided he must be telling the truth.

"Are . . . are you all right?" she asked timidly, regretting her waspish tone earlier.

She tapped the pencil in a rapid beat against the formica countertop and watched Petey staring into his tiny mirror on the bars of the cage, love-struck with his own image.

"Well, my forehead hit the rear-view mirror and they had to put ten stitches in it. My back is kinda sore, but I guess I'll live." He paused for a minute, as if there were something else he wanted to tell her. "I could use a night's rest to recuperate, though . . ." He laughed weakly.

"Oh, dear. I'm really sorry, Gene. And I'm sorry I jumped to conclusions, too. I really sounded like a witch." She blushed. *Witch or bitch?* "I do apologize but it looked as if you wanted to call

our date off. I was really mad. Disappointed."
Edna bit her bottom lip nervously and drew
small stars on the post-it. The tip of the pencil
broke off and she traded it for a black ball-
point pen.

"Yes, I know what it must've looked like and
I'm truly sorry," he answered. "Edna, I just want
you to know, I'll never stand you up again. And
this wasn't Helen's idea, either. I've noticed you
shopping in the Safeway a couple of other times,
and I never got up the gumption to speak to you.
I'm a gutless wonder. I was uh . . . thrilled when
you hit me in the tuckus with your shopping
cart."

His voice sounded heartbreakingly sincere and
a thin spark of hope bloomed in Edna's heart like
a ray of brilliant sunshine, spilling over a future
she'd always dreamed of. This man sounded as
if it mattered so much to him that she believe
him.

As if *she* mattered so much.

Edna felt her heart thumping faster with nervous excitement. The tiny stars she was sketching
changed to miniature hearts scrawled across the
pad in a lilting wave.

"I . . . I don't know what to say," she admitted,
feeling self-conscious.

"Say you'll forgive me . . . and that you'll go to
the movies with me tomorrow night?" he suggested, his voice impossibly boyish and eager.

Petey cawed softly and pecked at his beak's
reflection in the plastic mirror.

"Do you think you'll feel up to it by then?" she

asked, stalling for time. How could she possibly go on a date by tomorrow night? Her legs were sliced up like ribbons! Claw marks ran across her cheek, two long scrapes from the cheekbone down to her neck. Not a snowball's chance in hell of disguising them. He'd ask questions and then she'd be up against the wall, forced to either hide the truth or to tell what he would perceive as a wild, implausible tale. Shit, he'd think she was a crazy loon.

Two hot tears slid down Edna's face, stinging it.

"Sure I will. That is, if you don't mind dating a guy with black thread running across one eyelid and a few other battle scars," he joked, sounding happy, ecstatic that she'd forgiven him.

Battle scars. Cripes, he didn't know the half of it! She looked like she'd been dumped into a cage with ten hungry lions. It sounded as if it would benefit them both to stay the hell home and recuperate.

"I—I—" Edna stuttered, not knowing what to say. "I can't. I just *can't*. Not right now, Gene. Maybe later, but not tomorrow night." She gulped back tears and her voice was thick with emotion. Would he wait a few more days or think she was giving him the brush-off because he'd stood her up? The hearts on Edna's pad dissolved into small triangular pyramids composed of severe slash marks.

He took a moment to digest this turn of events. "Well . . . but why not?" he then asked, hurt creeping into his voice.

Trapped, like a jackrabbit trying to escape a wired-up coon hound, Edna thought, panicking.

"I can't." Two sticky tears trailed down her cheeks and she winced from the pain in her face. She drew a few hateful psychotic slashes on the pad. "Not right *now*."

"Hey, what's wrong, Edna?" His voice softened as he sensed something had upset her, something he knew nothing of.

She remained silent, wiping tears off her face with the back of her hand, trying desperately to think of a viable excuse, but her mind was a total blank. The cat had her so stressed out it was becoming hard to think rationally—or to think at all.

"Please tell me. Maybe I can help."

His concern caused her to blurt it out abruptly, almost against her will, as if she'd known him for years, as if he was an old friend. He *felt* like an old friend. She felt some weird cosmic tie to him, corny as it sounded. It was as if they were meant to be together.

"I . . . I just can't right now, Gene. I uh, I'm having a problem. This is going to sound so ridiculously stupid, I know. This uh . . . cat . . . this cat in my neighborhood has been bothering me." Edna drew stick figures of fangs as she talked.

"A cat? What *kind* of cat?" Gene's voice sounded strangled.

"Well . . . it's, uh, just an ordinary stray alley cat. Mangy old thing. A black cat. It's been hanging around the house, that's all. Bothering me. Being a pest."

Her voice quaked anxiously and the words seemed to hang in the air as she sensed a tidal wave of tension flowing across the wire from Gene's end. He thought it was bullshit, no doubt. Some cock-and-bull story she'd invented.

She wondered if she should tell him the whole sordid tale or just shut up while she was ahead. Two more tears danced across her cheeks. She replaced the pen in the cup, crunched up the paper, and threw it in the trash.

Petey leaped up on his red plastic swing and rocked until the bells on the edge of it jingled wildly.

"What do you mean, 'bothering you'?" Gene seemed to sniff out her hesitation with an uncanny accuracy. His voice was stilted with a harsh edge she hadn't heard before.

"Soul mates." The words ran screaming through Edna's brain. Maybe those romance novels weren't so laughable, after all. Maybe there were such things. This man seemed to *know* she was making light of the situation with the cat.

"How?" Gene interrupted her reverie. "*How* has it bothered you, Edna? Edna, are you there?"

Her voice gave a ragged hitch when she spoke. "Oh, it started off by trampling through my azalea bushes, doing harmless things. But then . . ." She fought off a sudden fierce deluge of tears. Suddenly she wanted to tell him all of it. She *needed* to tell him. He was so sympathetic and maybe he'd have some clever idea of how to fight the demon.

"Then what? Come on, please tell me, Edna. I want to help," he pleaded with consternation.

"It attacked me." She gulped. "That's why I don't want to go out with you tomorrow night. I want to wait until the scratches heal. It just attacked me, for no reason at all . . ." Her voice turned to a whimper as he gasped with shock.

"How bad is it, Edna? Are you all right? My God, I can't believe it did that. Can't believe it would be that damned aggressive. It's a black cat, you say?" He swallowed roughly.

"I'll be fine. It really scratched up my legs, though. And my cheek has a couple of claw marks on it. I look like an escapee from a grade-B horror flick." She laughed weakly. "I didn't want you to see . . ." She sniffled and pulled a paper towel off the roll on the table to blow her nose on. "It was a big black cat. Ugly. The ugliest damned critter you've ever seen."

"Oh Jesus," he breathed softly. "How did it happen? Where?" He was full of questions now, firing them at her one right after the other in a taut, urgent tone.

And she'd been scared he wouldn't take her seriously! Or scared he'd chuckle politely and say something like, "Oh, Edna, don't tell me you're scared of a little pussycat? You? A grown woman?"

"It just leaped out at me as I came up the front porch. Just jumped at me out of nowhere and started biting and clawing." Her voice cracked. She had to watch herself here. She couldn't tell him about the locket or about what she thought the cat was. If she told him her dead husband's soul inhabited an alley cat's body, the man would think she was mad. He'd find himself a girlfriend who had all her ducks in a row. Someone who could function in the real world, not a gibbering, spaced-out idiot who was forever stuck in la-la land.

Something like that had to wait. Even if she *did* think he might be her soul mate.

"Good God! I've never heard of such a thing, for an ordinary cat to do that without any provocation . . . It's—it's weird, Edna. Is this the first time it's attacked you?"

"No," she admitted, sensing he'd demand to know the truth if she hedged. She was galled at the swiftness with which their relationship was developing. She felt as if she were catapulting headlong into an intimacy with him that was amazing, almost as if she'd known him from a previous life. If she believed in that sort of thing.

"He attacked me once before. Scratched my legs a little." She already seemed to know what his reaction would be.

A dead silence greeted her.

"I'm coming over there, Edna." His voice was pugnacious and headstrong when he finally spoke. "Please let me," he added, as though dimly recalling that it was proper etiquette to ask permission first. "This is weirder than you think. A lot weirder! We've got to do something about the dirty bastard. Tonight. Pardon my French." He sounded angry and frightened for her safety.

But what the hell was he talking about, saying it was a "lot weirder" than she thought?

"One more question, Edna. Did this black cat have crooked eyes, one kinda lower than the other? Really fucked up? Pardon my language again."

Edna could forgive his use of the obscenity. After all, she had used it herself to describe the cat. Fucked up was the perfect description of the cat's eyes. If she looked up the phrase in Webster's, she'd probably find a sketch of the beast grinning, big as life. But how did Gene know it had fucked-up eyes? She wondered.

"Yes, but—"

"I'm coming over," he cut in aggressively.

"Well, all right," she relented. "But how did you know about its eyes? Why don't you just wait until tomorrow, Gene? You've been in a car accident, for God's sake. You need to rest and recuperate—"

"Tonight." His voice was as bellicose as an insistent bulldog. "Before it gets a chance to hurt you again. Besides, it's not all that late."

"But how did you know it had fucked-up eyes?" she yelped, then covered her mouth up as if she'd been stung. Edna hardly ever swore but she did now almost constantly ever since the cat had shown up.

"I'll explain when I get there."

Edna agreed and proceeded to give him directions to her house.

After she hung up, she slipped into a decent

houserobe, flicked the porch light on and collapsed into the recliner to wait for him, wild-eyed and weary.

He had a lot of explaining to do.

Chapter Thirty-one

Gene slid the telephone back on its hook, pushed a few quarters into a nearby vending machine to buy two packs of cheese-and-peanut butter crackers, and left the Emergency Room in a huff, pushing his white cotton shirt back down into his pants.

It was 10:25 at night, but Gene didn't give a damn. He was filled with a disquieting sense of urgency about Edna and the cat. He was sure it was the same evil black sonofabitch that had caused him to have the accident. It hadn't hurt him any, thank God, but it had lunged at him from the back seat of the car and caused him to lose control of the steering wheel. He'd crashed into a brown Volkswagen and did a good job of denting its fender. The owner, a man near his own age, was fuming mad, but unharmed. Where the black cat had gone afterwards, he didn't know. One minute he'd seen black fur flying toward him, felt sharp talons scratching the hell out of one arm. The next minute he'd been thrown forward violently from the impact of rear-ending the Volkswagen.

And the cat had disappeared into thin air. Gene supposed it had leaped out the window to safety.

"God, she'll think I'm crazy, wanting to come over there now," he mumbled, wagging his head as he unlocked his car and got inside.

Gene couldn't explain the overpowering sense of protectiveness he felt toward Edna. He barely knew her. It was nuts to be worried sick about someone you didn't even know, wasn't it? Someone you'd only mooned over from afar as she picked out grapes at the supermarket? Someone he'd only spoken to a few times? Yet he felt this strong compulsion that he *must* go to her house, that the cat might strike again. Something odd was happening here. The same goddamn cat attacking them both. He couldn't explain it, but he could feel a chilling sense of foreboding that told him to go to her right now.

This very night. This very *minute*.

He clicked the ignition on. The right headlight was out and he'd messed up his own fender a little as well as the other guy's, but it was no big deal.

He leaned forward a little to squint into the rear-view mirror. He looked like holy hell. His left eyelid was puffy and laced with black thread, like some rag doll sewn together badly at the seams. The small of his back ached a little, too.

Teach him to wear a seatbelt, he guessed. He'd only been going about thirty miles an hour, but that was enough to do some damage.

"Oh, this is romantic as hell." He grinned ruefully at his face in the mirror. "A real memorable first date." He hoped she didn't think this was some dumb-ass ploy to come to her home and seduce her. But he wasn't really worried because he knew she felt it, too—this *tie* between them. She knew better than to think he just wanted to jump her bones. Not that her body wasn't nice, but it was her heart he really wanted.

He pulled out of the hospital parking lot and fished one package of the crackers out of his shirt pocket.

It had begun to rain during the more than two hours he'd been in the Emergency Room. He cut the wipers on, cursing a little at the loud, annoying click they made.

"Ah, the hell with it," he growled impatiently, turning the wipers back off. The damn clicking noise was getting on his nerves. He was all keyed up, anyway.

He had to think. Just what the hell could he do about the cat tonight? Not a damn thing, probably. The animal would certainly have the good sense to make itself scarce during a heavy rainstorm. It wasn't stupid. Just mean as hell!

He followed Edna's directions to the house, beginning to feel silly over his dogged insistence at seeing her tonight. After all, it *was* raining. The sonofabitchin' cat wouldn't show up. Not unless the fat little bugger wanted to get its whiskers waterlogged.

Gene chuckled a little and pried the last cheese-and-peanut butter cracker free of the cellophane as he pulled up to a red light.

Well, at least he could make sure Edna was all right. He had a strange feeling she'd tried to diminish the severity of the cat's attack. She had sounded so damned frightened yet she'd staunchly maintained that the cat just "scratched" her. He'd make sure she was okay. Then leave. He didn't want her thinking he was some pigheaded nut or some suave Casanova. He had nothing but honorable intentions toward Edna Wilkins.

He broke open the other package of crackers and polished them off, then turned onto Edna's street, clicking the wipers on again, forcing himself to ignore the whining, squeaking click as best he could.

Eight-four-zero-one. The number of her house wouldn't be too hard to find since he could only see two houses on the street. The first one said 8403, so the other one had to be Edna's. He slowed down to a cruise and crawled slowly past 8403.

It was as black as the ace of spades, but Edna left the porch light on for him. Her house was an attractive small red brick with white shutters, a chimney, and a flat neat lawn with azalea bushes flanking the front porch.

He cut his headlight off and eased his car into her driveway behind her car, as the gravel crunched crisply beneath his tires. A nagging, icy premonition hit him from out of the blue, that this was not such a hot idea. But he was already here now, damnit. He might as well go inside, or she'd really think he was some kind of screwball, coming all the way to her house—from the Emergency Room, no less—and then turning around and leaving. Naturally, she would've heard him pull up with that damned gravel snapping and popping.

"Shit," he mumbled, rubbing the back of his neck, wondering if he had whiplash.

He groaned and stepped out of the car into the windy whistling drizzle, watching small gusts buffeting the branches of the pine tree beside the driveway. He lifted a hand to protect his stitches from getting soaked. The gusts increased, spitting out a chilly drizzle that made him shiver and wonder how the weather could have changed so much in just three hours. The wind scooped up leaves from Edna's lawn and whirled them around with a sucking, howling noise like a banshee wailing.

"Good Christ, it's dark as a pit out here." He crossed the driveway, slick wet gravelstones pulling and sucking at his feet like hundreds of tiny, hungry apparitions. His black leather loafers skated slickly against the stones as if he were gliding across ice cubes.

"Jesus, it's like wading through quicksand." He gulped, nearly losing his balance.

Finally, he stepped up onto the concrete porch, pushed the doorbell once, and slid his shoes against the rubber doormat several times. He didn't want her to think he was some stupid clod who tracked in mud on the carpet. He was eager to make a good impression. He didn't want to get off to a bad start.

As if he hadn't already! Christ, he looked like a Halloween ghoul, sporting this purplish swelled-up eye. And she'd think he was some obnoxious, domineering asshole, the way he'd insisted on coming here.

Gene shivered as cold raindrops trickled down the neck of his white cotton shirt and matted his hair and forearms. He pressed the doorbell again, still shielding his wounded eye with one hand, like a soldier doing a half-assed salute. A deluged philodendron was at one end of the porch.

Suddenly the front door jerked open and Edna was looking up at him with luminous, frightened hazel eyes, an expression of intense relief on her face. She looked at him as if he'd rescued her from a fate worse than death.

Suddenly he was very glad he'd come and he knew she was, too. Shit, yes.

And he saw that he wasn't the only one who was covered with battle scars, either, for their first date. Edna stood against the doorframe, sagging limply, screaming-red blood oozing from a dozen deep claw marks on her legs. Her cheek bore two angry red gashes that made his stomach twist with rage. And he'd thought his eye was bad! Edna looked ten times worse.

Gene sucked in his breath in a raspy whoop, shock rendering him speechless, and wondered just what kind of savage, heartless monster this "common alley cat" was.

The wind and rain moaned and whined behind him like a dark apparition whistling a ghostly melody.

Chapter Thirty-two

Edna saw the silver Volvo drive up through her vantage point at the living-room window, leaning over the back of the recliner as she peeked through the slats of the Venetian blinds.

She watched anxiously as Gene walked up onto the porch, half expecting the cat to materialize magically from the deathly black shadows that loomed around the house, flickering and darting like capering ghosts.

Gene's hair was soaked with rain, the strand of gray falling in a wet limp curl across his forehead. For some strange reason, he appeared to be shading his eyes with his hand. His white cotton shirt clung to his muscular shoulders, showing his skin. He was already soaked! The rain was coming down in buckets, fat glistening drops that slid down his face and neck. The wind ruffled through his hair and shook leaves off the pine tree in the driveway.

Edna hopped up from the armchair to open the door before he drowned.

"Oh, Gene, I'm so glad to see you," she cried. Her heart lifted buoyantly at the sight of him, bedraggled mess though he was. She felt like hugging him.

He kept his hand above his eyes and squinted at her. His mouth dropped open in shock as his eyes traveled over her figure.

"Oh, Edna, my God," he croaked. A raindrop dripped from the tip of the gray curl onto the tip of his nose, hanging there. His white shirt was spattered with raindrops along the collar, the sleeves already wringing wet.

The wind whipped through his hair again and Edna suddenly got that tingly, heightened sense of awareness, a profound intuition that something was not right. The yawning blackness of night behind him seemed full of an evil malice.

"Well, don't just stand there. Come on inside," she yelped in her nervousness, putting out a hand to grab his sleeve.

She had to get him inside. Something was going to happen! It wasn't safe out there.

Gene lifted a foot to step over the threshold.

Too late, Edna caught a flash of movement, a hazy blur to her left from the direction of the azalea bush. The bush jiggled as if someone were shaking it and something sprang free, fast as lighting, a creature of the night, a creature of death.

Edna's eyes bulged.

With a high, hellish whine of fury, the fat black cat leaped from the bush onto Gene's back, tearing and clawing and hissing, finding purchase by digging its sharp talons into the material of his shirt. Its long fluffy tail stood erect, the hairs standing out as if electrified.

Its front claws were a blur of frenzied motion, hooking into the stitches above Gene's eye, ripping tender, already-wounded flesh apart and leaving bright blood spurting in gushes down Gene's rain-soaked, terrified face.

"Sssssss!" The cat acknowledged Edna's presence, then turned back to its work. Its black ears, slick with rain, were tight against its skull like small triangular bat's wings as black as the pits of hell. Its head bobbed up and down with small, quick movements as it bit and tore avidly with demonic blood lust. Shredding, ripping, gutting.

Gene moaned in agony and cried out, stumbling to the sidewalk below the porch as he fought the beast, pinwheeling his arms like a helicopter in a vain effort to grab hold of its lethal black body. But the cat was smart. It kept its back feet firmly latched to Gene's back, entrenched in the white cotton with a death hold and bent its upper body over his face, making it nearly impossible for Gene to twist his arms back to grab it.

My God, how cunning it is, Edna thought. She let out a scream of horror, her eyes blank as she stood transfixed by the nightmarish scene.

"Aaaah!"

Gene's cry of pure anguish jolted her into action. She stared frantically around the living room, her eyes like a madwoman's, searching for something to use as a weapon against the lunatic creature.

Outside, the rain had lessened a little, no longer pelting down with a loud, drumming sound, but the wind had risen, making a low moaning noise, as if it fully sympathized with Gene's plight.

Her eyes fell on a wooden-handled umbrella close to the door, leaning against the wall. She seized it and sprang toward the cat, fueled by a powerful surge of adrenaline born of sheer terror. Gene lay unconscious on the sidewalk, blood streaming from his ravaged eye, oozing from his throat, covering his thin summer shirt. The cat still had its ears flattened tight against its misshapen skull, busily working at Gene's jugular, hideously clawing in a two-handed motion, like a squirrel burying a nut.

Edna felt a huge wave of nausea turn her stomach, clutching at the doorframe for support. It meant to kill him, she realized, shocked. Her heart beat out a crazy tattoo and a little scream escaped her lips. It wanted to kill them *both*! The thought sent her into a blinding fury.

"I'll kill you. I won't let you hurt him" Edna hissed at it through clenched teeth, the cords of her neck standing out, straining with rage.

The cat raised its ink-black, glistening skull and faced her suddenly and she could see its luminescent eyes shining in the porch light, glowing, burning with a malice that had survived the grave.

Edna rushed forward, stumbling down the concrete porch steps, holding the umbrella firmly in a white-knuckled grip, ready to strike at it. Before it killed Gene!

Suddenly it rose from its prey on the sidewalk, took two slow sinuous steps toward her with an arrogant, mocking gait, and threw back its angular head to hiss at her, an endless cry that sounded blood-chillingly human. Its huge, jagged fangs gleamed like needles. Spittle mixed with Gene's blood smeared its horrible face, covering its twitching whiskers, and oozed down from its hateful lips. A rabid, frothy foam of madness seeped slowly from its mouth to its chin.

It cocked its head and glared at her. "Hssssss," it whispered again, and the eerie sound seemed like an invitation, as if it were urging her to come and do battle with it—so it could rip out *her* jugular. It took another slow, bold step toward her.

Edna stood frozen with fear, rooted to the spot like a wooden doll. Her hand clutching the umbrella shook visibly, the bones in her hand moving like a dancing skeleton's limbs, and the sweet smell of blood and raindrops filled the night air.

It took another mocking step in her direction, slowly, ever so slowly, looking her dead in the eye with its hypnotic, dreadful gaze that made her blood freeze. She very nearly dropped the umbrella, then held it tighter, but she couldn't seem to make herself move. Her arms and feet felt like lead and she breathed so rapidly she felt in danger of hyperventilating.

It's as though it can read my mind, she thought, meeting its gaze, unable to look away. *As though it's telling me it is James, telling me it wants its revenge, that it means to have it*!

Edna gulped back a bitter, sour bile that filled her throat and felt her legs go weak, as her knees knocked together in a sporadic rhythm. It was deliberately taunting her, reveling in her terror. Her hand holding the umbrella shook spasmodically, trembling and bouncing as if she had no control over it.

"Mrawwwwwr!" The cat bared its teeth, fixing her with a sinister rictal grin, and made teasing, biting motions with its fangs, thick saliva dripping through its blood-soaked whiskers. Its evil, hooded eyes shone hollowly up at her, full of an unspoken accusation that turned her blood to ice.

The sonofabitch was giving her a preview of his plans, opening and closing its mouth like that! Showing her its fine teeth, all the way back to its goddam tonsils, as if to say "See, Edna, old girl, this is what's gonna rip the life right out of your body! Take a good look!"

"J–James!" she wailed, cold fear gripping her heart like a steely fist. "Don't . . . please don't!" Sweat mixed with raindrops trickled down her face and she shivered spastically beneath the soggy, wrinkled robe. A bolt of white lightning seared the sky, throwing the cat's outline into an eerie, unearthly illumination that made her gasp.

It raised its lips in a feral snarl and uttered a low, growling noise deep in the back of its throat, like the noise of a primitive jungle beast before it lunges at its helpless prey, moving in for the kill. It raised a paw up in the air and showed her its talons, extending them slowly, theatrically.

It was coming for her, she realized. *Now*.

Edna forced motion into her lifeless arms and swung the umbrella in an arc, gripping it two-handed like some drunken baseball player bellying up to home plate to take a good swing at the ball. And, oh, how Edna prayed for a home run!

Edna prayed hard, mumbling and crying at the same time. Rain water matted down her permanent against her face in wet slippery tendrils as she prayed that she could hit its terrible head— which *was* roughly the same size of a goddamn baseball, she thought, an insane giggle bubbling up from her throat. Oh, how she'd like to knock its fucking triangular head right off! She hoped she would, prayed she would, with all her heart. Because if she *didn't*, if she failed to hit that home run, it was going to kill them both. Right here and now!

The blow connected with the ugly beast's right paw. A good, solid connection, though she hadn't managed to knock its stupid head off. It squealed a high-pitched keening moan of outrage and its freaky eyes widened with surprise, then blinked dumbly at her, awestruck.

"Didn't think I could do it, huh? Didja, James?" she cackled hysterically, half-blinded now by the rain streaming down her face. Her hair hung in bouncy wet ringlets around her head and the hem of her robe clung damply to her legs. "Didn't think I had it in me, huh?" She threw back her head and laughed raucously as a crack of lightning punctuated her words. Gone was the fear, the mindless panic. Edna was ready to fight the mean sonofabitch.

"Well, I'll show *you*, James. I'll show you!" she rasped, feeling her oats now. She'd struck it once. She'd hurt it!

She brought the umbrella down swiftly once more, while it was still stunned and gaping at her, and smacked its tailbone with a thump as it finally took flight across the rain-soaked grass. Edna smoothed a strand of soggy hair behind her ear. She held the umbrella poised, ready to fight should it change its course to spring at her again.

Thunder rumbled and a bolt of white lightning shook the sky, accenting the dark, twisted form of the cat. Its eyes glittered unnaturally like hot molten coal as it fixed her with a final menacing glare. It paused briefly in the middle of the lawn, peeled back its blood-ringed lips and threw back its head to howl once, a tortured cry which promised Edna it would return.

"Just try it!" Edna shrieked, shaking a fist at it, not caring that the rain was streaming down her robe now, rendering it as shapeless as a corpse's shroud. "Just you try it!" Her voice thrummed with fury, then dissolved into a broken whimper. "I'll score a home run next time, you son of a bitch," she vowed. "I'll knock your damned head right off!"

Her throat was raw. She tossed her head so that her hair flopped backward, out of her eyes. She was sick and tired of being intimidated by the creature. She would fight it, not cower from it! She'd stand up for herself, as she never had with James *before* he'd died. It wasn't too late.

She lunged forward a couple of steps and flung the umbrella at its hideous black body, tossing it like a deadly spear. It yelped loudly as the umbrella struck its back and then fled off down the street, the deformed torso bouncing unevenly up and down with a deranged, mad tilt.

Edna slumped to the sidewalk near Gene's inert body and sobbed her heart out as the wind whistled its shrill melody through the pine tree and shadows danced against the house like black demons performing a funeral rite.

Chapter Thirty-three

Edna called 911, and they put her on hold for an eternity, then delayed her with questions while Gene lay out on the sidewalk, semiconscious, bleeding like a stuck pig. She hadn't had a clue what to do for him. Before calling 911, half-hysterical, she'd run inside and grabbed a cold cloth to lay gently over his eye, not sure if that was the right thing to do, and then rushed back inside to call for help.

She knew the ambulance would take forever, and she vaguely recalled Janet's teenage brother, Doug, lugging his boom box down the street a few months ago. Some absurd rap song blared from it. Something about 911. Oh, yes, now she remembered. "Nine-eleven is a joke." That was it. And wasn't that the truth!

Outside again, waiting for the ambulance, Edna sank down on the concrete beside Gene, crooning soft words of encouragement while a steady drizzle beat down on them. Whether he heard her, she didn't know. He didn't move or speak.

She wiped at the scratched and caked blood on his neck with another cloth, blotted thick blood pouring from his cheek. His eye looked frightening, a lethal gouge with pulpy, flowing blood that turned her stomach, like something from a horror show. She could not stand to look at it. She'd always hated gory things; it made her sick with revulsion.

Finally the ambulance arrived a million years later, it seemed to Edna. They eased Gene's body onto a stretcher, placed him carefully inside the ambulance and left, the red light whirling drunkenly. The wild *whoop-whooping* idiot noise screamed through the dark rainy night, announcing the tragedy.

Nine-eleven *was* a joke. If she'd had her wits about her, Edna could have easily gotten him to the hospital faster in her own car. But there was no cause to chastise herself, she supposed. He'd only been half-conscious and she wouldn't have been able to rouse him. And she certainly couldn't lift his heavy bulk herself and carry him to the car. He was a big man, probably 6'2" or 6'3".

She'd stood there huddled against the rain, staring after the ambulance, still in shock over all that had happened, shaking like a leaf.

She hadn't gone to the hospital with him, though she'd wanted to. Before he'd lost consciousness, he had spoken severely to her, begging her not to.

"Stay in the house, Edna," he'd pleaded in a voice groggy and slurred with pain. "Lock all the doors and windows . . . I'll kill it when I come back . . . Don't try to fight it, Edna . . ." Then he'd gasped and sank into unconsciousness, only uttering an occasional low moan of agony.

But it looked as if Gene wasn't coming back. No time soon, anyway.

Two hours after the ambulance had gone screaming off into the night, a doctor from the Holy Cross Hospital called Edna to say they were admitting Gene. He had a laceration of the cornea and his eye would require an operation, which was scheduled for Monday morning.

Edna hung up the telephone and an icy, hopeless shudder convulsed her body. She laid her head down on the kitchen counter and moaned. She was sick at heart over what had happened to Gene. If only he hadn't insisted on coming to her house! The doctor had assured her that his eye would be fine, he would not lose the sight in it, but she felt hollow and numb with grief nevertheless.

She lifted her head up off the counter and wiped her face off with a paper napkin.

She guessed the accursed cat had her right where it wanted her now—alone. James had very cleverly cut Gene out of the picture.

"Well, no matter," she said, jumping up off the stool to pace the kitchen like a restless, caged tiger. She would get her own revenge for what it had done to Gene and the trauma it had inflicted on her.

She went back outside in her rubber thongs to scoop up the umbrella, which was dripping wet from laying on the soggy grass after she'd flung it at the cat. She shook it off, tapping it against the sidewalk curtly, and went over to Gene's car to make sure its doors were locked. The front fender was dented and one of the headlights had been punched out.

My God, she thought, what a night poor Gene had had!

She jerked the door open on the front passenger side and reached in to pop the lock. Something fell out onto the white gravel and she bent to pick it up.

Roses . . . half a dozen of them mixed with baby's breath in green tissue paper. Edna let out a ragged little sob and hugged them to her chest, then ran back inside, her thongs slapping against the concrete sidewalk.

After she'd put the roses in a vase, she cracked open a bottle of white wine and poured herself a thimbleful, just to calm her frayed nerves.

"I'll kill that cat myself—if it's the *last* thing I do!" she said, lifting the wineglass in a toast, as if making a secret covenant between herself and James.

She wanted to do it. In fact, she itched for the confrontation.

Chapter Thirty-four

Sleep seemed impossible. Every time she shut her eyes, visions of the cat rose before her: a feline specter, its fangs shining, bathed in blood; its narrowed eyes glaring at her just the way James's had at the last, seething with accusations and burning hotly with a demented desire for revenge that had not lessened with death.

The rain pounded down on the roof steadily like a relentless drumbeat until Edna had to rise and put a pot on the bathroom floor where the roof always leaked during heavy storms.

When this madness is over, she thought, *I'll get that stupid roof repaired*.

By three in the morning the pot was half-full of rain water and she got up to empty it, groaning with weariness. She felt like a truck had run over her. Her legs ached, her cheek ached. Finally, as she got back into bed, the rain seemed to slacken off.

She drifted off and managed to get a few hours of sleep, awakening again four hours later. She stumbled back into the bathroom, dumped out the remainder of the rain water, and cleansed her wounds with hydrogen peroxide, wincing as the liquid foamed and her eyes watered from her smarting face.

She was worried sick about Gene. The operation was scheduled for Monday morning at eleven and Edna intended to do some housework, pick up Janet's mail, and go to the hospital to visit him. It was the least she could do.

She put on a loose paisley cotton jumper and some tan leather sandals, combed her hair, and did her teeth.

When she went into the kitchen, Petey was hopping around the bottom of the cage, strewing out feathers and generally making a fuss. His food dish was nearly empty.

"Okay, okay. I'm hungry, too," she said, opening a walnut cupboard to get his seed out. She ran fresh water and gave him a large refill of birdseed and he seemed content.

After a breakfast of buttered toast and scrambled eggs, Edna mopped the kitchen floor and cleaned the bathroom fixtures.

At nine-thirty, she grabbed her car keys and exited the house, after checking each window to be sure it was closed and locked. The rainstorm from the previous evening had given way to a gorgeous, sunny day. The sun was a huge golden disc in the sky, beating down with pulsing rays of warmth.

"I *have* to mow this damn lawn," she said, crossing the driveway toward Janet's house. If she didn't do something about the lawn soon, the grass would be up to her butt.

She looked in Janet's mailbox and took out a few envelopes and headed back to her car. She threw the mail in her bag and then started up the Cavalier. She backed it out carefully, moving it far to one side and around Gene's car. She had one arm on the back of the passenger seat and her head twisted around behind her. She had to watch closely so that she didn't back into the small ditch at the end of the driveway beside the curb. Suddenly she got a prickly feeling on the back of her scalp and that undeniable, intuitive feeling that something was not right.

She turned her head back around and shifted the car into the drive position, sucking in her breath with a whispery gasp. The black cat stood proudly on the front hood of the car, facing her, its front paws perfectly parallel, like an elegant majestic ebony statue.

"Oh, s–shit," she stuttered. Her heart began to race at a galloping, crazy patter; her chin trembled like a toddler ready to whine. She lifted a shaky hand to cover her mouth. It was looking at her, poised there, just staring a hole right through her.

Don't be a chickenshit wimp, Edna. Do something! a part of her advised. *For God's sweet sake, do something!*

She didn't know what to do at first, as it sat there grinning at her, wearing a complacent, gloating expression that caused her blood to boil. It was right in front of the windshield wipers and it took her breath away to see the monster so devastatingly close—only a foot away from her face with a thin pane of glass separating them.

"I'll bump it off!" she spat fiercely, her eyes blazing at it through the window.

It hadn't moved a muscle. It remained sitting there with its dark mocking face, glowering at her spitefully.

She stepped on the accelerator and braced herself as she almost immediately stepped on the brakes. She gritted her teeth and swore softly. The bastard still wore its calm grin, though she could see it digging its long nails to grasp the base of the windshield wiper.

The sonofabitch meant to ride with her! To cause her to have an accident. Yes, it would like that!

She pressed the accelerator again, rode a few yards, and abruptly slammed the brakes on. It didn't phase the creature at all.

It hooked its claws harder around the windshield wiper and hunkered down, a wide, horrible grin plastered across its face. It moved its head forward and gently nosed the windshield directly in front of her, as if to call attention to its cleverness. Edna wanted to scream and howl and, above all, she wished she could take her eyes off it, but it was dead ahead of her. She had to look at it if she wanted to watch where she was going. Obviously, it intended to cling to the wipers and ride the vehicle, no matter what. Well, she would show it!

"Ride 'em, *cowboy*—you son of a bitch," Edna hissed, narrowing her eyes at it.

The car lurched forward and she instantly stomped on the brakes, bracing herself as the brakes squealed and her head nearly crashed against the window. The cat squealed, too; in fact, it screamed right in tune with the brakes, creating a ghastly, hair-raising duet. Its talons scratched a long screeching mark the length of the car as its fat body was hurled abruptly off the car, and into the street.

Edna didn't know what happened to the blasphemous creature next because she was too busy throwing the car into park after she moved it up a few yards into the driveway. She leaped out, flopping her purse on her shoulder, and made a mad dash for the house. She heard it emit an enraged howl, but as she tore across the lawn there was silence. She could only hope it had run off.

Luck was with her this time as she slid the key into the front door and it sprang open immediately.

She stayed inside with the door locked and bolted, sitting on the couch like a zombie, watching TV and brooding.

That night she dreamed about the cat, seeing its mocking face as it rode the car, its back hunched stiffly, its claws clinging to the wipers for dear life, like a deranged cowboy riding a bucking bronco.

Chapter Thirty-five

The next morning Edna's legs were fire-engine red. She crawled out of bed to wash them off and then poured the last droplets of hydrogen peroxide over her calves, plunking the empty bottle into the trash can. She made a mental note to get more. She fished a couple of gauze bandages out of the box. It was empty, too.

"Crap." Now she would *have* to go to the store today, that was all there was to it. She couldn't just cower in a corner, for fear of encountering that hellcat. She couldn't let it hold power over her like that. She needed food, too. Milk, eggs, and bread. The basics. And something to munch on, like potato chips. She pawed through the medicine cabinet for a minute or two, hunting for a bottle of rubbing alcohol she'd thought was there, but it was gone.

She might as well go shopping now and get it over with. She sighed. No way was she going to sit in the house and let that cat call the shots. The hell with that noise. Besides, she still wanted to visit Gene.

She picked out a pair of knee-length green shorts and a green-and-white cotton blouse. It was already hot and humid. The weatherman had declared it would reach nearly one hundred degrees today. Edna pushed her feet into a pair of tan canvas summer shoes and went to the dresser to fetch her car keys.

The gold locket twinkled merrily up at her from where she'd left it on top of the jewelry box. She picked it up to place it back inside the box, hesitated, and then changed her mind.

Why not? she asked herself defiantly, clasping the locket around her neck. Surely lightning wouldn't strike twice in the same place. If the dastardly animal tried to yank it off her throat, she would kill it. James wouldn't confiscate it from her again. She wouldn't allow it.

Just as she picked up her purse, the phone rang. Thinking it might be Gene, she rushed toward it, flinging her purse and car keys down on the coffee table on top of a magazine.

"Hello?" she said.

"Hiya," drawled Helen's nasal twang, too loud in Edna's ear. "How'd that hot date of yours go, girl? When are you two lovebirds gettin' married?" She let out the familiar donkey-bray ending in a wheezing snort.

288

Hellcat

"Very funny, Helen," Edna answered, quickly losing patience. She plopped down on the couch beside her purse and parked her feet on the corner of the coffee table. The last thing she needed right now was to be interrogated by Helen about her love life. Her nonexistent love life. "I didn't *go* on a date," she said, taking a diabolical glee in bursting Helen's bubble of romantic voyeurism.

"Huh? Well, why not? You change your mind about him or what? Listen, Edna Wilkins, he's a real good catch—" Helen launched into a sing-songy lecture, but Edna cut her off before she got rolling.

"He was in a car accident. A minor one." Edna adjusted a crooked pine cone in the bowl on the coffee table. "He's fine, but we've postponed the date, of course. Uh . . . Helen, I'm in kind of a hurry. I'll call you in a couple of weeks, after we've gone on a date, okay?" Her voice sounded strained. Promising to call Helen later on was the best tactic she could think of to put her off; she certainly couldn't tell her about the cat. It would require all sorts of awkward explanations that would only frighten Helen.

"Well, Gawd, that's too bad. Glad he's all right. I hope he didn't mess up his car too bad. Edna, you be sure to call me after you go out with him, ya hear?" Helen's voice was disappointed and sad.

"Oh, I will. And his car's okay. The fender's a little dented and one headlight is out, that's all. No big deal."

"And, Edna, don't let this one get away. Take i᷄
from me, he's a real winner. And you're not gettin̄
any younger either, Ed. Pardon me fer bein' sᴏ
blunt, don't mean to hurt your feelin's . . ." Heleṇ
lowered her voice conspiratorially as if confiding
a deep dark secret.

Edna bit her tongue hard to keep from telling
Helen that she, too, was no spring chicken.

"I appreciate your concern, Helen. Good-byᴇ
now. Call you in a couple of weeks." Edna prayed
that Helen would get the hint that she wanted tᴏ
be left alone, at least until she solved the problem̄
of the cat.

She sure didn't need any visitors until theṇ
God, what if Helen came barging in for a visiᵗ
and the cat attacked her? Edna couldn't stand
another scene like that; she couldn't bear it. Better that Helen should be ticked off at her thaṇ
have her eyes clawed out. She couldn't chancᴇ
her friend being attacked and seriously injured,
like Gene had been. For the time being, Heleṇ
would simply have to suffer her rudeness.

"Well . . . okay." Helen's voice sounded like a̱
wounded little girl pouting as she agreed.

Edna replaced the receiver and grabbed heṛ
purse and keys again. Then she walked quicklʸ
around the house to double check the windows.
In the kitchen she took a quick peep inside the
refrigerator to see what she needed to buy at the
Super Fresh. She grabbed the post-it pad from̄
the kitchen counter and jotted the food items
down on it before she forgot them. Of course, she
included a new *TV Guide* and the new *Examiner*.

Edna was ashamed to read such a tacky paper, but it was fun. Just like the romances. She supposed there were a lot of "closet" *Examiner* fans. She jammed the list in the side zipper of her purse, saw Janet's mail and put it on the counter. She headed for the front door, perspiration already covering her forehead. Petey screeched defiantly and hopped to the edge of his cage.

"Oh, yeah. Birdseed, too. Thanks for reminding me." Edna laughed and scratched it on the bottom of the list.

She stopped to cut on the fan. If only she had thought of getting the air conditioner before the summer had arrived. It would be a real hotbox by the time she got back, but it was better than worrying herself into a conniption fit over the cat, wondering if it could somehow squeeze its way inside a window, and hurt Petey. She just hoped the bird didn't melt before she returned.

Edna pulled the front door open and stepped out into the unnaturally bright June sunlight. An unearthly calm seemed to have descended upon the atmosphere, as if it were a still-life portrait and, for no reason at all, Edna was suddenly consumed by acute terror. Her pulse raced as a tight sensation of panic overwhelmed her, and her stomach twisted into a hard ball of apprehension.

Something is watching me.

The words hummed and buzzed inside her brain, sending up a red-flag danger alert. Her eyes moved fearfully across the lawn, searching for a dark shape. The tall grass swayed a little in the slight breeze, along with dandelions half a foot high. Was it only her imagination, or was something making a soft rustling noise in the direction of the azalea bush to her left?

"My God, I'm getting paranoid as hell," she mumbled. She walked out to the edge of the porch and took another nervous look around.

Nothing moved in the yard, but her heart began to hammer and caper erratically.

"Mrawwwwrrr!" The primal scream broke through the still air like a shotgun blast, setting off an unleashed chain of terror within Edna. Her heart plummeted and she couldn't seem to inhale.

Out of nowhere, a flash of black fur hurled itself from the top of the azalea bush to materialize on the concrete sidewalk directly in front of Edna. She stood sticklike, frozen into immobility, gaping at it in a horrified, sick daze. Her heartbeat jumped and rolled into an irregular, arrhythmic pattern as she stared down into its menacing, slitted eyes, bent on mindless destruction.

Move, you idiot, move, she thought. *Turn and run back inside before it's too late, before it rips you apart!*

But she couldn't move. Her legs felt like soupy jelly, boneless and liquid. Made of mush. Two shaky rubber bands of muscle, unable to support her. Perspiration glazed her upper lip in a fine sheen, cold and clammy, and her throat was like sandpaper. Her pounding heart felt as if it would burst from her chest and explode.

"Hssss!" It skinned its thin, dreadful lips back and hissed up at her, its eyes shining with an evil, Satanic power. It seemed to say, "I'm coming for you now, you stupid twit! Coming for you. Gonna go for the jugular this time. Not gonna let up until your blood is splashed across this sidewalk like the Red Sea."

Its ebony fur stood out stiffly from its body and its back hunched upward, bowed like some cartoon Halloween cat, its monstrous talons extended and quivering. Its eye seemed hazy and hooded with a dark insanity.

"Ssss!" It hissed its susurrant, malevolent death song once more, its eyes turning fiery and determined as it lowered its body into a taut, feline coil, hunkering low on its haunches as it made ready to spring.

Edna's scalp crawled with fear, icicles of chill bumps sprang up on her arms, and she began to pant as if an elephant were parked on her rib cage, suffocating her.

Run, you fool! screamed a guardian angel in her head, fearing for her life. She sprang into action, released from her trance. She fumbled clumsily for the doorknob behind her with one trembling hand, still facing the hideous, mad creature. She was scared to turn her back on it.

It opened its mouth wide, showing a cavernous gulf of pointed fangs, and moved into position to lunge at her. Madness glowed in its narrowed eyes, and spittle seeped down its chin.

Edna clawed desperately for the elusive doorknob, her fingernails raking at the door like a corpse trying to claw its way out of a dim corroded coffin. She yanked it open at last, simultaneously stepping backward into the doorframe.

She spun her body around like a whiplash and slammed the wood door shut so hard it clattered on its hinges. She was panting like an old dog that had run too long a race, whooping and gasping.

Out of the corner of her eye, she'd seen it hurl its fat black body toward the door, ramming it like some terrible missile of destruction, its head *thrown* backward, its teeth poised, its claws lifted, eager for destruction. But it hadn't gotten her! Instead, its thick, fibrous body smacked the door with a solid thud that was soul-satisfying.

The minute the door had clicked shut and she'd heard the thump, sounding its defeat, a line from an old Clint Eastwood movie flashed through her brain. "Go ahead. Make my day."

Her day had just been *made*, all right, by the sound of the beast's body striking wood, instead of her jugular.

Edna sagged weakly against the inside of the door, as her nerves jangled with fright and her pulse askew with terror. She let out a low, keening moan as she listened to the scraping trail of claws running down the outside of the door. The sound made her hackles rise.

"Eeee!" It wailed with rage that its attempt on her life had been foiled. It dragged its talons against the door, faster and faster, raining down its fury.

Edna cried out and covered her ears against the horrible sound. "Oh, sweet Jesus. Holy Mother of God, help me," she wept, crumpling to the floor in a lifeless heap, her body throbbing and shaking violently against the chilling noise.

Chapter Thirty-six

Edna prepared a cup of hot camomile tea, kicked off her canvas sandals, and sank down onto the flowered couch. Fifteen minutes after she'd slammed the door, her heart was still pounding out a weak, thready rhythm.

It had scraped its claws against the door for a full five minutes or more, nearly sending her to the brink of insanity as she realized each scratch had been meant for her.

She talked to herself, tried to convince herself not to let the cat intimidate her. She couldn't stay cooped up in the house forever. She had to check Janet's mail, see Gene at the hospital. She needed groceries, needed hydrogen peroxide for the wounds that abomination had inflicted. She had to go out that door sometime.

The teacup jittered and clattered against the dish in nervous rhythm as she set it back down. Her hands still trembled from the terrifying encounter.

James had the advantage now, all right. She was all alone in the house, except for Petey. Her only neighbor was on vacation, leaving the street dark and secluded. She was totally isolated—perfect for its needs.

And the cat had cunningly eliminated Gene, her only ally. The dog/cat catcher was out. So were the cops. The rat poison had failed, too.

Stalemate.

She was left to fend for herself, to plot some scheme to get rid of it. She was trapped inside her own home, too damned scared to leave. Too paranoid it would strike again, the minute she opened the door. And the next time she might not be so lucky. Just look at her now. She looked like a damned truckload of wild panthers had chewed her up and spit her back out again, literally covered with claw marks. She had a chilly premonition that next time, James would get his revenge. He'd kill her and it would be a bloody, gruesome battle to the death.

Edna was in a quandary. She didn't know what to do except sit on her rump and play this sordid waiting game. The damned cat had to leave sometime, didn't it? To hunt for food, if nothing else. Surely it couldn't hold this stakeout on her house forever.

"But then again it's not of this world, maybe it *can*," she whispered, biting back her panic.

Maybe it could afford to wait forever. Maybe all the nourishment the ghoulish thing required was human blood and suffering. Perhaps that was its sustenance.

Edna drank the rest of her tea and stretched her legs out on the couch. She had to turn her mind from such morbid thoughts. She had to keep her wits about her, to force herself to maintain a positive, hopeful attitude. Or all was lost.

She had to destroy it—before it destroyed her.

The picture of her pointing a gun and blowing the disgusting creature's head off was clearly etched in her mind.

Chapter Thirty-seven

All day long Helen thought that Edna had sounded weird on the phone. Scared, actually. Her voice was kind of shaky and tight as a drum, giving out with these monosyllabic replies. Oh, she wasn't a chatterbox like yours truly, but still, it wasn't like Edna to be so abrupt and Helen was worried.

She thought maybe she'd take a ride on over to Edna's house and see how she was. See if everything was okay. Edna'd said she would call in a couple of weeks—and that was strange, too. Normally, Edna was only too glad to talk, unless she had something special to do, or was on her way out. To her knowledge, Edna had few friends and no family, and seemed happy to receive an occasional phone call from her.

Helen wanted to tell her about her wild date with Freddy last night. She'd gone to the fair to see the demolition derby with him. They'd eaten a lot of garbage stuff: cotton candy; a couple of half-raw hot dogs with chili and onions; candy apples on a stick; and a funnel cake with all that gross sweet sugar on it.

As a result, Freddy had upchucked in her lap as they rode the ferris wheel. Right at the crest of the ride, at the very top, he'd let loose, barfing his guts up so suddenly he hadn't even time to turn his head. Her lime-green slacks caught the worst of it and, though she'd run to the ladies room quickly, she couldn't get the sour stink out of it. The odor had made her feel like losing her lunch, too.

Freddy had still felt ill when she came out of the ladies room, and wanted to go home. He looked green-faced and sickish.

"Probably a bad hot dog," he'd snorted, leading her by the hand toward the car.

"Hot dog, hell! It was all that sweet crap that did it. Just the thought of what we ate is enough to make me throw up. Surprised I didn't toss my cookies, too, 'cept I have a cast-iron stomach." Helen had patted her stomach and giggled.

And the smell of vomit from her lime-green slacks had very nearly made her throw up. They had to ride with all the car windows down because of the sickening fumes.

She had hung her head out the side of the car to get a breath of fresh air, glad to inhale it, even though it wreaked havoc with her French twist.

Hellcat

Helen was sorry they'd had to leave the fair so soon. Friday, when she'd gone with Skipper, all he'd wanted to do was gape bug-eyed at the female mud wrestlers all night long, the rascal.

So Freddy'd taken her home early, still a little green around the gills, pleading a bellyache. She'd given him a quick peck on the lips—neither of them felt a bit amorous, what with the stench of vomit—and had come inside to watch Arsenio Hall and gave her slacks a good washing with disinfectant. Some Saturday night, but what could she do?

She'd sat up late watching Arsenio and then an old movie with Fred Astaire, and slept late this morning.

Now she wondered about Edna. She thought she'd trek on over there, just to say hi and see why she'd sounded so weird. She wouldn't call first; she had an idea Edna would tell her everything was just ducky, no need to worry about her. She'd just run over on the spur of the moment. Stay fifteen minutes, that's all, to get this odd feeling out of her system. This odd feeling that something was wrong.

Helen got into her ten-year-old Chevy Vega, cranked up the air conditioning as high as it could go, and pulled off her stiletto heels to lay them in the passenger seat. Helen always drove bare-footed, partly because she always wore three- or four-inch heels, partly just because she liked to.

The trip to Edna's took only ten minutes. As she stopped for the red light at Holloway Road,

303

she saw an enormous scraggly black cat sitting on the curb.

Was it her imagination, or did the cat stare at her, with a fixed, unblinking gaze? It was creepy the way it stared at her. She reached for her purse and pulled out a cigarette, punching in the car's lighter.

Jesus, it was ugly, and something about it nagged at her. She thought maybe she'd seen it before, but couldn't remember where. She lit the cigarette and puffed on it a little. The cat was still there, its eyes focused on her and what a pair of eyeballs it had! Suddenly everything clicked into place and she remembered that she'd seen this same incredibly ugly black cat sitting against the outside of the window at the Safeway when Edna and Gene had come in. It had waited until they came out of the store, then she'd seen it snooping around, following Gene right out of the parking lot. It was crazy.

Helen sucked on the cigarette, tapped the ashes off into the ashtray, and parked it there. The red light changed and she spun around the corner, noting that the cat seemed to lope down the sidewalk right with her, in the direction she was going. It was ugly as homemade sin.

She went slowly down Holloway Road, the speed limit being only twenty-five miles, and let the car window down to get a whiff of the honeysuckle. She adored the honeysuckle that grew down this road, covering the side of the narrow street with its beautiful lemon-yellow blossoms. The opposite side of the street had gorgeous dogwood trees. Edna lived in such a picturesque, pretty little section of town. Helen sighed, wishing for the millionth time that she could afford a cute little house like Edna's, instead of her dumpy, one-bedroom run-down condo with no closet space at all, and a living room the size of a postage stamp.

She rode slowly along, daydreaming, and taking in the pretty scenery, puffing on the cigarette. She flicked it out the car window and noticed, at the same time, that the damned cat was still trailing behind her, on the road now. It had moved off the sidewalk and was jogging alongside her, parallel to the car. Every once in awhile it crooked its head and hissed up at her.

The son of a bitch. What the hell did it think it was doing, skulking around after Gene and then her like this? It was some ballsy goddamn animal, she thought, tagging after her. Now it had moved very close to the driver's door, near the front left wheel, racing right along with her, periodically raising its horrible head to shoot a dirty look up at her.

Helen got mad. She didn't understand why it would want to do this, but it gave her the creeps. She leaned her head partially out the window to shout down at it. "Get away, you bold son of a bitch! Get away!"

To her amazement, it gave a little hop up in the air and showed her a big dirty yellow claw, as well as a good pair of fangs, leaping up so close she could practically kiss it.

Helen jerked her head back inside the window so fast she caused the car to swerve madly. *Good thing this is a tiny little back-road two-laner nobody travels*, she thought, as nervous sweat ran down her forehead. She pulled the steering wheel to the left. She'd halfway run off the road smack into a honeysuckle bush. Then she straightened the car out, twisting her head to catch sight of where the S.O.B. had gone. It had nearly run her off the road! She gritted her teeth and thrust her jaw forward, mad as hell. This sucker was no sweet little kitty-cat.

If it comes at me again, I'll give it the heel of my goddamn shoe, she thought, grabbing hold of her pink high heel on the passenger seat. *See how it likes that!* She held the shoe up with her right hand, poised and ready to let the sorry sonofabitch have it full blast. She'd show the nervy beast it better not mess with Helen Townsend. Helen Townsend knew how to fight.

She guided the car back to the middle of the road and spied it hurrying back toward her, its black legs a fast blur of movement. She sucked in her breath raggedly with surprise. It was running directly in front of the car and she was going to hit the crazy-assed thing if it continued! Much as it had angered her, she didn't want to kill it. Hell, it was a living thing and Helen didn't hold with killing any living thing if she could help it. Even a mean sonofabitch like this.

It held its mouth open in a weird sneer and continued to waltz directly in front of the car, keeping its eyes pinned right on Helen's. Her hand shaking on the wheel, she swerved to the left to miss it. It darted to the right for a moment as she straightened the car out, and stood perfectly still in the center of the road as if waiting for her to start the game again.

"Your move now," it seemed to grin up at her, and its eyes glowed. Fear trickled down Helen's spine and her throat closed up into a dry, husky sandhill. She did not relinquish her grip on the high heel, however, but continued to steer the car one-handed, using the butt of her other hand to help out when needed.

Jesus, it's crazy, it's insane. It doesn't care if I do hit it! The idea dawned on her suddenly, stunning her. Because it was true. The cat-and-mouse game seemed to be rejuvenating it. It seemed to be deriving a strange thrill out of this dangerous game.

This scared Helen shitless because she sensed that this was no ordinary cat. Something bizarre was going on here, something she wanted no part of.

She pulled the car to the right and, sure enough, it lunged to the right, its black legs pinwheeling through the air toward the front fender. She instinctively crashed the brakes on to avoid hitting it and rammed the heel of one hand against the horn. But the sound of the horn and the squeal of the brakes didn't deter it. She barely missed hitting it as she swerved and ran off the black asphalt pavement, coming to a stop with half a honeysuckle bush bursting through the open passenger window, raining golden petals down on the seat.

Gnats and bumblebees buzzed and droned angrily, upset by the ruckus. Helen swore and yanked the gearshift into reverse, backing out with a loud squeal of the tires, as the black cat sat grinning at the side of the road, anxiously awaiting her next move.

"Ball's in your court, Helen old girl," it seemed to be saying, taunting her. Its pink tongue flicked out to lick its lips and it blinked, sitting stolidly on the asphalt waiting for the game to continue, relishing the moment, jeering at her.

"I'll give you a game, damn your black hide!" Helen spat through gritted teeth. She jerked the car back into drive and started forward, not giving a good goddamn now if she *did* hit it. The sonofabitch was *begging* her to hit its ass, wasn't it? So why should *she* care?

It leaped to its feet and sprang at the wheels of the car. It was instinctive for her to strive not to hit any living thing, no matter what she'd said and Helen threw on the brakes, this time crashing into the honeysuckle and coming to rest against a wooden fence.

Thank God she hadn't actually hit the fence, just sort of sidled up to it. This creature was trying its damndest to cause her to have an accident, she realized, as a cold sweat beaded her upper lip. That was the object of this sinister game they were playing. She saw that now.

Well, she was going to get free of it, if it was the last thing she did. No shit-eatin' kitty-cat was going to buffalo Helen Townsend like this. Nosirree.

She glanced at the road. The black cat was right smack in the middle of it, up on its hind legs hopping around, doing some kind of victory dance, shuffling around in tiny, fast circles.

I can't believe I'm seein' this, she thought, and her mouth dropped open.

Quick as a wink, she backed out of the bushes, shutting her nostrils at the cloying scent of honeysuckle. The car was full of blossoms now and buzzing gnats to add to the confusion. She shot forward. She weaved once like a drunken hell-for-leather joy rider, to avoid hitting the animal. Then it pranced alongside as it had done before, loping parallel to the front wheel beneath her window, snarling up at her, its ears flattened against its skull.

"Rawwwwwr!" It gnashed its teeth. Honeysuckle blossoms clung to its back and a tiny twig from the bushes decorated its left ear.

She'd show this sucker what a stiletto heel could do, if it didn't get its ass moving. "Get away," she hissed down at it, careful not to put her head very far out the window. "I'm warning you!" Her heartbeat galloped rapidly and her breath came out in a shallow whine.

God Almighty, those eyes!

Helen's head pounded, sweat ran slickly down into her eyes, and a gnat batted against her nose and buzzed in her ear. She felt like she was about to faint. The animal took a flying leap suddenly, charging at the open window, grinding its teeth, but they clicked together on thin air as Helen jerked her head backward from the window. Its open claw hooked against the window.

Jesus God, it's tryin' to take a bite out of me. It was out for blood! She transferred the stiletto heel from her right hand to her left, well below the window where it couldn't see what she was up to.

It did a neat half pirouette into the air and tried to clamp a claw on the bottom of the window frame again, but failed.

It wanted to get into the car with her. That was obviously what it was trying to do. Helen gulped back a sob and crazily recalled the old adage, "Never let 'em see you sweat." Well, no way was this ballsy bastard going to see her shaking in her boots. No way. She'd see it in hell first.

A yellow butterfly fluttered through the window of the car and out the other side, and a bird sang sorrowfully in the distance, trilling out a mournful rejoinder to their macabre cat-and-mouse game.

It snatched up a paw on the doorframe again, trying to find purchase on the ledge so it could lift its body up and get inside. Helen could feel its breath blast against her face; that was how close it was. The smell was foul and rotten, what she'd imagine the odor to be like if she were a bystander at an autopsy, watching a human body sliced up from stem to stern, viciously gutted.

Helen, with her cast-iron stomach, feared she would vomit. *But not before I knock the livin' hell outta him*! her brain screamed the vital instruction. *Not before! Not before I knock his goddamn fangs out his asshole*! Then she could vomit. Then she could allow herself to rest on her laurels. But not a minute before.

It pirouetted again, a graceful feline ballerina, and swiped a claw across her arm. Blood jetted out. Helen tried to keep from swooning at the terrible ancient maggot-breath it exuded. Its fat black body bumped the side of the car as it fell back down from the jump and Helen was quick to move. She clutched the heel as if her life depended on it—and maybe it *did*.

She flicked her arm out the window in one liquid motion and brought it crashing down against the beast's neck. The stiletto heel made a sickening crunching sound against the back of its jaw, but it was hard to tell if its jaw or neck had taken the brunt of the blow.

"Rawwwwwrrreeee!" It howled like a tiger in the throes of a seizure and fell to the ground, but not before a talon snaked upward and jabbed a hole in Helen's forearm with a slicing, cutting motion. Blood oozed out, thick and fast, and it hurt like hell but she was okay. Okay to drive. And get the hell out of here!

She screeched to a stop and grabbed a couple of paper napkins from the glove compartment to press against her bloody wounds, keeping one eye on the cat.

It just laid there, slumped against the asphalt pavement. She squinted her eyes to see if its chest rose and fell, but it looked perfectly still. She had a dull, pounding headache, felt half sick with nausea. There was a pool of blood around the cat and she wondered if she'd killed it.

She patted the napkins against her arm. It only bled for a minute. The cat lay unmoving in the hot sun, the bright rays dancing across its gleaming fur. Its chest didn't move an inch.

I killed it, thought Helen, without a trace of remorse.

Her shoe lay on the ground right beside the cat. She didn't give a shit. She certainly wasn't going to retrieve it. She didn't know why not. It looked like it was dead, but she just had a spooky feeling about the cat, didn't want to be anywhere near the devil.

The hell with the shoe, just go, something told her.

She wiped the blood off her arm, twisted the paper napkin up into a ball, and pushed it into the small trash bag hanging off the dashboard.

Stinkin' honeysuckle buds all through the car, she thought. *I'll go home and clean it out . . . worry about Edna later. I've got to put somethin' on these cuts.*

She took another paper napkin and wiped the sweat off her face, then put the car into gear. The cat was dead, wasn't it? It hadn't moved all this time—and they *were* her favorite shoes. Why the hell not get the shoe? She could just kinda ride slowly, real slowly, right by it, let the door open just a small crack and reach right down and grab that shoe up. In nothing flat. It wouldn't take a minute.

Hell, they were the only goddamn pair she *hadn't* bought at the thrift store. She'd paid thirty-five dollars for those suckers.

Was she really scared of a dead cat? Helen grinned. That was dumb as shit. Of course she wasn't scared of it. She shook her head and started up the car, eyeing the cat steadily, swiping at the sweat on her lip. It lay in a black, sagging heap, blood ringing its head like someone had outlined it in red magic marker. A gnat zinged noisily in her right ear and she shook her head and batted it away.

She eased the car ever so slowly toward the cat and she thought she would choke from the smell of blood and honeysuckle and rotted decayed flesh. She sidled the car up to where it lay, carefully, beginning to have niggling doubts about her mission.

But what the hell? It lay still as a goddamn corpse, didn't it? She wasn't going to let it best her and go slinking off into the sunset like a whipped puppy. It was only a cat.

She inched the car forward, squelching the impulse to run over its body ruthlessly, repeatedly like a bloodthirsty gunsel. It was stone-dead. Why did it need running over? That was an odd thought.

She cracked the car door open an inch. Thankfully the Chevy Vega sat close to the ground anyway, as if the car had hunkered down when it had traveled over the assembly line. Helen remembered how much she'd bitched over its low-slung body when she'd first bought it ten years ago.

"Feels like my ass is dragging the ground!" she'd griped. And it did. It was so damned close to the ground, she could bend over from the driver's seat and touch the pavement if she wanted to. Without even straining herself. Every damned time she went over a speed bump, the cotton-pickin' muffler scraped the ground and the impact damn near caused her head to bump against the ceiling. It was a low-slung little buggy and now Helen was grateful for that.

For once, it would come in mighty handy. She'd ease on up beside that cat, edge the door open a few inches, reach down and pluck that shoe up with no problem.

Except that when she got parallel to the cat's body, she stretched the door open several inches and looked at the sun glinting down on the cat. Was its leg twitching?

"Ummph." Helen bent from the torso, one red polished nail fingering the tip of the shoe. She couldn't seem to hook onto it. She half gagged at the awful smell surrounding the cat like a stinking, diseased shroud.

A nervous tic pulled at Helen's right eye. She peered closer. Was its chest heaving? Or was she turning into a Timid Tillie?

A wasp zoomed down onto the patch of blood around the cat's head to inspect it, sniffed a second, then buzzed away.

Hellcat

Helen could hear her younger brother, Al, egging her on, whispering to her in her head: "Don't be a squeamish, gutless wonder, Helen. Get your goddamn shoe! Gonna let that ugly-as-sin shitheel of a kitty-cat stop ya?" She could almost hear him snort with disgust.

Al had never let anyone intimidate him. Anyone or any*thing*. And he'd taught his older sister, Helen, to do the same.

"Aaah," she grunted, bending farther over. She caught the tip of the shoe between two long fingernails and lifted it up swiftly. She also caught an unwelcome whiff of that ungodly smell, like a thousand outhouses overflowing with day-old excrement.

A big bird flew overhead, swooping down a little as if it entertained the notion of taking a nose dive through the blood on the pavement. It cawed loudly in a raspy gravelly voice that sounded like a harbinger of doom, then it quickly swooped up sky-bound, as if the scene below were too terrible to get close to. Helen thought maybe it was a crow or a vulture.

After she got a firm grip on the shoe, she tossed it into the car with a plop against the gearshift. Before she could slam the door shut, the cat flicked its eyes open and she felt a gut-wrenching wave of revulsion swim over her as she gaped down into its glittering eyes.

It was alive. She'd known it! Playing possum all the while.

"Oh, no, oh holy sheeeeit," Helen snorted. She slammed the door shut and pushed her bare foot against the accelerator simultaneously as the cat's black claw snapped upward at her, its talon scraping the edge of the door. She'd missed crunching it by a hair.

"Oh, you son of a bitch!" she screamed in a quaky trembling wail. "I damn near amputated your fuckin' claw. Damn near! Wish to God I *had*." Helen whinnied a hysterical, bubbling laugh at the top of her lungs as she made a Keystone-Cops-type U-turn in the middle of the road. The car scraped past the honeysuckle bushes, this time traveling so fast she got a little souvenir to take home. A big chunk of vine and blossoms had cut off at the nub and landed in the passenger seat.

At least she could smell something good on the trip home, she thought. She deserved it after that outhouse smell of the cat's breath!

Helen stomped on it, putting the old pedal to the metal, tires shrieking across the asphalt, and heaved a giant, shuddering sigh of relief.

Overhead, she noticed the big black bird, dipping down and then up again, perusing the scene. Maybe it had been waiting for her bones to pick over and gnaw on, she thought. Maybe it was making a bet with itself over just whose bones it would feast on—hers or the cat's. And there for a while, it had looked like the cat was the winner. But she'd bested it. And that was all that counted.

She rode home blasting the radio. Soft rock music had a calming effect on her, and if she ever needed calming, it was right now. The cat had her all shook up. It had gouged her arm and scared the living shit out of her.

She wanted to go home. She'd visit Edna when her arm got better, and tell her about the weird thing that had happened with the cat. But she probably wouldn't believe a word of it. Shit, Helen didn't believe it herself. But at least she had her shoe and a sprig of honeysuckle. And at least she'd managed to wound that horrible, vile demonic animal. It had bled and that meant she'd gouged it somehow, somewhere. She hoped to hell it was in pain.

"It'll know better than to mess with Helen Townsend again," she sniffed, pushing her lower lip out sullenly. But her chin trembled, and her body shook nervously in spite of her bravado.

And if it ever was fool enough to mess with her again, she'd be pleased to give it more of the same.

Helen Townsend knew how to fight, all right. She'd been raised in the hills of West Virginia with three hillbilly brothers who socked and punched and beat the hell out of each other when they were bored. Just to see who could best who. What else was there to do when you lived on top of a frigging mountain, for God's sake?

In the rear-view mirror as she sped off, she glimpsed the cat sitting there in the middle of the road and the image of it seemed to blur and tremble. Maybe it was the way the sun shone down on it. But Helen imagined its face seemed to waver and change and flicker and for one wild instant it looked just like a man's face instead of a cat's.

Helen looked again and it was just a black cat sitting there, mad as hell that she'd left it behind in a cloud of dust, mad that it hadn't gotten to eat her alive like it had wanted to.

As she turned the corner off Holloway Road and back onto East Highway, she dared to peek at it again and its strange triangular skull did its odd shape-shifting routine again. A man glared out at her with frightening dark burning eyes.

Helen squinted at the road ahead and didn't look back, thanking God it showed no signs of following her.

"Sweet Jeezus, I must be a lot more shook up than I thought," she murmured, running a hand through her hair.

Either that or the cloying scent of the honeysuckle was downright hallucinogenic.

Chapter Thirty-eight

After calling the hospital and learning that Gene was in surgery, Edna prayed that his eye operation would be successful. She fixed herself a cup of herbal tea and clicked on the TV to watch the Donahue show, and took up her post on the couch once more. She munched a couple of half-stale pecan shortbread cookies as she threw her feet up on the corner of the coffee table.

Phil was monumentally boring this morning. Anyway, his frantic scurrying up and down the aisles with his coattails flapping, as if in a race to see how many people he could give a shot at the microphone, was really getting on her nerves. Did he have to run like that? He rushed up to as many people as possible, yet once he thrust the mike under their chins, he seemed fidgety and anxious for them to finish, antsy to get to another person before they'd hardly said a few words. They could never speak fast enough to suit him.

She was sick of Phil today and she wandered into the bedroom, exchanged her nightgown for a thin, billowing sleeveless tent dress, indubitably the dowdiest thing she owned. But she didn't give a damn. She certainly wasn't expecting company, that was for sure, and it was by far the coolest garment she had and it didn't irritate the scratches on her legs.

The temperature in the house had already reached a sweltering ninety-seven degrees and it was unbearable. She was afraid to open the windows even a little, too frightened the cat might somehow wedge its fat torso inside when she wasn't looking.

She put on her scuffy blue thongs and meandered back through the hallway to the living room, then arranged both box fans so that they strategically pointed toward the couch.

She felt exhausted, spent from nervous tension. Damn it, she needed to just sit and vegetate for a while, to become the quintessential couch potato. Relax. Before she had a nervous breakdown. She could read those other romances she had stashed away for a rainy day. Reading always relaxed her.

Hell, if she got really desperate, she could always finish that damn afghan she'd begun a year ago and never finished. Cooking was out, since it was already stifling in the house. Just turning the oven on would probably cause her to become delirious and pass out.

She got a wet cloth from the kitchen and dusted off the blades of the fans, then clicked them on.

"I can outwait you, James," she muttered, her chin thrust forward aggressively in her determination. "I always could."

But what if it stays? her brain nagged. *What if it stays outside the house until all the food is scarfed up, until I'm sitting here on my duff, licking crumbs from the bottom of a bag of cookies? Then what'll I do? What if it stays until I've damn near sweated myself into a fucking coma? And how will I ever explain to Janet why I couldn't check her mail?*

Then what?

"Yeah, then what, ya stupid twit?" she could almost hear James ask in his brittle, mean voice.

Edna went into the kitchen and jerked open the pantry door to examine its contents, scooting the trashcan further away from the louvered doors.

"Why, there's plenty of food in here," she told Petey, who was craning his neck to watch her. There were a lot of canned vegetables on the shelf. A can of tunafish, two cans of chicken noodle soup, and about a million cellophane packages of Oodles o' Noodles. Two brand-new boxes of birdseed sat on the floor in the corner. Well, she hadn't needed to buy it, after all. So Petey was in luck.

"I might have to turn vegetarian for a while but I have plenty to eat," she reiterated, and slammed the pantry door shut. "No need to freak out." She might have to wind up eating Oodles o' Noodles for breakfast, lunch, and dinner, but she'd be all right.

She wiped a thin film of perspiration off her upper lip and wondered if she dared open just one window. It was hot as hell. Dare she slide the kitchen window open just a bit?

"No. The living room would be better. I can watchdog it as I read," she said. God, it was frightening how much she'd taken to chattering aloud to herself, like a panic-stricken magpie.

The cat had done that. The cat was turning her into a raving lunatic, a blithering, gibbering, motor-mouthed fool, afraid of her own shadow. *Not a pretty sight*, thought Edna grimly, hysterical laughter bubbling to the surface.

"Why, I'll probably be mad as a confounded hatter by the time this is over," she said, and then cackled until tears welled up in her eyes. As she wiped the moisture from her eyes with one finger, that uneasy, disturbing feeling washed over her, an intuitive certainty that another presence was near. An ominous, threatening presence.

But could she trust it—or was it just her paranoia?

Oh, this was terrific. Now she was jumping at shadows *inside* the house, as well.

She went through to the living room, her blue thongs slapping dully against the linoleum. *Get a grip, Edna,* she thought, *or they'll be carting you off to the funny farm soon.*

As she approached the couch, the fans gusted her tent dress high into the air. It was like walking through a wind tunnel. But she couldn't shake the feeling of foreboding and sweat began to stream copiously down her forehead like a burgeoning waterfall, despite the fans. This was nervous sweat, not from the heat, she thought, and her palms turned moist with a panicky clamminess.

She leaned over the green armchair to fiddle with the Venetian blind cord, having finally resolved to crack the window just a few inches. The skin on her nape crawled and prickled with dread, vibrating with a secret knowledge of some unknown, imminent horror.

Just stop it! she commanded herself fiercely. She was going to stop this foolishness and sit herself down on the couch to make out a check for the telephone bill and her credit card bills. She would keep busy. That was the ticket.

She flipped the blinds open and fell back, uttering a shrill squeak of terror that sounded like a mouse in distress, choking for breath, her hand before her protectively shielding her face.

The black cat sat perched on the outside of the windowsill, its tail wrapped neatly around its plump, shaggy body, its face pressed tight against the glass with ghoulish glee. It lifted its odd, pyramid-shaped skull to snarl and gnash its teeth at her, its eyes slitted with hatred, signifying evil intent.

Edna sucked in her breath with a whistling, petrified gasp, and her face turned a sick, doughy white.

Brown. Its eyes are brown now, she thought dully. But that was impossible, wasn't it? They had been *green* before, just like any other cat. She was dead certain of it. Then she did a double take.

Chocolate-brown eyes—just like James's!—bored down at her, through her, reveling in her bewilderment, shining with triumphant mockery. Bits of leaves and clumps of dirt clung to its back, stiff and crusty, like a corpse that had crawled from its grave. Though it was unlikely, Edna could swear she smelled a rank, rotting odor permeate the air, and her stomach heaved rebelliously with a sickening nausea.

How could a smell seep through a locked window? But it was there. A pungent, fetid aroma of decomposing, stinking bodies rose up into the air, choking her, suffocating her with its cloying thickness.

Edna sucked and wheezed to pull air into her lungs, like someone having a bad asthma attack. A cold sweat drenched her temples and oozed down from her upper lip until she could taste its salty moisture.

"G–get out of here! Go away, James!" she screamed, her voice a thready, croaking rumble. She bent to fumble for the Venetian blind cord, groping and clawing at the windowsill frantically, her nails making a clacking sound like two skeletons engaged in a fist fight.

It opened its mouth wide to hiss at her and she glimpsed fresh droplets of blood on its stark white fangs, dripping against the pane in a soggy mess. It lifted one huge claw and raked at the blood, spreading it, wiping it, swirling it round and round against the window in a vague pattern.

Oh, sweet Jesus, what was it doing? Painting the window red with blood, just for fun?

Edna clawed and scrabbled futilely for the cord, too horrified to break her steady gaze from the animal, hesitant to look down for the cord. A nerve pulsed dully in her forehead. Her fingers felt like chunks of heavy metal, as though she were moving in slow motion, treading through a dense, sucking quicksand that wanted to swallow her up.

At last she managed to grab hold of the cord, her eyes never wavering from those chocolate-brown ones that mocked her, held her in morbid, rapt fascination. Those same eyes—those very same identical chocolate-brown eyes—had once proposed marriage to her. She remembered how she'd kidded James about his eyes being such a deep, dark brown when they had first met. She'd made some silly remark about how incredibly brown his eyes were. Dark velvety brown.

"Shit-brown. Is that what you're trying to say?" he'd laughed, his eyes sparkling, staring down at her with that handsome tanned face. God, that jet-black hair of his had reminded her of Rock Hudson! Such a shy waif she'd been back then. She'd blushed furiously with embarrassment, unable to speak a word.

And he'd laughed at her nervousness, replying, "Yeah. I'm so fulla shit, even my eyes are brown. That's what they all say."

And hadn't *that* turned out to be the stinking, God-awful truth?

And now, now she was staring into those same shit-brown eyes.

And now she'd figured out what the pattern of blood streaks meant. There was a pattern to the puzzle. She jerked the cord hard and sent the blinds crashing down to the windowsill with a deafening thud, then fell against the recliner, sobbing brokenly at what she'd seen, the horror of it. Her entire body convulsed with a spasmodic tremble that she was powerless to control.

The brown-eyed demon had smeared the droplets of blood into a perfect *J* on the windowpane.

"Hung up on his own goddamn initial!" she hooted, laughing with a hysteria that verged on insanity.

Chapter Thirty-nine

Gene was groggy and loaded with anesthesia, but he kept praying for Edna, praying she had listened to him and wasn't trying to fight the cat alone. It would make mincemeat of her. That was what it probably wanted, for her to try to attack it, so it could demolish her like an elephant squashing a peanut.

As they wheeled him down the hall from the operating room on the rattling hospital gurney, Gene felt like he was floating, drifting off to Never-Never Land, but he was dimly aware he was babbling a bunch of nonsense, a weird bunch of drug-induced jabberwocky that didn't make a bit of sense. And it was all about Edna.

"Sshh, take it easy," someone said, a big monster in white with a face that shifted shapes, and patted him on the shoulder.

He continued to blabber, telling them all about Edna and the cat, the goddamn evil cat that had almost torn his eye out of his head, the cat that was the cause of all this pain and misery. The cat that was going to *kill* Edna!

He had to call her . . . had to call her . . . tomorrow. He sank weakly into the black hole of sleep, muttering Edna's name incoherently and dispensing sagacious tips on how to fight the cat more effectively.

Chapter Forty

Edna sat up late, huddling on the couch in a fetal position, her legs drawn up underneath the tent dress. She stared sightlessly at old movies on the tube, hardly aware of what it was she was watching.

She dozed off for a few hours and woke to find a gray, overcast new morning, with bunches of thick gray clouds floating across a dull white sky.

Her throat felt dry and congested; she'd foolishly fallen asleep with the fans blasting air across her.

She yawned and rose to turn them off, grunting a little at the stiffness in her joints. An Epsom Salt bath, that was the ticket. Her African violet on the end table looked bone-dry, like it had been growing in a desert somewhere and she went to the kitchen for some water.

She poured a cup across its withered petals and gathered up a couple of brown dead leaves from the dirt and trashed them. Then she plodded wearily to the bathroom like a worn-out old mare, turned on the bathtub faucets, and pulled the tent dress over her head.

"Oh God, no," she moaned, catching sight of the deep red gashes lining her calves. The ones she'd had no gauze bandages to cover appeared just a shade too red and puffy, perhaps on the verge of infection.

"That's all I need," she lamented, leaning over the sink to inspect the scratches on her cheek in the medicine-cabinet mirror. They looked passable. No cause for concern.

Cursing softly, she slid the medicine cabinet open wider and prowled among its contents to locate a bottle of rubbing alcohol. There was an old bottle of cough syrup that looked sticky and corroded which she dumped into the trashcan. Also a lot of aspirin bottles, some eye drops, and a half-eaten package of antacid tablets. But no alcohol.

"Damn Sam!" she swore, and hunkered down to a squatting position to yank open the walnut cabinets beneath the sink. She pilfered through the toilet paper, feminine-hygiene products, hair dryers, hair spray, and cleaning liquids, but found no alcohol or hydrogen peroxide, no stray box of bandages.

"Well, shit," she hissed, grunting back up to a standing position.

She eased gingerly into the bathtub and dumped half a box of Epsom Salt into the water which was the last of it.

Oh God, it felt divine . . .

She stayed in the tub until her skin puckered up like a prune, thinking of the cat's ambushing her trip to the store and to the hospital. She brooded, trying to decide on a plan of action, some brilliant strategical move that would bring the battle with the cat to an end, before the irritation on her calves blossomed into a full-blown infection that would require medical attention. She couldn't stop thinking about the gun laying on the shelf in her bedroom closet.

Chapter Forty-one

Edna wondered how Gene was doing, but decided to wait for him to call her when he felt able. She certainly hadn't been up to it. She hoped he wasn't concerned about his car. That was the least of his worries. She also thought about Janet's mail sitting in the box across the street. Well, there was nothing she could do. She barely got her own and she wasn't about to go and get Janet's. She'd just tell her she'd been sick and hadn't gone out at all.

After throwing a load of laundry into the washer, Edna opened a can of vegetable beef soup and heated it, tossing in a few saltine crackers. She went to the couch and set the bowl on the coffee table.

As she started to eat, she could swear she'd

heard a horn honking down the street, although who on earth would be honking was beyond her. Janet was at Ocean City with her lover for the week so the street should be deserted, unless Edna had a visitor.

She went to the front door and pushed aside the white curtains to peek out. The street was still. No car in sight. Three or four birds were hopping around on the bird feeder pecking at seeds.

"Hmm . . . that's strange," she mumbled, and sank back onto the couch to eat her soup. After finishing it, she put the laundry into the dryer and settled down with a new book, *Love's Sweet Promise*, a saccharine-sweet story, though it had its redeeming qualities.

She was almost halfway through the book, and halfway through a large box of cheese crackers she'd scrambled from the back of the cupboard, when the phone rang. She reached across the arm of the couch to pick up the phone from the end table.

"Edna?" It was Gene's voice, sounding thin and weak.

"Gene! I didn't expect to hear from you so soon," Edna gasped, jerking upright on the couch, aware of how worn out he sounded. The novel fell to the floor and Edna scooped it up and laid it on the coffee table. "How did the surgery go? Are you all right?"

"I'm fine, just a little tired. But, Edna, are you all right? What's happening there? Listen, I . . . I know there's more to this than you're telling me, about the cat . . ." he stuttered in a scratchy voice.

Edna didn't want to worry him, and was loathe to tell him everything about the cat but, remarkably, she found herself spilling out the rest of the story, telling him everything, knowing how irrational and insane she sounded. She couldn't believe she was telling this man—this near stranger—things she hadn't told a soul and didn't dare to tell anyone.

And Gene listened wordlessly, a captive audience, occasionally muttering expressions of incredulity or an angry grunt over all that she'd suffered. At the end of her tale, Edna broke down and wept softly, all the misery building up into an explosion of sobbing she couldn't control. Her breath came in fast, ragged chuffs like that of a kid who'd skinned a knee. She was embarrassed by it at first, but then too relieved to care. It felt so good to get it off her chest.

He comforted her, told her he believed everything she'd said. That made her weep all the more, at the sheer miracle of being believed after relating such an amazing story. Edna thought he was kind and tolerant.

"Edna, now I have a few crazy things to tell *you*," he said in a grim, tight-lipped voice.

Edna wiped at her eyes with a tissue from the end table and warned Petey to shush. He was making such a fuss in the kitchen, shrieking and chirping.

"Go on," she said. "Sorry for the interruption.

My bird is squawking its head off."

"Remember you wanted to know how I knew what the cat's eyes looked like? Well, the damned thing knocked a glass into my hot tub a few days ago and I cut my foot on it. It came up to my car at the grocery store the day I met you—"

"No!" Edna cried.

"There's more. It, uh, smeared some blood around on the deck beside the hot tub. Now brace yourself! At the time I saw it, I thought it looked like a letter *J*. So I know that you're not losing your mind, Edna. This is really happening, and we've got to deal with it."

Edna liked the way he said "we've" got to deal with it. After all that he'd been through, he still wanted to help her.

All the good ones aren't married, she thought. *Here is a good guy right here—and he cares about me. He wants to help me.*

Her eyes welled with tears. God, this situation was turning her into a weeping fool, spouting maudlin tears at every turn. She reached for another tissue and blew her nose softly so he wouldn't hear. He'd think she was a big cry baby.

"My God, I . . . I just can't believe it," she said. "What is he trying to do?"

"Edna, Edna listen to me," he said, patiently waiting for her to pull herself together. "You've got to stay inside that house. Promise me you will! Just sit tight." He sounded frantic with worry; his voice was gruff, full of concern.

"All right," she said, not sure if she really meant

336

it. She wanted to appease him, set his mind at ease. He'd been through an operation. He shouldn't be worrying himself sick about her; he needed to be focusing on his own recovery. "All right, I will. Don't worry about me. I wanted you to know that your car's fine. You can pick it up whenever you're feeling up to it. By the way, when will you be getting out of the hospital?"

"Soon, I think. I'm doing good enough to complain about the lousy food and all that stuff. But I have to have some eye therapy before they discharge me," he said, and then bombarded her with questions about James.

Edna surprised herself once more, giving him answers she'd never told anyone else, confiding in him easily and telling how she wished James dead and her belief that she had killed him. They seemed to talk like two old friends, with a rare camaraderie and an instant rapport that she couldn't explain.

"Edna, you've got to stop blaming yourself," he said when she'd finished. "Don't you see? He killed himself. You're riddled with guilt over something that was never your fault in any way. So you threatened to shoot him. You said yourself you were just running off at the mouth, just angry. So what? Any wife who caught her husband in bed with another woman would say one hell of a lot of things she didn't mean."

Edna whimpered softly, hot tears tumbling down her cheeks. Every kind thing he said seemed to set her off, grinding out a fresh bucket of tears.

"Edna," he whispered gently, as if to drum the sense of it into her brain, "*he* knows you didn't mean it. Shit, you even said you'd never fired a damned gun in your whole life. That son of a bitch *knew* you wouldn't hurt a fly. Do you hear me? It wasn't your fault, hon. For Christ's sake, give yourself a break! Do you hear me?"

She heard him all right, but she was bawling like a baby, the words of absolution turning her into a useless pile of mush. It was a minute or so before she was able to speak again.

"Give yourself a break. Stop beating yourself up over it, Edna," he reiterated. "Okay?" His voice was soft and tender then.

"Y–yes," she gulped, hiccuping little sobs. "B–but I fed him all the wrong foods . . . on purpose—"

"He would've eaten that crap, anyway, from what you've told me. Or smoked himself to death," he interrupted.

"I—I practically *forced* Nadine on him. I *told* her to go for him. A sin. A sin the way I used a simple person like that . . ." Her sobs broke out anew as guilt nagged at her.

"Used! Hah! Maybe you shouldn't have done that, but she sure as hell sounded like a nymphomaniac to me. It would've happened, *anyway*. Don't you see? You're putting yourself down for nothing. Letting it eat at you for nothing. She was a tramp and he screwed around on you all through your marriage. From day one. Why would he suddenly behave like some chaste priest?" thundered Gene, his dander up now as he tried to drum some sense into her. "The man would have seduced her, anyway. Or she would've come onto him, since balling men was a hobby of hers! Oh hell, sorry, Edna, for speaking like that, but it just makes me furious!"

Edna became silent, wiping at her eyes with the soggy tissue, ruminating over all that he'd said. And it was true. James would have done all those things despite her. When had she *ever* had any control over thickheaded, stubborn-as-a-bull James? When had he *ever* listened to a single word she'd uttered? Or to anyone, for that matter?

"I guess . . . you're right, but I still feel so bad that I played a part in it, that I set him up with Nadine . . ."

"I tell you, it isn't your *fault*. You've got to stop dwelling on it," he said adamantly.

"I'll try . . . God, you must be exhausted, Gene." She sighed wearily, floundering for another tissue. She checked her watch. "Good grief, we've talked for nearly an hour!" She blew her nose. "Gene, do you really believe it's James? Is it possible? But we've both seen its damned initial. I don't understand."

He paused a minute to think, then spoke slowly, in somber, thoughtful tones. "You know we both can't be crazy, Edna. I've seen for myself that that *thing* isn't natural. It's a monster. It's supernatural. Just be careful, Edna. *And don't go outside*. The instant I get out of here, I'll be knocking at your door. Just hang in there."

"Don't worry about me, Gene. Just you worry about getting better. God, what a nightmare this has been for you. The accident and then the cat attacking—" Her voice caught. "I'm just so damned sorry, I can't tell you . . . and I want to apologize for not calling the ambulance right away. I was fighting that hellcat, chasing after it with an umbrella and couldn't call immediately. Then, when I did, it seemed to take forever . . ."

"That's not your fault, either, Edna. *I* was the hard-headed son of a bitch who insisted on coming to your house, remember? And I'm not afraid of James. He won't scare me away from you." His voice sounded tough and determined.

Edna hoped he was right.

"Take care of yourself, Gene. Hurry up and recuperate. And I'll call you tomorrow."

"I'm workin' on it. We'll make that movie yet, Edna."

They hung up and Edna collapsed against the couch, exhausted mentally from all that he'd related to her about the cat's evil high jinks. She was dismayed that the cat had tracked him to his home, horrified that it had been present at the Safeway, too.

Just how long had it been stalking them?

She shuddered and buried her nose back in the novel. An imaginary world seemed the only safe one at the moment.

Chapter Forty-two

Gene hardly slept a wink that night in the hospital, as he dreamed fitfully of Edna and that wretched cat. The fucking evil cat was dancing on her grave. The damn thing had on a black top hat and tails and carried a cane. It wore a pair of those old-fashioned white shoes that men wore a long time ago, with the buttons on the side. And white gloves, no less. Making a real fashion statement, the bastard was.

It cavorted and pirouetted in concentric circles across Edna's grave, shuffling with plenty of shuckin' and jivin', giving it one of those good ole Fred Astaire/Gene Kelly-type soft-shoe numbers.

It ended this hot little number by tipping its gleaming black top hat and giving a broad, sappy wink, its whiskers twitching as it gloated. It was a likable enough image—if you were into soft-shoe numbers—until Gene's mind panned in closely and saw its blood-saturated lips and pseudo-smile which, in fact, was a barely concealed grimace of stark hatred. One eye was crazed and milky, and its lids drooped at half-mast like a man who'd been without sleep for a week.

And was that a tiny ragged bit of human flesh riding the tip of its whisker, just hanging there?

Gene cried out in his sleep and broke out in a cold sweat, his body trembling like he was doing a fast, uncoordinated shimmy. But the dream continued.

The cat danced and danced, twirling like a top gone wild, spinning around until Gene thought he would go mad from watching it, all the time grinning at him, the grin a thin disguise, a feral snarl lurking just beneath the surface. It tapped its black cane smartly against the tombstone and, with one lithe movement, leaped atop the stone and continued tapping. It never missed a beat, moving from the ole soft-shoe into a gung-ho tap routine. It threw the white gloves rhythmically from side to side, its fingers splayed, really getting hokey now and grinning from ear to ear.

Gene could see that it was having a ball. And didn't that nice tombstone make a fine platform for a tap dancer? Sounded out each and every tap just as clear as a bell.

It hopped off and landed on the grass in front of the gray tombstone, flipped its black hat into the air, and commenced shaking it to and fro. It just reeked of hoopla and ballyhoo, so hokey now that he couldn't bear to watch it without groaning.

Gene trembled in his sleep, and suddenly the cat's face began to change. It wavered briefly like a flickering lantern and glowed with a dim, bluish light that vibrated. Gene looked again and the cat's face was gone. It was a man. A dark-eyed man standing there, glowering furiously at him, seething with madness, and making no bones about how much he hated Gene.

The scene flickered again and fizzled out.

Then Gene saw the cat, skipping this time, round and round the grave gaily, like a cute little kitty-cat, coyly clutching the cane and moving it back and forth in rhythm. *Dancing on Edna's grave.*

Oh God, God, God! Even through his sleep-filled consciousness, the overt symbolism hit him like a fist in the gut.

Gene could clearly see the big gray-white tombstone looming behind the cat, larger than life. He could see the clear perfect letters on it that spelled out "Edna Wilkins."

Gene let out a blood-curdling yell, until the root of his tongue vibrated against the back of his throat.

"Oh, Edna . . . Jesus, Edna *stay inside*," Gene murmured, tossing restlessly, gripping the white hospital sheet in a steely clench.

A nurse entered the room, then went for a sleeping pill after assuring him everything would be fine. But Gene had his doubts. The nurse knew nothing of the black cat and what it was capable of.

She should thank her lucky stars, he thought.

Chapter Forty-three

Edna scavenged through the walnut cupboards again while "Night Court" blared forth from the TV in the living room.

She did a jubilant little victory dance across the kitchen linoleum in a zigzag pattern. Petey twisted his head in a quirky motion like he thought she was nuts, as his blue feathers stood awry.

"Oh, Petey, you'd dance, too, if you'd just latched onto a package of shortbread cookies, you little bugger." She laughed, waving the bag in the air.

Especially if you were facing being cooped up here and forced to eat a lifetime supply of Oodles o' Noodles, she added to herself.

Cookies and romance novels went together like

a horse and buggy, she'd found. She ripped the package open eagerly and lay down across the couch with a book.

After meeting a man like Gene Martin, she'd decided the mushy love stories weren't so farfetched after all. If a man like Gene existed, who was kind and supportive, there had to be more like him somewhere. They couldn't all have become extinct.

Men weren't all selfish, heartless, and lazy like James. And just because she'd picked a rotten apple once did not mean she'd make the same foolish mistake again.

She finished *Love's Sweet Promise* rapidly, whizzing right through it and dwelling on the juicy parts. She grew misty-eyed at the sappy ending, and regretfully laid it on the coffee table next to the cookie wrapper. She was rationing herself with the cookies. She'd only eaten three.

There was nothing good on TV tonight, not one decent movie. She wished she'd bought cable, but then again, when the salesman had come around a year ago, she'd still been pinching pennies like a fiend.

That left housework (yuck), or that nasty half-finished afghan that she kept putting off. Sighing she rose to go dig out the balls of yarn from the back of the linen closet. Suddenly a cataclysmic bolt of pain ripped through her jaw on the upper right, stopping her dead in her tracks with a horrendous pain like knives twisting in the side of her face.

"Ooooo!" she moaned, raising a hand to cup

her face. She staggered against the wall in the hallway. "Good God, not this!" It was an old, familiar pain. It hadn't been all that long since she'd had an abscessed tooth and the blinding pain was something she hadn't forgotten.

She recalled how the dentist had warned her about the one on the upper right becoming abscessed.

"Oh holy shit, not *now*!" she wailed as the pain seared through her mouth again, like someone stabbing her with a thousand sharpened butcher knives. Mercifully, it ended a minute later, leaving her standing in the hallway, gasping as she clutched her jaw.

But for how long? The other abscessed tooth, she remembered, hurt like hell, but the pain came and went alternately, coming at her in avalanches, allowing a blessed respite of minutes, hours, sometimes even days, in between the painful sieges.

"Not like most folks," the dentist had confided, wagging his head in bafflement. "You're an odd duck, Edna." She was an unusual patient, he explained, on two counts: The way the pain was intermittent in the abscessed tooth, as well as needing so many shots of novocaine when he worked on her. A real weirdo. "You're a lucky one, Edna," he'd said. "Most folks are walking the floor, moaning and groaning. It's a steady pain. There are no 'rest breaks'."

But would she luck out this time?

If the pain stayed with her, became totally unbearable, she'd be forced to leave the house.

She'd *have* to go to the dentist. And go out that front door. *And the cat be damned!*

She rubbed her jaw as the pain diminished as quickly as it had come, leaving her feeling drained. She pushed herself back up from the wall, and muttered, "Keep busy. I gotta find something to do, or I'll be bouncing off the walls soon."

She got the sack of yarn balls and a few granny squares she'd crocheted, tossed it on the couch, then went to the kitchen and slugged down two aspirins. Just as insurance. In case it hit her again.

Before she'd gotten halfway back to the couch, the pain gripped her again, intense and devastating, like a rattlesnake's incisors biting into her jaw, chewing off a big chunk. She sucked in her breath, bracing herself until the excruciating wave subsided.

"Oh . . . God. Maybe a hot compress . . ." she mumbled shakily.

She ran steaming hot water across a washcloth and held it clamped tightly to her jaw with one hand, rolling her eyes at Petey, who was eyeing her curiously, no doubt wondering why his mistress was doing so much moaning and groaning.

"Oh, hurry up, aspirin!" she grunted, rocking back and forth on her heels as the daggers sliced through her jaw again. The heat felt good. It gave some small amount of relief and it was the best she could do.

She glanced up at the kitchen wall clock. Eight-thirty.

"Gonna be a long night, Pete," she told the parakeet. "A loooong, hard night."

She sat down on the couch and crocheted half a granny square, but got bored and antsy. Besides, she couldn't hold the washcloth on her jaw if she crocheted. The pain had abated, but she got zapped by a good, strong twinge occasionally and she wanted to be prepared.

She watched a rerun of a sitcom, fighting a compelling urge to look out the window, just to see if she could glimpse the cat. Finally, her curiosity got the better of her. A part of her was scared to death of seeing it, yet she also felt this terrible, undeniable compulsion to check.

She laid the warm washcloth down in a bowl on the coffee table and crept to the living-room window, peeping furtively through the blinds, her hazel eyes wide with fear.

But she saw nothing, save the dark, still night. Janet's house across the street lay in deep black shadows, with no light shining at all. And Edna felt guilty again about not picking up Janet's mail. A fat gray squirrel darted up the trunk of the pine tree in Edna's front yard and she gasped slightly at the sudden, quick movement.

She checked the kitchen window then, but saw nothing except a few fireflies avariciously hovering near the azalea bushes. She moved slowly down the hallway to peep out the bathroom window. Nothing. Her jaw emitted a vague, low-key warning ache and she almost turned back to the living room and the comfort of the hot washcloth. But a niggling uneasiness drove her on to check the very last windows in her bedroom. If it was nearby, she had to know! She couldn't rest easy until she did.

"I'm being ridiculous. It's gone. Please, God, let it be gone for *good* . . ." She yanked the Venetian blinds apart on the east side of the bedroom and saw nothing outside except a yawning black abyss of darkness.

"See!" she chastised herself, a note of hope creeping into her voice. "You're just getting paranoid, that's all." Maybe it had gone. Maybe she'd even hallucinated those maleficent brown eyes, hallucinated this whole damn nightmare.

Sure. But had Gene hallucinated the things that had happened to him, too?

Feeling silly, like some gauche amateur sleuth, she moved across the bedroom on tiptoe to gaze through the blinds on the west side of the room.

The night seemed uncommonly still and very dark, and there was no cat outside to leer at her, or even a fat gray squirrel.

Just a message for her, written in blood, scrawled across the windowpane in a sloppy, uncoordinated hand, barely legible.

"You murderer," it said.

Edna collapsed.

Chapter Forty-four

Gene sat up in his hospital bed and eyed the dinner tray with a sour, sulky expression. Meat loaf, mashed potatoes, green beans, and some sort of unidentifiable dessert he supposed was pudding. Rice pudding? Who could really tell?

It was a brownish, soupy slop and he sure as shit had no intention of eating it. The green beans looked slimy and anemic, the mashed potatoes watery and gritty, and he had absolutely no comment on the frightening tan object that was supposed to be a slice of meat loaf.

He couldn't wait to get out of this hellhole. And his first stop would be a fucking Burger King. The next stop would be Edna's house . . . to demolish that murderous, hideous beast that was responsible for putting him here.

He picked up a fork and toyed idly with the green beans, staring up at the news on a TV that was suspended from the ceiling in a corner of the room, not really listening.

Jesus, how he cringed at the thought of going to sleep at night. He couldn't get any rest at all. Every goddamn time he shut his eyes and tried to drift off, he was assaulted by brutal nightmares about Edna and the cat.

He was afraid to go to sleep. It was a regular *Nightmare on Elm Street*.

Chapter Forty-five

That did it. She was going to kill it. With the gun. The gun she couldn't bring herself to use all through these past torturous days and nights. The very same gun, in fact, that she'd threatened to shoot James with the night she'd found him with Nadine. How ironic!

"Poetic justice," Edna whispered in a shaky voice. It would be justice, all right. Oh, the irony of it—the *exact same gun*, having to kill the *same person twice* with it. It was a scenario that should have sprung from the brain of some freaked-out psycho. Not ordinary Edna Wilkins, who was as plain as a cornfield.

It was all too much for her. She could feel an untamed hysteria bubbling up inside her chest like a hot, roiling cauldron. But did she want to laugh or cry her eyes out? That was the question. The cat was driving her to insanity. She meant to kill the damn thing, if it was the last thing she did. She couldn't stay trapped in this house, cooped up forever, like a sitting duck, chowing down noodles and canned green beans and letting her scratch marks fester from the lack of rubbing alcohol.

And her tooth was abscessed. It wouldn't be very long before she was howling with pain like a mad animal foaming at the mouth. Even if it *was* intermittent pain, soon she'd be incapable of bearing it. And there were only three aspirins left!

"I'm gonna kill the s.o.b. and be done with it," she announced to her clothes closet, staring dully at the top shelf where the gun lay. A nervous tic in her eye twitched sporadically.

Edna reached up and fished the gun from high off the closet shelf, standing on tiptoe. Her hands shook as she lifted it down and sat perched on the edge of the bed. Just staring.

Oh, it was all fine and dandy, getting the courage, the moxie finally to kill it, but what was she supposed to do? Step onto the front porch, brandishing the firearm, and coo, "Here, puss" sweetly, begging it to show itself? Begging it to attack again, begging it to carve her gizzard out, begging it to rip her eyes from their sockets, like a pair of soft, rotted grapes. . . .

Stop it! Just stop it! she mentally reprimanded herself, blinking and rubbing her hand across her face. She sat mesmerized by the gun, staring down at it in her lap, wondering if she could actually bring herself to fire it at the cat. Could she hit it? She'd never fired a gun before in her whole life; in fact, she hated them. It would have to be a close target, all right. She certainly didn't stand a chance in a million of hitting it from afar, that was for sure.

"I'll be lucky if I don't shoot my own damned foot off," she muttered, looking at the cold, dark metal gleaming in the light from the ginger jar lamp on her nightstand.

Even the sight of the gun was gruesome; it revulsed her.

She checked the barrel to make sure it was loaded, then laid it gently inside the nightstand drawer with a timid, shaking hand. She lay down in the bed, snuggling up underneath the thin sheet.

She had a feeling she wouldn't have to wait very long before the cat came to *her*.

Chapter Forty-six

A phantasmagoria of fiery, earth-shattering pain singing through her lower cheekbone brought Edna instantly awake with a loud howl of agony.

Her eyes snapped open abruptly.

"Oooh, ah God help me . . ." she crooned helplessly, clutching her jaw two-handed, rolling over atop the striped pillowcase and back again fitfully. Tears stung her eyes. Helluva lot of good crying would do. She couldn't leave the damned house to go to the dentist!

With the cat stalking her, she was trapped like some helpless invalid, like a bird in a cage. Utterly at its mercy.

What was worse? Having the abscessed tooth or having your goddamn eyes ripped out of their sockets?

Then she remembered the gun in the night-stand, her grisly ace in the hole. There was an alternative.

"Oh, I'm gonna get you, James!" she wailed as the pain roared through her mouth.

"Oh Jesus, Joseph, and Mary, make it go awaaaaay!" she screamed, throwing the sheet across the bed. She fled to the kitchen like a wild thing and downed two aspirins with a glass of lukewarm water. One aspirin left. Big deal.

"*One* won't do a fucking thing!" she cried. It wouldn't even phase this kind of pain, a red-hot surge of agony that she could feel all the way down to her aching toenails.

This was major agony. Big-time stuff, causing her to shout vulgar invectives and to scream like a madwoman. Showed you what a little pain could do, a gut-gnawing, crushing pain so strong it knocked the breath right out of your lungs in a big brutal whoosh. Showed you what a little fear could do, too. It could bring you to your knees, by God. You didn't much give a damn how foul-mouthed you were when you had a cockeyed cat with murderous inclinations breathing down the back of your neck, stalking you like some feline private-eye.

She drank the rest of the water, slamming the glass down on the counter to grab her jaw with both hands as another mind-numbing pain hit.

"Eeee!" she yelped, hopping up and down on her toes. The sound frightened Petey and he began to squawk in commiseration, trotting frenetically across his wooden perch with a vengeance.

Edna began to think how the cunning cat now had the upper hand. It had left claw marks all over her body, practically. She was a physical wreck. And she didn't intend to sit here like a vegetable and endure an abscessed tooth on top of all that, just for fear of it. The hell with it!

She traipsed back into the bedroom, drew the gun out of its hiding place, and laid it on the bed, blinking down at it wide-eyed.

Let the sorry sonofabitch attack. She would attack it right back! She would show it how it was done, by God. She would fight the beast. She was weary of being a sitting duck, just sitting around on her butt, waiting until it showed up to terrorize her or maim her. Or *kill* her.

If James Wilkins had risen up from his grave like some eerie, devilish specter and was looking for a fight, then goddamn his ugly hide, she'd give him one. She would stand up to him. For once in her life.

She'd always knuckled under to James like some simpering willowy sycophant. A spineless jellyfish, bowing and scraping to him. She'd always given in, cowed by his dominant, overbearing personality and extreme selfishness. But she would fight him now. And she intended to *win*.

Edna took up the gun with her trembling hand, the nervous tic jerking her eye spastically, and proceeded to the front door. Her eyes shone with an odd mixture of stark terror and a white-hot anger.

No one was going to intimidate her, not ever again, and certainly not this little twerp of an alley cat.

All her adult life James had intimidated her and all her adult life she'd meekly accepted it. She'd been a mealy-mouthed cowardly yes-man, done whatever he wanted, sacrificed everything. It was high time for a showdown.

Edna felt her skin crawl as if tiny insects scurried across her flesh. Every cell of her body was on red alert as she opened the front door cautiously, and stepped out into the eerie moonlit yard.

Chapter Forty-seven

The night was deadly still, taking on a surreal aspect. A pale yellow moon, impossibly large, hung low to the earth, and backlit the stark branches of the oak tree, like inky-black witches' talons raking the sky.

The tiny front porch light spread odd shadows, tall and dark, looming against the brick house like skeletons.

Edna's throat felt tight and choked. Her heart thumped dully in her chest. Intuition told her to go toward the back of the house, holding the gun out before her, two-handed, like she'd seen in the movies.

She stepped slowly, timidly across the driveway, the stones crunching beneath her feet. She wore a light, knee-length nightgown and a breeze flapped the hem of it. She'd put on her sneakers, the better to flee if flight became necessary.

The atmosphere seemed filled with a suffocating, leaden density and nothing moved, not even a squirrel. She saw no fireflies, no bird, no creature of any kind. It was as if they'd received some message that the cat was lurking nearby, a message that had traveled like wildfire throughout the animal kingdom.

Her heart pumped a crazy, lurching rhythm at the thought. A vein pulsated in her forehead with a thick, dull throbbing, and she felt her stomach twist with fear. She winced suddenly and gulped down a silent groan as another hot jolt of pain ripped through her cheekbone.

Oh, God, please don't let this fucking tooth bother me now. Not now, Lord! You can let it bring me to my knees later, but not right now, she pleaded silently.

Edna's ankle twisted as she lost her balance on the loose gravel. Her hip thudded dully against the hood of Gene's car.

"Shit!" she whispered vehemently, regaining her balance. She'd have a bruised hip for sure tomorrow morning. That is, if she lived to see the end of this hellish night.

She took one step forward and something skittered across the hood of Gene's car in a slithering, twisting motion, accented by the patter of tiny feet, claws striking metal crisply.

Edna spun around, legs apart, gripping the gun before her, Rambo-fashion.

A beady-eyed rat sat quivering atop the Volvo, staring at her with its round marble eyes, its whiskers twitching, its snout atremble as it sniffed the air. Then it jumped off and raced into the street.

Edna half collapsed against the fender in relief, fighting the urge to let out a shrill donkey whinny, just like Helen.

Some Rambo I'd make, she thought. *I practically go into cardiac arrest at the sight of a rodent.*

She drew a deep breath and set off for the back yard again, as her sneakers slid furtively through the soft, tall grass. She kept her eyes wide and alert, searching out all the shadows, paralyzed with terror that the cat would jump her and tear her apart, going for her eyes or jugular, like it had done to Gene. Her pulse beat like a small, frightened robin. The gun shook in her hand and she forced her attention to it, fighting to hold it up properly.

She mustn't give in to her fear. She had to fight, fight for all she was worth. Maybe she could clobber it with the gun, if need be. Surely a good sharp blow with the hard metal could render it unconscious, if not actually kill it.

She took mincing, old-lady, shuffling steps through the grass, rounding the corner of the house beside her tiny rock garden, her apprehension growing with every step. An electric charge zinged through the night air, and she had a gut feeling she was not alone. She could feel an ominous presence nearby. She grew vaguely dizzy, half-disoriented with fear, her nerves jangling to the breaking point like a guitar string stretched taut.

You can do it, Edna, coached the courageous tough-cookie side of her. *Just keep sliding those fucking sneakers. Find the ugly bastard and kill it. And for Christ's sake, don't let go of the gun!*

She gripped the gun with all her might. Gripped it until her fingers felt numb. She chewed her bottom lip, a bad habit when she was under pressure.

A soft screeching noise came from the azalea bushes in back of her, cutting through the too-silent night like a reverberating whipcrack. Edna spun around, her heart in her throat, ready to fire.

Go, Rambo, go! She wanted to throw back her head and cackle hysterically, but that would have to wait. She felt on the verge of madness. What the hell was she *laughing* about? Was she going crazy?

The bushes rustled and twitched and susurrated, like ghosts trading eerie whispered secrets in the depths of hell. But it was only a cardinal perched on top of the bush, cocking its small head quizzically toward her.

She expelled a shaky gust of air and moved forward to the back yard where the shadows turned deep opaque black, charged with sinister possibilities.

Edna's molar flared suddenly with a fierce, fleeting throb. She bit back a yelp, and tiny mute sobs escaped from her lips.

Hold that damned gun straight! The terse command blasted through her consciousness. *Slide those sneakers*!

But she was fearful, all at once, of going into the back yard. It was far too dark. How could she ever hope to see the black cat, before it spied her? Its body was jet-black, the color of the night, the color of the ominous shadows that lurked there. It would blend right in with its surroundings, the perfect camouflage. She wouldn't stand a chance.

Edna paused and contemplated turning back before it was too late. What on earth was she doing out here at one-thirty in the goddamn morning, in the pitch dark? Had the pain from her tooth caused her to lose her common sense?

The wind picked up, sending its ululant whine whispering through the pine trees and bushes. A terrible, grotesquely gory vision of the cat's eyes came to mind and she could see its fangs, long and lethal, dripping fresh blood.

She decided to turn back; it was wise. This was absurd. She was just asking for trouble, just begging it to attack her. She'd go back inside, take the last aspirin, and hunt for the creature tomorrow, in the safety of daylight. Like a sensible person.

Oh, what a lily-livered chickenshit coward you are, Edna Wilkins! hounded the courageous, hell-for-leather Ramboish side of her that had been anxious for a dirty confrontation.

But she didn't give a damn. She was too frightened. This was just too risky. She had the short end of the stick; the cat laid claim to all the advantages. It was like a dark, dank bottomless pit out here, a suffocating black abyss that promised trouble.

She could almost *smell* the cat's presence. The hairs against the back of her scalp stood erect and the nervous tic in her eye jittered double time as a cold fear sluiced through her.

A low, whistling wind rushed through the oak tree and shook its limbs, making macabre shadows play across the lawn like legions of tiny demons sprinting.

"I'm going back," she whispered in a dry croak, and trembled as a shrill breeze lifted her nightgown and swirled it about her figure like an apparition capering in its shroud.

The instant she lowered the .32 snub-nosed gun and took a step forward, it was on her.

Chapter Forty-eight

The black cat flung its heavy, solid body from the highest branches of the oak tree with a screaming, cawing cry of victory, the weight of its body squashing the breath out of Edna with a dull thump. She fell face forward, her jaw striking the ground, solidly crunching, revving up the pain from the abscess into high gear.

"Eeeee!" Edna let loose a howling, yodelling scream of agony and fury intermixed, but tightened her grip on the gun, which she'd somehow managed to cling to despite the sneak attack.

The black cat was a blustering, raging flurry of activity, ripping at the back of her neck with its long spiky talons, spewing droplets of blood across the grass with a reckless abandon. Its hot sour breath against the back of her neck, the stink from it, caused her belly to churn with nausea.

"No, no!" yelled Edna, her pulse skittering, her face a doughy sickish chalk-white, her heart leaping to her throat with horror. Its claws felt like butcher knives shredding her tender, vulnerable flesh into trails of blood-soaked ribbons. Her sneakers thrashed a mad, furious drumbeat against the grass in rebellion.

"No!" She uttered a single, guttural cry and flipped over with a quick, snapping motion onto her back, the tall grass brushing her face, nearly smothering her.

Why didn't ya mow the lawwwwwn, ya stupid, air-headed twit? Bet you'd have mowed it if you'd guessed you'd be hugging the fucking ground, getting a snoot-full of ragweed and dandelion spores—ya stupid twit!

Too late now, too late, she thought numbly.

The beast whined with outrage and neatly slid out from under Edna in the nick of time, preparing to launch itself at her face, its claws extended and eager to draw blood.

Her heart hammered with horror. Her insides did a sickish, kaleidoscopic somersault while the grass tickled her ears. The odor of mold and decay filled the air.

Hit it. Hit it right now—hurry up, you dummy! a voice in her head instructed, like an impatient schoolteacher advising the class dunce.

She slung the butt of the gun at its great furry neck with all her might, as her rage and terror lent a hyped-up adrenaline to the blow. The chocolate-brown eyes glared at her from their gross, crookedly-positioned sockets, heightening the atmosphere of insanity and pure evil that surrounded it like a vampire's dark cloak. It peeled back slick lips to show her its teeth oozing blood and a stench akin to the smell of graves and rotting cadavers emanated from its gaping mouth.

The blow landed as it lifted its claws in mid-air, keening its victory with an ungodly, chilling glee. She could hear a soft, *whumping* crack when the gun met bone, somewhere in the vicinity of its shoulderblade. She felt dizzy with relief, consumed by a dim, weak vertigo.

The cat slumped and sagged onto the grass, lying limply on its side, still mewling with anger over her conquest. She could not tell if she'd mortally wounded the beast. And she wasn't waiting around to find out.

She seized the moment to leap to her feet and to bolt inside the house. Her nightgown flounced in the breeze, and her feet flew madly across the ground as she goose-stepped rapidly, chuffing and hitching for breath. Her side ached and her jawbone felt like liquid fire from the flowering abscess.

She whizzed through the front door, threw the dead-bolt, and fell onto the couch, as her breath whooshed out of her lungs in one great ragged gust. Blood streamed down the back of her neck and through her hair, forming a sticky, matted mess. She sat perfectly still for a minute to compose herself, letting her rapid, shallow breathing subside.

But this time Edna didn't fall apart like a gelatinous, quaking mass of jelly. She didn't even whimper or sob. She walked calmly to the living-room window, lifted the Venetian blinds just a wee bit and, with slow deliberation, stroked a message of her own onto the windowpane.

"One last 'love note' from me to you, James." She smiled, reaching to the back of her neck. She swabbed blood from her nape onto her finger and wrote: "You're dead."

Then she took a hot shower and stepped into a clean, cool nightgown after discarding the bloody one into the trash. *The blood spots will never come out. I might as well trash it,* she thought.

She napped fitfully for only a couple of hours, writhing across the rumpled mattress. The dratted tooth awoke her at almost five in the morning with a torturous, breathtaking pang. As she rose to get a hot compress for it, she thought she heard a noise in the ominously silent house.

Her heartbeat capering arrhythmically, she grabbed the gun out of the nightstand and crept cautiously through the house on tiptoe, like a super sleuth checking everything out. But she could find no cause for alarm. Everything appeared normal.

"I probably just imagined it. I'm nervous, jumping at shadows," she said, and lay back down. But she decided to park the gun on the nightstand beneath the ginger jar lamp, at the ready, rather than inside it as she'd done previously. Just as a precaution. She didn't want to be caught with her pants down.

Lord, as hard as she'd smacked the creature with the butt of the gun, surely it had died. She could not believe that it had survived the hard blow she'd dealt. Impossible. Tomorrow she'd call Gene and tell him she'd gotten rid of it herself. She could still see it in her mind—crumpled on the dark lawn in the back yard, lying immobile, not stirring a single muscle, still as death. It *had* to be dead.

And tomorrow she'd pay the dentist a visit and get her tooth taken care of before she went wild with pain. And she'd buy herself some god-damn hydrogen peroxide and gauze bandages, before the gashes blossomed into a full-blown infection; they were already halfway there. She'd even get herself some food and a brand-new *TV Guide* and check Janet's mail. Things were looking up.

Edna slept, feeling cloaked in a blanket of safety like a babe nestled in its mother's arms, reassured and comforted as she reminded herself of the powerful blow she'd given the animal.

She dreamed dark dreams, restless and fitful, of tiny kittens, their paws joined, their pointed demon faces pulled into rictused mocking grins, spinning around and around the red brick rambler in a mad, celebratory dance of death.

And every last one of the little sons of bitches had tootsie-roll-brown eyes, and droplets of blood fizzled at the corners of their rapacious, cavernous mouths.

And they chanted her name, over and over again.

Chapter Forty-nine

She didn't call Gene that day, after all.

What she did do all day was sit like a stone against the flowered couch, rarely moving, not eating, feeling herself sinking into the realms of madness.

Her jaw ached cruelly, transforming her face into a blurred mask of agony. The wounds from the brand-new scratches on the other side of her face already looked reddened and puffy, near infection. She'd had no medicine to apply to them at all. Her body took turns at hurting—first her cheekbone and then the cat wounds—in a weird, brutal point-counterpoint melody of agony.

Tears streamed down her face several times during the day, burning her wounds, but there were no huffing, breathless sobs of misery. She was like a zombie in a trance. She didn't read a book or speak to Petey or watch TV. The telephone rang at two different times and she sat right beside it, unmoving like a block of concrete.

At midnight, she rose from the couch, drank a cup of water, and gobbled down some noodles. Then she resumed her position on the couch, tucking her legs up underneath the thin cotton nightgown.

She was scared. She didn't know which she was more frightened of: losing her mind, or the cat's next attack. Both were quite possible and very likely. For that morning, she had gazed out the Venetian blinds in her bedroom, like a convict staring dully through prison bars, fully expecting to see the black cat's inert body in a heap on the grass, near the redwood fence.

But it was gone.

Chapter Fifty

Gene was thrilled. He was going home the day after tomorrow. His therapy and healing had gone well and he would return once a week on an out-patient basis until his therapy was complete. "Praise the Lord!" he felt like bawling, though he wasn't especially religious.

"Burger King, here I come!" was what he actually shouted when the doctor told him.

He'd tried to call Edna twice, but got no answer. He wondered where she was. He wanted to tell her the good news, to tell her to hang in there. And to tell her, again, to stay the hell inside. Too late now. He supposed she was out shopping. Damn it, why hadn't she listened to him?

He pushed the worry out of his mind and tried to get some sleep. He had to get his strength back for his big day. The minute he was released he'd get a cheese whopper with fries and a chocolate milkshake. Then would come the good part. He'd see Edna again and kill that long-tailed son of a bitch.

Chapter Fifty-one

"Paper or plastic?" Helen inquired of the gaunt young man in pleated pants as he tossed some frozen french fries and a loaf of Italian bread on the counter.

"Paper," he said rather abruptly.

That was what she liked, a man who knew what he wanted.

He started giving her the eye and she thought of telling him he was much too young for her, not that she wasn't tempted. He was a good-looking little bugger. And wasn't that the thing these days, to date a guy who was young enough to be your son? This one had a cute butt and a wallet chock-full of twenties and a few hundred dollar bills, she noted.

Helen grinned wider. What the hell? He might

be young, but he was old enough to make up his own mind about her, wasn't he? If he wanted to date a cradle-robber, that was *his* business.

Besides, she was on the outs with Skipper and needed a new fellow to fill his shoes as her "spare." Just Freddy wasn't enough. It was her firm policy to have a spare. Skipper had apparently fallen in love with one of those nasty mud wrestlers, of all things, the shithead.

She flirted with the kid awhile and he flirted right back with a thrilled, ecstatic gleam in his eye. Oh, yes, she thought, he'd do, all right. He had the hots for her, and had it bad. He had a nice personality to boot.

Helen scribbled her phone number on his brown paper bag with a wink and dumped the french fries and bread inside.

"Gimme a call sometime," she breathed so only he would hear. His pupils widened and he nodded mutely.

After the man left, Helen thought about her trip to Edna's the other day. Her arm was still sore from where that rotten sonofabitchin' cat had scratched her, but she was determined to go see Edna tomorrow, anyway.

They could laugh their heads off over what an insane incident it had been with the cat, birddogging her car like it had, just begging to get squashed.

It was funny—now that it was over, that is.

She shuddered.

Chapter Fifty-two

Edna was dreaming and in the dream she fancied she heard a dull, flat thump issuing from the living room, perhaps from the fireplace. She fancied she heard the dim sound of nails clacking against the parquet floor of the hallway which led to her bedroom.

She forced this vaguely disturbing dream from her thoughts and made way for a light, happy dream of Gene. Gene and herself, their hands sweetly joined, strolled through high grass (Mow the lawn, mow the lawn, mow the goddam lawwwwn. Should've done it!) dotted with yellow sunflowers on a hillside.

A romantic, happy dream, a dream she could lose herself in forever. But something nagged at her, a dull gripping panic biting at her consciousness, refusing to let go. It demanded her urgent attention, whispering to her to remember the *other* dream—the dream about the scrambling, rumbling, skittering noises from the direction of the fireplace. *The damper.* Dear God in heaven *no*! her mind roared as in the dream she envisioned a fat black cat squiggling around, twisting and turning, until it weaseled its way down the damper into the house.

The chilling picture raced through her subconscious with knifelike clarity for an instant, then was forgotten as a half doze took her weary body and carried it away.

Edna sighed and rolled restlessly onto her back. The back of her wrist brushed against the gun on the nightstand to her right.

Morbid, hateful dreams swirled and eddied into her subconscious with a frightening vividness. A miasma of death pervaded the landscape of her dreams, featuring a macabre kaleidoscope of grinning, evil ghouls.

Edna dreamed deeply and in the dream she smelled the fetid, festering odor of the cat, felt its hot putrid decaying breath in her face, slurping and whispering, felt its burdensome weight on her chest, suffocating her, drowning her, weighing her down, pinning her solidly to the bed. She fancied her eyes snapped open abruptly in the dream, and she saw the cat's face hovering close above her own, its marquis-shaped pupils gleaming like ebony daggers.

Except it was *James's* face, too, superimposed over the cat's skull like a bad film negative. One instant it was the cat's, its teeth gleaming in the hallway light, frothy whitish foam spilling from its mouth. The next instant it was James's face as he sunk to the floor from his fatal heart attack.

Edna dreamed she heard it utter a low, primal hiss, announcing its presence, wanting her to know, needing her knowledge, her awareness, so it could witness her helpless terror and glean joy from it.

Except this wasn't a dream.

"It's not a dream, not a dream! Wake up, you stupid goddamn chowderheaded, dumbass twit!" The words screamed at her in James's voice, sounding like a booming death knell.

Edna kicked off the sheet. It landed on the floor in a heap. The dream took on a bizarre, fantastic, surreal aspect and the temperature in the bedroom seemed to dip to a bone-chilling iciness like some dark, dank dungeon. Edna's hand groped the mattress for the missing sheet with no success, then was still.

And then Edna's eyes flew open, already knowing what they would see. An overwhelming, dizzying sense of claustrophobia descended upon her at the sight of it on her chest. It felt as though the creature weighed one thousand pounds, pressing down, down, down, squeezing the precious air from her lungs, suffocating her. Terror ripped like a deadly sword through her heart. She stared at it, eye to eye. Chocolate-brown to hazel.

The mauve-and-gray bedroom took on the ambience of a cold, gruesome death chamber as she gaped at the dark outline of the cat, backlit by the hallway light.

As though in a hypnotic trance, Edna's fingers began to work desperately, her knuckles twitching, scrabbling across the nightstand like a crab to reach the gun.

The creature's terrible eyes were crazed and unfocused, as if it were in a psychotic daze. Whitish frothy foam dribbled copiously down its jowls as it opened and closed its fangs in a wickedly demonstrative biting motion. Its soured breath sickened her, sending her head reeling with an attack of vertigo.

Edna couldn't force motion into her limbs; she was petrified at the nearness of it. Her stomach heaved and she fought to draw air into her parched lungs. It snarled then and uttered a long, low hissing sound like a rattlesnake spitting saliva, its whiskers twitching with bloody anticipation. She must have struck it across the shoulderblade the previous night and the blow had grazed one eye, for it was covered with sticky caked blood that streaked across its scruffy black fur clear down its snout.

"Sssssss," it mewled, its jowls drizzling saliva and froth down onto her neck, like hot acid stinging her skin. It raised one ragged paw and extended its claws. In a flash, it began to rake the claws lightly, slowly, down her jugular, teasing her like a cat with a mouse, basking in her terror. Its fetid, filthy breath blew out in a gurgle against her face, making a wet whistling sound that was obscene.

This was her worst nightmare scenario: trapped. Alone in the house with it.

Edna wanted to swoon at the acrid stink. She felt her hand bump against the gun, sending it crashing onto the floor, out of her grasp.

"Ah God, help me, help me—" she choked, terror squeezing her heart in a murderous vise. There was no time to think of what to do next, unless she wanted to lie here like a lifeless mannequin as it tore her throat out and ripped at her eyes like some vulturous, greedy bird jerking juicy worms from the ground.

She had to fight back, had to. . . .

Like a reflex action, Edna balled up one fist and took a deep breath, then punched the nasty black fur as hard as she could, giving a high-pitched rebel yell of fury, like a soldier engaged in deadly guerrilla warfare. The beast screamed with pain and its claws shot outward, hooking into her nipple through the paper-thin nightgown, rocking Edna with a heinous pain.

She arched her back and howled in tune with the animal's primal cry, creating an ungodly duet for a minute. Its huge body flew through the air, taking a minute tidbit of Edna's nipple with it, and smacked solidly into the Venetian blinds close beside the bed with a loud, thundering clatter. It rolled to a saggy heap beneath the window. The aloe plant on the windowsill crashed to the floor beside it, its clay pot cracking into a million jagged pieces, punctuating the already deafening cacophony.

Edna's heart fluttered and pounded madly.

"Oooooh . . ." She was barely aware that she was moaning and sucking for air. Oh, dear Lord, had it torn her nipple from her chest? She was afraid to look, but now was not the time, anyway. It was time to fight. Time for a showdown.

She threw her body into a roll and slid off the side of the mattress, grappling frenziedly for the gun, releasing its safety catch after a few shaky, quivering attempts. A clammy sweat trickled from her eyebrows down into her eyes, half-blinding her, despite the fact that the bedroom had turned into a chilly deep freeze. A spastic shudder shook her frame as pain rocketed through her jaw again with a grueling intensity.

"Oooooh . . . Have to kill it, have to h–h–hurry—"she stuttered. It would get up in a moment or two, and it would surely go for her jugular or the *other* nipple, as it had insinuated minutes ago, graphically demonstrating with its hooked claw, delicately rubbing it across her skin in that teasing, taunting motion.

Edna clutched the snub-nose with a panicky cold fear as she trained the gun on its still form. She peered across the top of the mattress from her crouched position on the floor. Its crusty, matted black fur was visible and it was an inert hump.

Oh, but she wasn't fool enough to trust *that*. She'd learned the hard way how inert humps can suddenly waltz off during the night, like it had in the back yard!

Hellcat

Edna willed her hand to stop shaking as she raised it and carefully took aim, her nostrils pinched against the vile terrible odor of death that permeated the freezing air.

It was freezing because there was a real live ghost in the room. Something that was already dead, a crime against nature, was in this room! Edna thought. She could feel her joints quivering as if they'd been dipped in snowflakes. She could feel her teeth wanting to clack like some stupid pair of toy false teeth that jumped around on a table in the dime store.

She steadied her hand, miraculously.

"You're dead," she whispered at its shapeless, shaggy form, and squeezed the trigger gently.

Nothing happened.

Then the black hulking shape rose, wobbling on its feet, staggering around to face her. James glared at her from across the bedroom. She could see his face so clearly now. Then the cat's evil grimace was superimposed over the image, blending and wavering and merging as one in a pale bluish aura. A glint of gold flickered sporadically from its neck in the hallway light.

The locket! It was wearing the damned locket around its throat.

"Holy Mother of God," Edna murmured, her voice faltering raggedly. She pulled the trigger once again, offering up a silent, fervent prayer. Her stomach roiled with anguish and her pulse jumped into a jagged, impossible rhythm.

The blast rang through the air with a stentorian, thundering roar and Edna reeled backward on her haunches from the impact, striking her shoulderblade against the nightstand.

The shot caught it in mid-air, as it prepared to launch itself at her. The beast's throat exploded into a million pieces, sending bone and ragged bits of flesh flying against the creamy mauve-colored walls which she'd just painted a month before. Its mocking triangular skull caromed back, crashing through the Venetian blinds and the windowpane like a flying softball, leaving its neck a ravaged bloody stump of pulpy, sickening flesh and veins. An awful corroded stink of mutilated bodies wafted outward and she half-gagged.

"There. There you are—*you stupid twit!*" screamed Edna, as hysteria engulfed her. She screamed it over and over again, liking the sound of herself calling *James* a stupid twit. She couldn't stop, but kept on until her throat was hoarse. Then she slumped against the bed and sobbed miserably, emptying herself of all the years of pain and suffering, and of all her pent-up hatred for James, until she felt like a dry, emotionless husk.

Chapter Fifty-three

Edna couldn't bear to look at the grotesque sight, but she couldn't leave its corpse there, either. Jagged splinters of glass from the shattered window lay strewn across its thick, still body, mixed with blood, a piece or two poking erectly out from its fur. The raw stump that had been its neck pumped blood out in thick, pulsating gobbets that matted and caked the dark black fur, dribbling down its chest.

Edna's eyes bulged as she regarded it. Impossibly, the golden locket remained entwined in the fur where its neck had been, awash with blood. Small splinters of bone jutted out haphazardly along the edge of the gutted stump.

She felt her gorge rise, bile creeping up the back of her throat, as she leaned gingerly across the windowpane and spied its head in the grass outside the window, its eyes glaring blindly up at her. They remained chocolate-brown. She shuddered, though the temperature in the room seemed to be rising to its normal range.

Oh, she'd scored a home run this time, all right, with her .32 snub-nose. She'd knocked its fucking head right off, as she had promised.

She trembled again, rubbing the goose bumps on her arms, and then let the blinds clatter down, loath to look upon its crazed eyes and the severed tendons and veins and soupy glistening bits of bone drenched in blood.

She flew into the bathroom in a desperate, jogging lope, and retched dry heaves, a runny hot acrid liquid that seemed to go on forever, while spasms shook her body. She couldn't face cleaning up that mess tonight. It would have to wait for morning.

She had stood up to James at last—and won.

But the grisly sight of that thing's head flying across the room was something she'd never forget; and that *sucking*, *whumping* sound its body had made as its head was torn from its neck—bones splitting, tendons gnashing, and veins snapping—was something she'd have nightmares about for a long time to come.

Chapter Fifty-four

Later the next day, after she'd cleaned up the sickening mess and drove to the dump to dispose of its corpse, Gene called, telling her that his therapy had gone well and that he was getting out of the hospital tomorrow.

"It's dead," she announced abruptly, her voice numb with exhaustion. "I . . . I shot it." She paced the kitchen floor as she spoke, running a hand wildly through her hair. Petey side-stepped in a fast, jittery dance back and forth across the wooden bar in his cage, matching her direction, fixing her with his beady eye.

"Oh Jesus, I wish *I* could've done it. I *wanted* to do it," he said. "Damn it, Edna, it could have hurt you!" His tone was gruff and tender and brought her close to tears.

"I'm perfectly all right. And you couldn't have wanted to kill it any more than I did!" she answered with a rueful laugh.

"Edna, you'd better get to the doctor. Let him look at those claw marks, okay?" Gene paused a moment. "I want you to be ready for a date, you hear me?"

Tears glistened in Edna's eyes. She had wondered if she'd ever *see* Gene Martin again at one point, when she was gunning down the cat, much less have an actual date with him.

"Okay," she croaked hoarsely, fighting her tears. "I—I've got an abscessed tooth, too, I'm afraid. It's been half killing me. Gotta have a hot date with my dentist first."

"Guess I don't mind playing second fiddle"— he paused—"so long as it's the dentist and not some other guy. I want you all to myself."

Edna blushed a deep, rosy scarlet and Petey poked fun at her with a loud shrieking cluck that sounded half human.

"Gene?"

"Yeah?"

"The cat . . . Before I shot it," she gulped, "I could see James's face, it *turned* into James's face. It was awful . . ." A tremor washed over her.

"Don't think about it, Edna. You've got to put it out of your mind. I saw it, too. You're not getting feeble-minded, let me assure you. I saw it do that in a dream. It moved and wiggled and then suddenly I was looking at the facial features of a man . . ." His voice trailed off.

"Let's not talk about it anymore, all right, Gene?"

"Okay. Good idea," he agreed. "Listen, lady, you just be ready for a movie. And dinner. Tomorrow night!"

"I will. More than ready. I'll get something done to this tooth by then. Hey, maybe we'll even twirl by the Safeway afterwards, give Helen the thrill of a lifetime?"

"Yeah. Let her see how great her matchmaking efforts turned out." He laughed affectionately.

Edna's heart fluttered crazily, but not from fear this time. It was the light, free feeling of joy that bubbled within her.

"Yes," she agreed in a husky voice that was near tears, the old shyness tugging at her.

"And one more thing."

"What?"

"Will you pick me up at *my house* this time in my car? And I'll drive you home."

She agreed heartily, with a little chuckle, no longer frightened of what the future held. Gene Martin was a kind and gentle man, a man who was caring and loving. They might have arguments, but Edna was certain he would never mistreat her, never be abusive; he was far too gentle-natured. And he'd never, ever, not in a million years, call her a stupid twit or physically abuse her.

There was goodness in the world, and love. And at last Edna Wilkins was ready to open herself to it, to let herself love again and be loved.

There was one secret she would keep herself, however, about slaying the cat, and she would never tell another living soul, not even Gene: That she'd made one hell of a good home run. Award-winning, in fact. It belonged right up there with those guys in the Baseball Hall of Fame, damn it.

Chapter Fifty-five

Edna felt ebullient, exuberant.

She'd suffered through another root canal, much to her chagrin and the dentist's sadistic delight. But now she was looking forward to her date with happy anticipation, having decided she deserved a brand-new dress, after the cat had ruined the pretty pink-flowered one she'd been so fond of.

So she'd paid the dentist's bill and dropped by the shopping center. There was just enough time for some serious shopping before she picked Gene up. She wanted something terribly feminine, a dress that would catch a man's heart. Something special to wear for their first date. Their first *real* date, that is. That cataclysmic nightmare that had occurred when he'd come to her house that terribly rainy night a week ago most definitely didn't count.

In no time she found the perfect dress. An unforgettable dress, virginal white, a light frilly cotton with tiny pearl buttons and puffed lacy sleeves. It had a long romantic skirt trimmed with the most beautiful lace she'd ever seen.

"Hell's bells," she seemed to hear Helen's braying voice echo in her ears, filled with envy. "It looks practically like a damn wedding gown, Ed."

And it sort of did, but she had a feeling Gene wouldn't mind that a bit. Edna sighed and flipped out her credit card, grinning fatuously at the clerk. She could hardly wait to get home and put it on.

She stepped outside the mall into the brilliant July sunlight, bemoaning the fact that her car had no air conditioning. Damned little hot box, she thought, aggravated.

"Well, guess bitching won't help." She sighed, clutching the shopping bag close to her. As she moved off the curb and headed toward lane sixteen, her heart thumped heavily. The heat seemed to make her sway dizzily, and she choked back a tiny scream that threatened to escape.

A black kitten was perched atop the rear of her car, its innocent eyes wide as it stared at her lugubriously, switching its fluffy tail slowly.

"Oh, don't be such a fool, Edna Wilkins," she whispered angrily to herself, clutching the bag tighter against her chest. "Why, it's just a little kitten. You can't be afraid of every single cat you see forever. There are millions of cats in this world. You can't freak out every time you see one. You can't become paranoid like this."

But it is black, her inner voice insisted.

She raised her chin high and walked steadily closer to the car, determined to gain control of herself. She fought a bout of hyperventilation by using a deep-breathing method, hoping the kitten would simply scamper away. She told herself it was pure nonsense to think what she was thinking.

But it was *black*—and it was sitting on *her* car! The thought hammered in her head.

"Shoo!" she called to it as she approached the car, and waved her shopping bag threateningly.

It screeched loudly and twisted its small head to gaze directly at her before it leaped down, and Edna's world closed in on her as she sank to the pavement.

One of its chocolate-brown eyes was set slightly lower than the other in its triangular, misshapen little skull.